Altered Creatures

Betrayed

Epic Fantasy Adventures
Santorray's Privations Series
Historical Date 4.0646.0901
(4th Age, 646th Year, 9th Month, 1st Day)

Altered Creatures
Betrayed
Epic Fantasy Adventures
Historical Date 4.0646.0901
Santorray's Privations Series
Book 3, Revision 3.00
www.AlteredCreatures.com

Printed in the United States of America

Dedication:
This book is dedicated to all the people that have made decisions that haunt us for the rest of our years. No matter how hard we try, we can't shake the damage we did as the pain and grief gnaws in our thoughts. Why is it we can forgive others, but it's so hard to forgive ourselves?

Acknowledgments:
My lovely wife, Tami, who has encouraged me to address issues head on.

My mother, who taught me how to confront others without being confrontational.

Our kids and grandkids who inspire me to be a better role model.

My dyslexia, for this gift has taught me compassion & empathy for others, drive to conquer my struggles, and creativity to survive outside the norm. What a wonderful set of life lessons to have.

Everyone who took the time to read my manuscript to help me work out the details and issues, as well as those who I council with on various aspects of the story. These include Tami Wedgeworth, JoAnn Cegon, Sarah Wedgeworth, Bob Cegon, Darci Knapp, Kelly Gochenaur, Pat Mulhern, and Andrew Kelleher

Your insight is greatly appreciated.

www.AlteredCreatures.com

AC's epic adventures continue with the following books:

Nums of Shoreview Series (Pre-Teen, Ages 9 to 12)
Stolen Orb (Book 1)
Unfair Trade (Book 2)
Slave Trade (Book 3)
Baka's Curse (Book 4)
Haunted Secrets (Book 5)
Rodent Buttes (Book 6)

Thorik Dain Series (Young Adult and Adult)
Treasure of Sorat (Prequel)
Fate of Thorik (Book 1)
Sacrifice of Ericc (Book 2)
Essence of Gluic (Book 3)
Rise of Rummon (Book 4)
Prey of Ambrosius (Book 5)
Plea of Avanda (Book 6)

Tilli of Kingsfoot Series (Adult)
Hidden Magic (Book 1)
Final Days (Book 2)

Santorray's Privations Series (Adult)
Betrayed
Hunted
Outraged

Look for other upcoming stories of
Santorray's Privations
Ambrosius
Tilli of Kingsfoot
Darkmere
Myth'Unday
Dragon & Del'Unday Wars
and more…

Altered Creatures

Betrayed

by

A.G. Wedgeworth

Historical Event		Published Novel
2nd Age Begins: Notarians Arrive		
Creation of Unday		
Training of E'rudites		
Creation of Notarian Structures		
Completion of Lu'Tythis Tower	**2nd Age**	TD5 Prey of Ambrosius
Fall of Notarians		TD6 Plea of Avanda
E'rudite & Alchemist War		SP5 Outraged
Mtn King Temple Established		TK1 Hidden Magic
Nomadic Living & Fighting		
Migration of the Ov'Unday		
Creation of Magical Items		TK2 Final Days
Creation of the Myth'Unday		
3rd Age Begins: Del'Unday Rule		
Del'Unday Expansion		
War of Del'Unday and Myth'Unday	**3rd Age**	
War of Del'Unday & Dragons		
Del'Unday Civil War		
Rise of the Alchemists		
Victor Dovenar's Revolution		
4th Age Begins: Dovenar 1st Wall		
7 Provinces Created in Kingdom		SP1 Exiled
Dovenar Kingdom Civil War		SP2 Captured
Assassination of Dovenar Knights		
Creation of the Grand Council	**4th Age**	SP3 Betrayed
Matriarch's Cleansing		SP4 Hunted
Destruction of the Grand Council		TD1 Fate of Thorik
Dovenar Provinces Secede		TD2 Sacrifice of Ericc
Reuniting against Del'Undays		TD3 Essence of Gluic
The Final Great Battle		TD4 Rise of Rummon
5th Age Begins: Frozen Lands		SP6 Defeated

Epic Fantasy

Prologue
Post Dovenar Civil War

It had been a few decades since the Civil War devastated the seven provinces of the Dovenar Kingdom, one of which had been totally flooded, never to be lived upon again. Most became fractured and leaderless as the local government officials attempted to hold them together.

Eastland was completely cut off from the rest of the provinces, placing them in great danger from the Altered Creatures. Southwind fell to the power of the Matriarch, but she allowed politicians to feign control. Greensbrook broke up into little farming communities, while Pelonthal stayed isolated from the rest of the world. Woodlen leaders took immediate control of their region with a heavy hand as their new ways separated the poor and the wealthy. Doven, the heart of the Dovenar Kingdom, stood firm with the old ways as they tried to rebuild what had been working for six-hundred years, but the unified kingdom was no more.

All of the provinces were now at risk of being invaded by the Altered Creatures. The most aggressive and savage of these creatures were the various species within the Del'Unday Clan, which were led by the blothruds.

In addition, the threat from the Civil War fighters was not over. Cursed, they continued the fight long after being killed. These undead armies roamed the lands causing havoc.

Humans had been broken up and isolated from each other. Those in small villages were on their own to survive. They had to establish their own rules and how they would enforce them. They had to protect themselves from invaders and deal with their own disasters. It was a dangerous time for humans and their allies.

Some cities, such as Brushtower, were key locations for trade and strength before the Civil War, but they had been so severely damaged by the battles that those who remained in them left most parts abandoned due to lack of resources to repair and rebuild them.

But as with the wildfire destroying a forest, new growth is imminent. Unfortunately for the broken provinces, most regions contained opportunistic individuals seeking to expand their power over the weakened civilization. The time was ripe for the vulnerable to be consumed by the thugs and predators who desired power.

It is at this time that our story begins…

Chapter 1

Undead Army

Creeping out of the morning fog, an army of the undead dragged itself forward. Flesh clung to bones as torn uniforms helped hold their bodies together. Broken bones and missing limbs were common in the ancient battalion, but these challenges did not stop them from trudging forward as a unified force.

Missing nearly half of his face due to the swipe of a sharp blade many years ago, their leader guided the troops with his one remaining eye. He sat high upon a massive four-legged undead chuttlebeast that slowly marched up the final hill before spotting the distant fortress they came to destroy.

In the vastness of the open mountain foothills stood a great structure of stone and metal protruding from the mountainside as though it had broken free of the earth around it to reveal its strength. Solid walls with slits for windows surrounded the upper levels, while razor-sharp metal shards were placed across the entire wall's surface as though a grand mirror had exploded and randomly embedded its pieces within the stones. It was a deadly place to enter unless one was permitted to use the formidable metal front doors.

The morning sun was soon to rise and overpower the light given from the lanterns that lined both sides of the drawbridge that laid flat over a trench in front of the fortress. A large waterfall splashed down at one side of the fortress and the water was quickly swept through the trench in front of the structure. The river raced to the far side of the fortress and then down another waterfall into the valley below. With the drawbridge down, the undead army viewed its opportunity to make its way across the open hillside and into the structure, before killing all those that lived within.

Once a mighty warrior, the leader of the undead stopped the lumbering chuttlebeast creature he was riding and studied his surroundings. He was missing one eye, but his dry stretched skin held onto his bones better than most of his troops. His Civil War military uniform helped hold him together as he led his fellow soldiers into battle. Once a proud family man, Korin Swiph had gone to war to protect his people, only to be betrayed by his leaders. Today he wished to take revenge for their actions.

Raising his broken sword high in the air, Korin spoke. "Stop!" He then watched his army come to a halt after feeling a deep vibration emanate from the leader's magical weapon. The sword that had been used to control the undead by their Alchemist masters. It was the very sword that his master had used to make a deep slice across his face and remove one of his eyes for disobedience before Korin took possession of the weapon and used it to kill that very Alchemist. He now hoped to use the weapon one last time to murder the leader that was the cause of his years of suffering. Giving one more review of his options, he lowered his damaged sword and pointed it at the drawbridge. "Attack!"

His forces felt the wave of energy from the sword and charged forward. The stampede of partially flesh-covered skeletons attempted to run down the slope; some with broken or missing legs fell and were trampled by the rest. Regardless, the majority raced forward down the long hill toward the distant fortress.

The ground shook from the pounding of footfalls as hundreds of partially flesh-covered feet and ragged boots stomped their way forward to the unsuspecting tenants that lived beyond the harsh walls. Korin Swiph followed behind on the chuttlebeast, as it took some time to move its enormous weight from a dead stop to a jog. Large sections of the creature had been eaten away by insects and pockets of maggots roamed within its muscles and fat. With nearly half of its bones exposed, it was surprising that it could move at all, let alone with a rider.

The undead leader did not care about the beast. It was his last mission. He knew the army would be seen crossing the open field, but he hoped the fortress guards would not have the time to prepare any strategy. His goal was simple: use his forces to make an opening so he could cross the drawbridge and get inside to end the life of his enemy.

It was then that the fortress doors flew open, and the captain of the guard stepped forward. Wearing studded leather armor, Kaya was a tough-looking woman who stepped out with unwavering determination in her eyes, eager to meet the approaching army. She carried a spear with a sharp blade on one end and a counterweight of a metal ball with spikes, known as a morning star, on the other end. Spinning the weapon, the blade and morning star twirled so fast they appeared to be a solid ring of metal. Effortlessly moving the whirling weapon from one hand to the other, she marched forward a few yards to assess the situation.

Behind her, a large blothrud, known as Santorray, stepped out of the fortress and onto the bridge. Standing nearly twice the height of the female warrior, he had a massive dragon head that rested upon the thick neck of an oversized muscular human torso covered with scars. His skin was blood red, and his red eyes had a bit of a glow. Thick, sharp spikes protected the back of his neck, his shoulder blades, and the backs of his elbows. All the spikes were scratched, and several were broken, revealing that their dark exterior lightened to a deep red inside. Covered in brown hair, Santorray's large wolf legs could easily carry twice the weight of his massive body as he stepped up near Kaya. Blothruds were the ultimate fighters, and this one was the best of the best.

"What in the name of Della Estovia is that?" she asked the blothrud as she tried to understand what she was seeing racing across the open field toward her.

Santorray knew right away what they were up against. "Looks like a wave of undead from the Dovenar Civil War." Grinning at her concern, he added, "If you're not ready for this, you can watch me from the tower and take notes."

Glaring up at him, she knew he was just trying to get her motivated. "I'll write a paper for you called 'How to Kill Dead People: An Action in Redundancy'."

A slight chuckle escaped the blothrud's dragon-like muzzle. "You're getting better at those jabs. At least you learned one thing from me."

Holding back a grin, she replied, "It was the only thing you knew that was teachable."

"Ouch," he said with a smile as he watched the oncoming army. "Looks like it's time for us to get this started."

"Agreed." Kaya nodded as she continued to fluidly spin her weapon around in her hands. In some way it helped her relax and think clearly. "I want you to stay here and guard the bridge to ensure none of them make it inside. I think we can handle this assault."

Santorray watched the horde of undead running toward them. "There is much more that I can teach you and your guards."

"I know, but you'll be leaving us soon and we must learn to deal with these issues without you. This will be a good test of our troops while you're still here to have our back." Snapping her spear to a motionless position, she began her march forward. As she did, a legion of leather-armored men and women marched through the doorway and across the bridge to follow her into battle.

Crossing his thick muscular arms in front of him, he stood up straight as he watched them prepare for battle. "There are a few things I can teach you about fighting the undead. Just let me know when you need my guidance," he called out to Kaya.

"I won't need it. We're prepared for this!" she yelled back to make sure her guards heard the reply. She then yelled to the leader of the archers, "Pax, be prepared for my signal!"

Santorray appeared skeptical. "Know your opponent, your objective, your capability, and your risk. Once you realize you need my help just give me a signal, like a wave of an arm."

With a grin, she shook her head as she moved into position. "Keep your eyes open, Santorray! It's time for me to teach you a few things!"

"Oh, this should be good," he said to himself.

Marching in formation, Kaya's men and women separated and then regrouped as they walked around and past the huge blothrud who stood in the center of the bridge as requested. Once beyond the trench, Kaya's army filed into place and made a half-circle row in front of the drawbridge to prevent the enemy from getting through. Should any of them sneak by, they would have to deal with Santorray.

Kaya's forces stood several layers deep as they prepared to fight. The men and women in the front line made a barrier with their shields with one hand, while holding short one-handed weapons with the other. Those that stood in the back rows lowered their long pikes in between the frontline's shields with the weapons' metal blades pointing at the enemy. The rows in the center carried a range of weapons that fitted each individual's preference and skillset. In addition to the guards on the field of battle, Kaya had instructed her archers to climb up in the fortress and prepare to fire their arrows from above.

Kaya had learned that there was no value in wasting her people's energy by racing up a hillside to meet an advancing enemy. Besides, it prevented them from having a strong line that protected the only vulnerable access point to their home. Preparing and waiting was her strategy, and it had always served her well.

Spinning her weapon around over her head in various patterns, she communicated her commands to Pax and his archers. They quickly loaded their arrows and aimed at an oncoming target. Once she snapped the spear into a vertical position, the archers fired their weapons.

Arrows flew out of the fortress windows and the whistling of the thin missiles raced overhead at the oncoming ancient army of the undead from Dovenar Civil War. It was the first strike at the front line and hopefully would stop enough of them to slow the rest.

The arrows landed on their targets, lodging into the chests, arms, and stomachs of the enemy with absolutely no effect. Aside from a slight hesitation from the impacts, they showed no signs of slowing.

Kaya was confused by the reaction and signaled for another volley of arrows to be launched. The second round had the same effect.

"Know your opponent!" Santorray yelled from the bridge.

Ignoring him, she prepared her guards for the rushing army. "Stand strong! Lean into those shields! Brace those pikes! Don't let them through!"

Her guards did as they were told as the ground rumbled from the oncoming horde of partially flesh-covered soldiers.

"Know your risk!" Santorray called to her again as he continued to stand on the bridge with his arms folded across his chest.

"We've got this!" she yelled back to him as the armies began to clash. "HOLD YOUR POSITIONS!"

The crashing sound of the undead slamming into the wall of shields was deafening as Kaya and her troops were pushed backward. Well-positioned pikes impaled enemy soldiers one after another until there were so many on each pike that Kaya's guards could not control their weapons. They were forced to release them or be pulled away from their position.

Gaps in Kaya's front line gave way for the enemy to fight their way toward the fortress. "Defend our home!" she yelled, as she launched herself forward to fill one of the openings.

Her men and women did as they were told and yelled back in unison, "Defend our home!"

Kaya reached the opening and was immediately attacked by one of the undead. With both hands, she thrust her spear forward into the Dovenar warrior. Her blade struck hard and ripped through his stomach and out his back. It was exactly what she wanted so she could move onto her next opponent.

The man screamed; however, he was only shoved back a bit and showed no signed of stopping his attack. The loss of his stomach did not seem to be a factor in his ability to fight, and he lunged at her.

Stepping back, Kaya pulled her spear out of her enemy and used the blade to stab him time and time again in his chest, in his arms, and even through his mouth and head. Nothing was working.

"Know your capability!" was heard from the blothrud who continued to observe her progress.

Spinning her spear around, she took the morning star end and began bashing her opponent over the head until his skull completely caved in. With a final whack to his face from the metal spiked ball, his head was completely removed, and he fell backward.

"It's their heads," she muttered as she was determining how to stop them. She could see her guards were having the same issue, so she began to shout new instructions. But before she did, a hand grabbed her leg and pulled her off her feet. Slapping the ground hard with her back, she found the headless Dovenar warrior crawling up on her to continue their fight. "No!" she said with a bit of denial as she struggled to believe her eyes.

Leaping forward, the headless man landed upon her as internal organs splatted out onto her and a thick, dark liquid from his neck ran down upon her face.

Attempting to push him off, her hands went right through his body, and she ended up holding handfuls of rotted flesh ripped from his body.

The battle continued around her. Her forces were having the same experiences. Nothing seemed to be working, and those on the ground were being stepped on.

Kaya was furious with the situation and pushed the Dovenar warrior over so that she was on top of him. Grabbing his arm, she ripped it off before standing back up and shoving her boot through his other shoulder to separate the other arm from his body. She then kicked her boot through the opening she had made with her spear, causing his chest to roll away from his pelvis and legs.

After her first undead was disassembled and unable to harm anyone, another undead attacked her from behind. She swung her first opponent's arm at the new enemy's face twice before she had time to reach for her own weapon. In doing so, she found that others were standing on it, so she began pushing them off to utilize it. By the time she was able to pull her spear off the ground, the second undead had come up to her from behind and swung his sword at her neck.

Turning, she found the enemy's blade racing down at her face, only to be stopped be a second blade from the side. The saber saving her was owned by someone she knew all too well.

"Know your objective," Santorray said as he pushed the undead's sword back far enough to decapitate the ancient man. The blothrud then kicked the Dovenar Warrior to the ground before glancing at Kaya. "You're welcome."

Kaya spun her weapon around and instinctively stood back-to-back with her friend. It was a fighting position they had practiced many times. "What are you doing here? We have this!"

Grabbing another undead warrior by the head, the blothrud crushed the skull with one hand while slicing off his legs with one stroke of his blade. "I'm pretty sure you gave me the signal to help."

Slapping the next threat with her morning star, she was starting to understand what was needed to stop the enemy from attacking. "What are you talking about?"

"I saw you waving an arm."

"It wasn't my arm! It was my enemy's!"

Santorray shrugged. "I didn't specify that it had to be yours."

"You just can't sit back and watch, can you?"

"It's against my nature," he said with a grin.

"Cut off their heads and arms!" she yelled to her guards as she continued to fight.

"That doesn't kill them," Santorray replied.

"Of course it does." Glancing down at the undead on the ground, she realized their legs were still kicking and the rolling heads were still biting at her people's ankles. "This is insane! How do we kill them?"

Santorray continued to casually deflect attacks and crush the warriors near him. "You can't."

Kaya was flabbergasted at the comment. She never expected to hear the mighty Santorray say such a thing. "How is this possible?" she asked while keeping up the fight.

"Know your opponents. During the Dovenar Civil War, this army was cursed by Darkmere's Alchemists to never die. They simply can't be killed."

Kaya accepted his words as truth. "Then we must retreat." Between swings of her spear's blade and morning star, she glanced back at the bridge to find it raised. "What have you done?"

"I ordered them to lift it."

"WHY?" She realized they were now stranded on the battlefield with no option to retreat.

"Know your risk," he reminded her. "I wasn't there to protect the bridge, so it was best to close it."

"But now we're trapped out here."

"Know your objective," he said to her as they continued to fight back-to-back.

She was not in the mood for his lessons but followed his lead anyway. "Our objective is to destroy this army."

"No, that is how you've chosen to meet the objective."

Kaya was frustrated as she kicked away a severed arm that grabbed her leg. "Our objective is to protect our home. Protect the fortress."

Santorray nodded even though he knew she was facing the other way. "Know your capabilities. What do we have that can accomplish this while knowing we can't kill them?"

"I don't think we can ask them to leave, nor can we scare them off."

"But you do have the capability and resources to dispose of them."

Kaya spun her weapon and decapitated another undead before working on his limbs. She took momentary glances around her to see what she had to help her. It was then that she glanced at the waterfall and then followed the flow of the water through the trench and over the next falls. "The river!" she yelled to her guards. "Remove whatever limbs you can and then push them into the river! They will be washed down into the distant valley. They can't walk back up here if they don't have legs!"

Busy alerting her men and women to the plan, Kaya did not see an undead soldier leaping past a few of her men until it was nearly too late. She pulled her spear forward, and the blade impaled him in the chest, which of course had little effect on the undead.

Making matters worse, the blade lodged between his ribs and became stuck in his body.

"Damn!" She grunted as she tugged and twisted her weapon to break it free. With her spear locked in his chest, she had no way of using it to fight off the additional undead as they filed their way in through the growing gaps in her force's front line. "Santorray! I need a blade!"

Without hesitation, he made one fluid movement, stabbing a Dovenar warrior in the face and then tossing his blade over his shoulder to her. "Heads up!"

With a quick glance up, she saw the hilt coming down toward her. Grabbing it, she utilized the momentum of its fall to swing out at her opponent. What she did not expect was that Santorray had left the head of an undead on the end of his sword. Regardless, it did not stop her as the two heads collided and brain matter sprayed out in every direction, including all over her face.

"Seriously? You couldn't have cleaned your blade before sharing?"

"I thought you'd appreciate the gift," he replied with a smile as he crushed the next warrior with his bare hands. "Now you can't say I've never given you anything."

"Well, I'm about to return the favor."

"Really? And what would that be?" Looking over his shoulder, he saw what she was talking about. The leader of the undead army was closing in on the front line while riding his large undead chuttlebeast.

Standing nearly eight feet tall at their shoulders, these massive four-legged beasts normally roamed the O'Sid Fields. Long, clumpy, matted wool covered a chuttlebeast's entire body, including its large cube-like head. This specific specimen was missing large chunks of its body and face, exposing the cracked bone structure underneath. It was a terrifying sight to see, but even more frightening was that it was racing forward, trampling the undead warriors in its way to reach Kaya's guards. The momentum and its mass could easily push everyone in its path into the river. The undead leader riding upon the beast wished to do as much damage as possible.

"Damn!" It was Santorray's time to say it. Knowing that he was the only one that had any chance of dealing with the oncoming creature, he pushed his way forward toward the chuttlebeast. "I hope you've been compromised enough..." he said under his breath as he pushed the Dovenar warriors out of his way, "...for me to shatter what's left of you!"

Kaya and her guards continued to remove at least one leg of each Dovenar soldier before pushing or tossing them into the river where they were quickly swept downstream and over the waterfall. The tactic was working, and they were starting to make quick gains from the strategy.

Swatting his arms back and forth to knock the undead out of his way, the blothrud increased his speed while the chuttlebeast did the same, and Korin struggled to hold on as they approached the frontline. They raced at full speed until the blothrud and chuttlebeast crashed head-to-head with a thunderous explosion of sounds and debris. Korin Swiph was thrown high over the frontlines, splashed into the raging river, and was washed away. Flesh and bones flew in every direction and rained down upon the landscape in a heavy spattering of droplets and chunks of body parts. Rotted organs and shards of broken bones littered the area as the dust slowly settled.

Kaya finished tossing another torso into the river before searching for Santorray's outcome. The carcass of the beast was splayed open as clumps of flesh hung onto the remaining bones of its giant ribcage. The skull of the massive creature was partially intact but was now resting where the creature's stomach once was. The blothrud had hit it so hard that the beast's head had been pushed back through its own body.

Searching for a sign of her friend's fate, she saw the chuttlebeast's skull begin to move and then rise out of the creature's distorted and devastated body. As it rose, Kaya could see the body of Santorray standing up and then lifting the beast's skull off his own head. It appeared that Santorray was dazed, but he would survive.

***

Hours later, music was played and battle songs were sung by Kaya and her team of men and women. The wounded had been cared for, and those who could celebrate did so with great pleasure.

Santorray raised the broken chuttlebeast skull, and everyone cheered at the victory for them all. They had beaten their enemy, protected their home, and sent their problems downstream. A grand celebration was in full force as they congratulated and teased one another about the events of the day. Life was good.

The blothrud hung the hideous skull on the wall. Clumps of wool were still stuck in the bone's cracks, and the jaw was completely missing. Despite the grotesque image, it was a trophy of the day. Santorray laughed as he sat back down to have a drink with the fighters.

Kaya walked over, hopped up, and sat on top of his table, nearly knocking over his mug. "I learned something about you today," she said with a loud and proud voice for all to hear.

Santorray chuckled as he looked out at the men and women who had overheard her. "Please enlighten us."

"You talk a big talk, but you can't measure up to your own words."

Her guards howled and laughed at her comment as they waited for him to respond.

One of the blothrud's eyebrows lifted as he glared at her. "I'm pretty sure I saved your life out there today."

"True," she said loudly for all to hear. "But you've told me and my team on many occasions that if anyone ever threatened your life, you'd cram their head up their backside."

Santorray laughed. "I stand by those words," he said as he pointed at a few of the men he had had past arguments with. "That includes you, Pax!" he said with a grin.

Kaya smiled. "And yet you were only able to cram that chuttlebeast's head down to his stomach! You completely missed his ass!"

A roar of laughter at the blothrud's expense filled the hall; even Santorray joined in.

Kaya then jumped upon the table, stood tall, and raised her goblet to make a speech. "To Santorray! The hero of the day! We have hated your training sessions, but you've made us better warriors for it!"

"Hear! Hear!" her guards yelled in agreement.

After taking a sip of her wine, she wiped away what was left on her lips. "To Santorray! You have left us mentally and physically stronger than when you first arrived. We will miss you!"

"Hear! Hear!" the crowd yelled again before Pax shouted, "But not too much!"

Laughter filled the hall as they continued the festive occasion.

Kaya kicked out her legs and landed on her butt with a bounce on the table directly in front of Santorray. "I wish you well, my friend." The new conversation was now between them and not to be loud or lighthearted about.

"Thanks, Kaya. But I haven't left on my final mission just yet."

Her smile became a bit solemn as she nodded. "I just got word from the master before I joined the celebration. His son is ready for his last lesson, and his nursemaid, Nutrix, has begun preparing for travel. You're leaving tomorrow morning on your final task. This may be the last time we see you."

"I see." A sense of disappointment was evident in his eyes.

"You're going to have to learn to step back and not to get involved this time."

"I know what's needed," he reassured her.

"It's not in your nature," she reminded him. "You must fight that blothrud urge of yours if you want this final mission to be successful."

"I will," he said in a cavalier tone. But upon seeing her skeptical facial response, he changed his attitude to be more sincere. "I will fight my instincts to resolve issues. The master's son must learn to do this on his own if I wish to be successful on this concluding mission."

Accepting his words, she lifted her goblet toward him. "It's been an honor."

Taking a deep breath, Santorray nodded and tapped his mug against her goblet. "The honor has been all mine."

Chapter 2
3 Months Later

The small peaceful woodland village of Bentree had quickly changed from a normally calm environment into absolute chaos hours after the sun had set on the thatch-roofed structures. A fight inside the local tavern caused an oil lantern to crash upon the wall. The flame chased the stream of oil up the wall, erupted within seconds, and quickly engulfed the entire establishment. Blazing fragments of debris drifted their way to the attached buildings. The dry wooden beams were welcome tinder to the hungry flames that spread without shame of gluttony.

Agitated at the sight before him, Santorray stood on the grassy knoll just outside of the small village. The thin lips along his dragon-like face lifted enough to expose his dangerous teeth. His muscles became tense down his thick dragon-like neck, across his wide muscular shoulders, and down his red human torso. Both of his giant wolf-like legs moved uneasily as he restrained himself from running in to provide rescue. Unfortunately, he knew it was too late. "I swear, when this mission is over, I'm going find myself a remote place in the forest, so I don't have to deal with people like him anymore," he grumbled to himself.

"You told him to accomplish his goals in his own way," Nutrix said. She was a large cat, about the size of a lioness. However, instead of hair she was covered in scales that she could alter to change their color. When done right, it allowed her to nearly blend in with her surroundings. Unfortunately, she was an elder brandercat who now struggled to have enough control to completely disappear.

"If he'd listened, he'd know my proven techniques would serve him well and minimize casualties." A low growl followed his comment as he stared out at the anarchy within the village.

Flames twisted high into the air above the roofs as locals desperately collected their belongings before escaping their homes. The fire swept across the village like a wind across the grasslands. There was no stopping the blaze as it flew from home to home and shop to shop.

"Make sure you're not taking out your aggression on him when the issue is your own," said Nutrix.

"My own?" He pointed at the flames. "In what way is this my doing?"

"Your attitude changes every time you're not physically involved in a mission. You become overly critical and intolerant. Yet you act completely different when you're on the battlefield with Kaya."

"She didn't burn down an entire village to gather answers to a few questions!" Santorray argued. "Besides, Kaya is willing to learn from me and fight by my side. It's nearly impossible to make a change without being involved in the actions taking place."

Nutrix was slightly disappointed in his reply. "You don't have to be someone's master or comrade to make a difference. You just need to care and be there for them."

A large blast shook the ground as one of the largest buildings exploded and its front wall tumbled forward into the main square. It was followed by a second and third blast as debris was sent soaring into the dirt streets. Flaming lumber struck and ignited more homes and the local stable, as every structure became involved. The village would be a total loss by the time the flames were extinguished.

Men and women ran for their lives. Some carried their children, some raced away on wagons filled with neighbors, while others fell in the streets and sobbed in despair at the sight of the destruction.

Clenching his fist, Santorray watched the tragic scene play out before him. He knew if he charged in to help, the locals would run in fear of him. Blothruds, like most Del'Unday, were seen as evil Altered Creatures in these parts. Even Nutrix would have been viewed as a threat. "I'm going to knock him so hard he won't wake up for a month. I'm done with him!"

"The harder you discipline him, the farther you push him away. He's not like you, but he can eventually learn if you hang on to your trust in him and let him grow at his own pace."

"Sometimes hanging on does more damage than letting go," he replied in a softer voice before they both became quiet. As they watcher the blazing village, the moon rose from behind the distant mountains. It was a somber reminder of how much he missed being away from everything and everyone. The more he got involved, the more drama seemed to overtake his life.

As the two Del'Unday stood silent, a silhouette of a short male human walked directly toward them from the out-of-control flames. The person was not running in fear like the villagers. Instead, he had the casual stride of someone who was confident in his actions.

"GIN!" Santorray roared at the sight of the young man approaching.

"Easy, Santorray." Nutrix stepped slightly forward and in front of him, even though she could not truly stop him if he wanted to charge forward. "Let's hear what he has to say before you crucify him."

The young man was in his early teens and dressed in dirty tan leather from his neck to his toes. An unruly mess of dark brown hair fell to his shoulders and covered most of his face. He intentionally hid his eyes behind his thick hair like a mask to give himself an advantage.

"MMMboy!" A deep rumble proceeded the word 'boy' in a way that gave it more weight. Santorray had learned that technique from his father without realizing it. "What have you done?"

As the young man got closer, it became apparent that he was leading another man by a rope which was tied around his wrists and his neck. Yanking on the rope, he forced the elder man to stumble forward to keep up with him. The bald man had several tattoos on his head and a scorched gray robe that was saturated with alcohol, and blood from their brawl. He was clearly intoxicated and unsure what was going on. "I succeeded in my task," Gin replied as he approached and pushed his captive to the ground before him.

The elder villager was cut and burned. His hands shook from the shock of what had happened and fear of what would happen next as he lay before the massive blothrud.

Santorray gazed down at the old man only for a moment before glaring back at Gin. "The task was NOT to destroy the village!" It was against a blothrud's instincts to hold back his anger, but Santorray forced himself to do so. "You have once again failed to use any of the skills I've taught you. You give no thought to what your actions will do and who will be affected by them. I don't understand why you refuse to employ the skills I have taught you!"

Tossing down the rope that was tied to his prisoner, Gin marched up to Santorray. It was rare indeed to witness a human standing comfortably next to any blothrud. To see this young man march aggressively toward this massive blothrud, who towered at least a yard over him, was unimaginable.

Nutrix stepped on the rope before the villager decided to make a run for it. Her growl to him kept the prisoner tight to the ground.

In a fit of anger, Gin pounded a fist into the side of Santorray's stomach several times. Although it had no effect on the blothrud, it made him feel better. "Damn you! No matter what I do, it's never good enough for you! I can't do what you do. I'm not a blothrud! I must find other ways to get things done. When I do, you have never told me you're proud of me for thinking on my feet or finding alternatives. I've never given up! I always find a way! Not once have you praised me for this!"

Santorray reached down with both hands and grabbed Gin, lifted him to eye level, and spun him around to face the village. "If you'd pull that hair out of your face, you'd see that you have destroyed the lives of every villager. Who knows how many didn't make it out alive? You're reckless!" After tossing him back to the ground, Santorray's hands became fists. "I'm not asking you to be a blothrud. I'm teaching you skills to accomplish your goals regardless of your species."

Rolling back up to his feet, Gin pointed at the villager he had captured. "I accomplished my goal!"

"Your father wants the Terra King stopped. The king's influence grows like a plague across these lands. As my final training session with you, I am to have you find out where he lives and what vulnerabilities he has so that your father can use this knowledge to bring the Terra King to justice." Peering down at the pathetic old man lying on the ground, Santorray shook his head. "This is not the Terra King. You have destroyed this village and sacrificed many lives for nothing."

"I didn't say he was the Terra King!" Pulling his sword out of its sheath, he pointed it at the blothrud to command respect. "I didn't ask for this mission, nor did I ask you to train me. That was a deal you and my father made. I understand his reasoning, but the only benefit you seem to get out of it is the opportunity to belittle me and set me up to fail." Wiping some sweat from his brow, he corrected his stance against his opponent. "You've been training me for years, and I have learned more than you give me credit for. I am no longer the child you originally took under your wing. I am an adult with years of experience, and I expect you to start treating me as such."

"An adult? Years of experience? Mboy, I was taught by the most powerful warriors in the lands. They beat me down to a bloody pile of flesh more times than I could count. But I crawled away, bound my wounds, and then got back up to fight them again and again until I was able to outmatch them. I was never praised for success, nor did I need to be. Warriors do not crave approval from others. We celebrate our victories and then move on. I have led crusades, wars, and missions that would give you nightmares. I am the only one who has ever stood up against the immortal Lord Ergrauth and lived to tell about it!" He paused as he gazed at his student. "I have decades upon decades of experience. You've only been alive for less than one and a half. Yet, you stand before me telling me you are fully trained?"

Gin's hair parted enough to expose his face, which was tight with frustration. "I'm not a child any longer. I've learned what I've needed. I demand you treat me with the respect I deserve."

Nutrix stepped in to try to calm the tension. "We are never too old to learn more. Perhaps we all could be more open to learning from each other."

Santorray stayed focused on the young man before him. "Know your opponent, the Terra King and his allies! Know your objective; learn the king's tactics and weaknesses. Understand your risks; you could be killed if they discover your plans. Utilize your capabilities; use your brain to find out what you can without alerting your opponent of your plans!" He pointed at the village's flames reaching high over the forest trees. "You have just sent your enemy a signal that you're here search for the Terra King! People in that tavern will tell others of your questions and your brawl that led to their homes being burnt down."

"I know all of that and I took the risk! It was mine to take!"

"Your mission was to gather intelligence so your father can stop the Terra King before his power grows beyond anyone's ability to stop him. You came back with a bar-rat of an old man who is not the Terra King nor a member of his key council. And in the process, you destroyed a village. What respect is deserved?"

The young man stood up straight. "You were the one who suggested I go into this village. We both knew the Terra King was not here for me to find. This wasted effort is on you, not me. However, this old man has the knowledge we need to find the Terra King. I felt it was worth enlisting him into our little happy family so he can lead us to the king. This way we don't have to continue to roam aimlessly across the countryside like we have been. His knowledge will save us months, but that's on me. Shall I free him so we can do it your way?"

"Mboy, you're fortunate I'm not my father. He would have struck you down by the end of that first sentence." Stretching his tense neck, Santorray continued, "Once again, your intent and goal were correct, but the end doesn't justify the means."

"It did this time. What you don't know is that these people are already under the Terra King's power. The village had already been infected and needed to be destroyed before it spread to the next village."

"That was not your mission, nor was it your call to make." Glancing at Nutrix, he could see her giving him a look that said he had made his point and needed to move on. Taking a deep breath, Santorray addressed his student's hostage, whose saturated clothes smelled of alcohol. "Where is the Terra King?"

"My name is Wittig. I'm the local—"

"I don't care who you are or what you do. Just tell me where the Terra King is!"

The tied-up man cowered back a bit before answering. "I don't know."

There was a moment of silence as Santorray slowly turned to Gin.

"I didn't say he knew where the Terra King was," Gin said before being questioned. "I said he has knowledge we need in order to find him."

Santorray growled at the villager before him. "What knowledge?"

Wittig crawled backward again in a weak attempt to distance himself from the blothrud. "I have children. Please, let me go." Between the fear of being mauled by the beast standing over him and being intoxicated, he struggled to stay focused.

Santorray placed one of his huge wolf-like feet onto the man's chest before extending his claws to press against the man's skin. "If you have any desire to see your family again, you will tell us what we need to know. Where is the Terra King?"

Feeling the claws starting to cut into his chest, Wittig screamed out a name. "Javolo!"

"Javolo? I've never heard of such a place." He pressed a bit harder onto the man's chest.

"It's not a place. It's a woman. She works directly for the Terra King. She arranges his travels and is the only one who knows where he will be at any given time."

"Where do we find her?"

Waiting for the pressure to relax was not working to his favor, so he needed to answer before the pressure was too tight to talk. "Javolo is often seen in the village of Sandwell. You should find her there. She knows everything there is to know about the Terra King." His final words trailed off as the pressure on his chest was too much to stand.

Santorray gave it some thought as he removed his foot from Wittig's body. "Untie him and set him free," he told his student.

"What? No!" Gin protested.

"What are your other options?" the blothrud replied. "Kill him for doing nothing more than being in the wrong place at the wrong time? Send him on his way."

Unhappy about the order, Gin moved the tip of his sword toward the man. "No. He's our prisoner."

"He's your prisoner. Not ours."

Gin was not willing to give in quite yet. "We need to take him with us."

"Why? He's an old drunk you found in a tavern."

The drunk old man interrupted their conversation. "My name is Wittig."

"We don't care!" Santorray and Gin said at the same time before returning to their conversation.

Gin pulled in closer to his teacher. "He could alert Javolo that we're coming."

"We can be there and gone long before he would even arrive to cause us issues. Besides, who's going to believe this old fool? I doubt he'll even remember us in the morning."

"All it would take is one person to feel it was worth warning the king's officials. People are stupid. They'll believe any rumor they hear. We can't take the chance."

Santorray sighed at the thought before turning back to the old man and nudging him. "Have you met Javolo?"

The old man's eyes nervously flickered. "Few are allowed to approach her and have a conversation with her, but I have seen her from a distance," he replied with a nod.

"In Sandwell?"

He nodded again.

"How far is it?"

"Less than a day's walk."

Santorray growled at the idea of dragging the man with them on their trek. "Gin?"

"Yes?"

"He's your responsibility. You can share your rations with him if you see fit. And I don't want to hear any of his complaints, so make sure you keep him quiet."

Gin gave an evil grin. "I could remove his tongue to ensure he won't speak."

"Mboy, why must you take things to extremes? You don't have to mutilate him. Just keep an eye on him."

Chapter 3
The Plan

Hours after leaving the village of Bentree, the travelers came to a stop and made camp in a small clearing within the forest. The campfire brushed its yellowish light on the surrounding trees as the blothrud, the brandercat, and the two humans prepared to rest for the night.

Gin finished tying Wittig up against a tree before pulling out a long knife from a sheath attached to one of his knee-high leather boots.

Wittig's eyes grew as the light from the campfire reflected off the clean and sharp blade that was being held about a foot away from his face. "What do you intend to do with that?"

Gin gave the old villager a devious smile. "I plan to use it to slice off some meat for my meal tonight." Moving the blade closer until it rested against Wittig's nose, he asked, "Where do you think I should start?"

Shaking with fear, the man attempted to pull away. "Please don't. I beg you!"

Gin coughed out a laugh at the man as he pulled the blade back before standing. "Too easy. You're such a coward." Turning, he headed to the campfire to test one of the rodents that was being cooked over the flames.

Baffled, the villager realized it only was a joke. "You're sick, boy. What's wrong with you?"

Gin stopped in his tracks and spun around. "What did you say?" He gave Wittig no time to respond before stepping back over and starting a verbal assault while waving the blade at Wittig. "You don't know me! You don't know what I've been through! I was born with a death sentence on my head, and I've had to spend my life learning how to stay alive. I didn't have the luxury of growing up like others and playing games with friends! My games were tests to see if I could survive an attack!" His face was flush with passion as he stood imposingly over the man. "So, if my joke caused you distress, it's because you have spent too many years sitting on a barstool not having to face life and death situations. It's because you're weak! It's not because I'm sick. It's because you're a coward!"

After taking a few deeps breaths to calm down, Gin lowered his blade and relaxed his stance. "You don't know me," he repeated. "And it's best that you don't get to know me." Turning, he walked back to the fire and stabbed one of the cooked sandrats with his blade and lifted it up out of the flames before marching off into the dark to eat alone.

Santorray and Nutrix had watched the entire event and knew it was best to let him play it out; otherwise the scene would have grown even bigger.

Thankful Gin had left, the old villager leaned back against the tree. "You two need to get that boy some help. He's insane."

Santorray shot the man an irritated glare. "Keep your mouth shut if you treasure your tongue staying intact."

Wittig stiffened up from the warning and opened his mouth to protest, but slowly closed it as he could tell the blothrud was not making an idle threat.

"I'll go talk to him," Nutrix said as she stood on all four legs and walked into the darkness, following Gin.

The young man had not walked far; just enough to give himself some privacy. Biting down on the flame-cooked sandrat, he pulled off a leg and began eating in peace.

"No one can understand what you've been through, Gin." Nutrix's calming voice was still a few yards away as she slowly approached. "Lashing out at others for not knowing only hurts your cause."

He found her words amusing. "How could it hurt what already is a disaster of a life?"

"Your life isn't a disaster."

"It sure feels like it." He took another bite of his meal before continuing. "Even my birth was a bad omen. How many children are cursed and told they will be murdered before becoming an adult? I wish I could just start my life over with a family that actually wanted me."

"Your father does want you, and he has done what he can to prevent your death from happening prematurely."

"I wouldn't have been cursed in the first place if it hadn't been for him."

She knew he blamed others for many issues, but Nutrix did not want to rehash that conversation with him again. "You're allowed to be angry or disappointed. You're allowed to be scared and even cry when needed. But if I've taught you anything, you know that you're not allowed to give up."

Gin swallowed his mouthful and sighed as he looked up at the moon. "Every day, Nutrix."

"Every day?"

"Yes. You've been with me every day of my life for as far back as I can remember."

"I have. I cared for you. I fed you. I have raised you."

Nodding, he kept his view up into the night's sky. "And every night I look up and wonder if this would be the last night that I would live to see the moon and the stars. Was it the last day that I would be comforted by you when I was scared? Was it my last day to become something special to someone?"

"You are something special. I know. I have been fortunate enough to have raised you."

"Yes, you have given your life to do so," he said as he turned and gazed out from under his long hair into her eyes. "But as much as I appreciate you and all that you have done for me, I have always felt completely abandoned."

"Why?"

A sad grin grew upon his face. "As you said, you raised me. Not my mother; she died giving birth to me. So, I basically killed her."

"Gin, you can't blame yourself for that."

He continued as though he did not hear her. "I wasn't raised by my father either. He was too busy with land disputes, conquests, and trying to govern his people."

"He has many important duties."

"I should have been one of those important duties." His voice was stressed but contained. "Once he knew I had no future chance to become an adult and oversee his lands and become his successor..." His words lodged in his throat as he attempted to cough the rest of his thoughts out. "...he tossed me to the side and waited for the day that he could hear of my curse being fulfilled."

"You know that's not true."

"Do I?" Gin's voice struck harder than before.

Nutrix took a moment to allow him to relax before she approached and lay down near him. She then motioned to him to sit and lean against her like he used to when he was a child.

Reluctant at first, he wrapped the remains of his meal in a cloth and sat beside her. Once there, it felt natural to lean up against her. "I miss this," he said quietly with closed eyes.

"I do as well, my child." Once comfortable, she continued, "Your father was very selective as to who would raise his son. In fact, I had to work very hard to be granted the opportunity."

"Really? You never told me that."

"It's true. From the moment I saw you as an infant, my motherly instincts kicked in and I fell in love. I knew you were something special, and I had to be a part of your life."

"Special? Even as an infant?"

"Yes; I can't exactly explain. I could tell there was an essence inside you that I had never felt before."

"An essence?"

"An old essence. As you know, upon death our souls are taken to the underworld of Della Estovia. However, sometimes our essence is instead passed on to a new life that is allowed to learn new lessons and complete unfinished tasks. You just seemed like an old soul from the moment I laid eyes on you. Perhaps your soul is here to resolve an issue."

A smile grew and then faded from his lips. "An old soul that has been cursed?"

She nodded. "We all have different paths to walk in this life. Yours might be to defeat this curse and go on to create great things or influence the world somehow."

"I doubt that."

"Don't. Your father has provided you with the finest caregivers in the land to ensure your health. He's provided the most scholarly educators to teach you how to survive nearly any situation. You've been trained to fight and defend yourself since you were old enough to walk. As if that wasn't enough, he hired the most powerful warrior in the land, who has spent the past several years passing on his knowledge to you."

"I am as prepared as I can be to fight off the threat when it occurs. But I still lack having a father who is there for me. You and Santorray are the closest thing I have to family, and you will be leaving me soon."

"True," she agreed with a slight bow of her head. "Once you have completed this mission, your father will take over the reins of your upbringing. He will teach you what he knows."

"I'll believe it when I see it."

"He has given his word that if you complete this last mission, he will do this."

"There is always one more mission or one more reason why he doesn't have time for me."

"Then don't give him one. Take what you've learned and finish this task so cleanly that he has no choice but to agree you are ready for him and have earned his time."

Nodding his head, he peered over at her eyes while still leaning up against her. "You're right. I will exceed his expectations and prove to him that I am worthy of standing by his side and learning his profession."

The two took the opportunity to relax together like old times and simply stared into the night sky as a slight breeze ruffled the leaves across the tops of the canopy.

Chapter 4
Sandwell

Pulling a branch out of the way, Santorray peered out from the woods to see a small farming village as the morning's light breeze carried the scent of freshly baked bread. As with most of the regional villages, this one had the same basic layout with a main street for shops and a tavern. Most had a stable for animals on one end, and most people lived above or behind where they worked. At least one water well was usually located on the main street and sometimes in the dead center of an open area as a central gathering place, which was true for this village. A few additional homes had been built nearby, showing that the population had been growing.

The most unusual component about this given village was the recent construction of a temple. Such buildings were expensive and usually only for large cities. Although this specific temple was rather small, and it had been positioned at the base of a large clamshell seating area. Extending from the front doors of the building, a stage had been built to provide a venue to address a large gathering.

"Gin!" Santorray called out to get his attention. "Bring the old man here." He continued to watch the locals go about their business while he waited for Gin to carry out his orders.

With ropes binding his ankles and wrists, the man was slowly prodded to the edge of the woods to see the village. "That's Sandwell," he coughed out from a dry throat. "That's where you'll find Javolo, when she's here."

"When she's here? She doesn't live here?"

Wittig, wishing for the umpteenth time that Gin would share some food or drink, squinted from the bright sun. "No. She doesn't stay in one place long. Nor does the Terra King. Her caravan comes here often and sometimes stays overnight." Feeling he had performed his function, he made a request. "May I now have some water or wine? A handful of bread would do nicely as well."

Ignoring the request, Santorray raised his muzzle into the air and pulled in a strong waft of various scents. "I don't smell any fresh wagon grease or faralopes needed to pull them. Where, specifically, does she stay?" Santorray asked. His gaze never left the community and landed upon the man making requests.

Wittig was impressed with the blothrud's ability to distinguish various smells from such a distance. "The Terra King's most faithful stay within that small temple. At sunset, the torches will be lit out front and the king's words will be read to the locals. If it's not Javolo, then it will be one of the king's other devoted followers."

"Every night?"

"Yes, they hold this ceremony at dusk each day," the old man replied. "That is all I know. Now please let me return to my family. I must see if they are safe."

Santorray gave his words some thought before responding. "Gin, escort your captive back to his village. We can't release him here to warn the locals. Hurry and return here before nightfall."

Shocked by the orders, Gin stood up straight. "I can't risk it. I must be here in time for the ceremony. Nutrix can take him back."

"Nutrix is getting too old for these long treks." The blothrud glanced from the brandercat to the old villager restrained by several ropes. "Besides, you brought him into this, so you will put him back where he belongs."

"This is my mission!" Gin raised his voice to assert his authority. "I will not miss my opportunity to prove my worth to my father while escorting a barstool squatter through the woods."

"Then I suggest you start moving if you plan to be back here in time for the ceremony."

"No! It's too far to walk to Bentree and return in time. I need to be the one to capture and interrogate Javolo, not you. I must prove my abilities to show my training is complete." Gin stood up straight with his shoulders pulled back. He clearly felt the need to fight for the opportunity before them.

Santorray studied his student for a few moments. "I respect your drive to carry out your mission. But you also need to honor your commitment to your hostage. Take him back and return here as quickly as possible. I will spend the day observing and identify any opportunities to enter the temple from the far side. When you return, we will discuss the options and you will carry out the plan. We don't even know if Javolo will arrive today, so we shall focus on cleaning up loose ends and surveillance so we can plan for your next step." Bowing his head slightly toward Gin, he continued, "This is your mission to prove your worth. I have no desire to take this from you, so get moving."

With a deep sigh, Gin knew the call had been made and quickly gathered rations for his journey, untied the ropes around Wittig's ankles, and then headed back the way they had come.

After watching them disappear into the distance, Nutrix eased her way up next to Santorray, who was still checking out the details of the village before them. "I'm not that old. I could have made that trip back to the last village."

"It wasn't about that. It's about learning to take responsibility. Gin had promised to set him free once he showed us this village. Releasing him here would allow the old man to enter this town and warn them. The boy must learn the ramifications of his actions and commitments."

"He's barely a teenager. You're expecting too much from him."

Santorray scoffed at the comment. "I was fighting in wars by the time I was his age."

"He's not a blothrud, nor is he one of the Del'Unday species. The Dark Oracle designed us to be ready for such things at an early age. And here we are, after thousands of years, still able to leave the nest within a decade."

Crossing his arms, he stood up a bit straighter with pride for the traits of his species.

"Gin is but a human," she reminded him. "Human children are helpless and frail for much longer than most species. It has only been during these past few years that he has grown to be emotionally and physically healthy enough to grow towards being self-reliant."

"Because of my training."

"Yes," she said with a nod. "You have molded him into a warrior."

"No, not yet. He still has much to learn."

"Agreed. But you must exercise patience, Santorray. You can only push him so far before he snaps."

Grinning at memories of his own training, he could see the stark differences. "When I was young, the goal of our trainers was to force us to snap. Once they broke us, it was our resilience and fortitude to fight back that made us warriors. We learned the important lessons from being struck down and having to climb back up on our own. That made us strong. Those times separated the strong from the weak." Puffing his chest out a bit, he recalled the successes of his past. "We learn more from rising up from failures than we do from being protected from danger."

Nutrix listened quietly before speaking. "I have never lived in our homelands, so I cannot speak to our ways. However, I've spent my life around humans, and they do not always react in the black and white ways that you suggest. They are complex creatures that can take a lifetime to learn how to control their feelings."

"He doesn't have a lifetime. Nor do I."

"Please be patient with Gin until his emotional growth catches up with his physical growth."

Lowering his muzzle, he lifted an eyebrow at her in curiosity.

"You suggest that the Del'Unday either overcome and become leaders or back down and become subservient, correct?"

Santorray nodded in agreement of the concept.

"A human, such as Gin, may react in those same ways you suggest. But when under pressure, they have been known to react in many other ways as well."

"Such as?"

"When broken, he could become bitter and resentful to the one who broke him. Instead of fighting to overcome and prove himself, he may fight even harder to become powerful enough to defeat his master or teacher out of revenge."

"Ah, he would fight for superiority. This is common within the Del'Unday. It's how we grow within our military ranks."

"No, he would not be looking to grow or to climb any ladder. It would be strictly out of anger and the desire to hurt you for breaking him."

"I have not seen this in Gin."

"I'm not saying he is at that point. But I am saying that if you push him too hard, this could be an outcome."

A slight grin lifted his right cheek. "Let him try. I am not afraid. It would be a good test of his skills."

Shaking her head, she was disappointed in the response. "Your concern should be that you would have lost the young man that you have been raising like a son. That's the danger I see before you, and I feel the icy blade of his disdain for your actions would burn within your soul for the rest of your years."

The softening of his facial muscles gave away that he was beginning to understand what Nutrix was trying to teach him.

Chapter 5
Taking Wittig Home

Several hours into his journey through the forest, Gin was getting nervous about making the entire round trip in time for him to see the ceremony in Sandwell. He had never seen the Terra King's rituals and was curious as to why people blindly followed a man that rarely made appearances over all the territory he controlled. However, Wittig moved at a slow pace, causing the trek to take longer than he had hoped. The likelihood of getting back in time was fading away.

"Stop!" Gin ordered the old man. "Give me one reason why I shouldn't slit your throat and be done with you so I can return to Sandwell?"

The man raised his tied hands up to protect himself. "I mean you no harm. I simply wish to return to my family." Famished and dehydrated, his labored breathing made the old man look more pathetic than he had the night before. "Untie me and I'll be of no burden to you any longer, freeing you to return in time for the ceremony. This way we both get the freedom we want."

Gin listened to his pleas and shook his head. "You know too much. I should just strike you down to ensure you will cause me no future issues."

"No!" The old man fell to his knees in front of Gin. "Please. I beg you to spare my life. I only wish to return to my family. Allow me the opportunity to spend time with my children. They are everything to me."

Gin longed for his own father to say such things about him. However, his warm feelings quickly changed to that of jealousy for he knew he would never have such a relationship. "I don't know if you even have children. You'd say anything to save your life. There is nothing stopping you from following me back and then alerting those in Sandwell."

"Withholding the nourishment I need has made that impossible. We are well over halfway home. I'd be fortunate to make it the rest of the way as it is. I haven't the strength to follow you back even if I wanted to."

Biting his lip as he thought, Gin finally took out his dagger and cut the ropes from Wittig's wrists. "Get out of here before I change my mind."

Without hesitation, the old man stood and stumbled through the forest and out of sight.

Gin was now free to return in time to see the celebration. He knew he did not carry out Santorray's order to escort the man all the way to his village, but Gin knew Santorray would never find out the truth. This was not the first time Gin felt he had outsmarted his teacher by getting what he wanted despite having to complete the task he was ordered to do. Once again, pleased with his intelligence, he turned the opposite way from the old man and started on his own hike.

He had not traveled long before Gin heard voices and the snorting of a faralope. Curious, he changed his heading slightly to investigate. He soon found a carriage that had been driving along a dirt path which crossed through the forest. The large two-legged faralope had been unhitched and was tied to a tree while the driver was attempting to repair one of the wheels.

Upon getting closer, Gin watched a radiant young woman step out from behind the carriage as she waited for the repairs to be completed. Dressed in fine clothes and adorned with several expensive bracelets and a necklace, it was obvious she was from a wealthy family. On the left side of her head, she had long blonde hair that flowed down her neck and over her back. She wore it tucked behind her ear which held an intriguing hexagonal earring. The right side of her head had been shaved clean and filled with tattoos of several shapes and designs. A circular earring with 4 inner circles hung from her right ear.

Enraptured by her beauty, Gin stood motionless, not realizing that while he was observing her, she too could see him.

"Hello," she called out to him.

Her words caused her driver to look up from his duties and grab a weapon to protect her. "What you be wantin' there, boy?" the driver yelled.

His rough voice snapped Gin out of his fixation on the lady, who appeared to be in her early twenties. "Nothing. I was just walking to Sandwell, and I overheard you."

"Be off with ya, then!" the driver insisted.

"Nonsense," she said before Gin could leave. "We could use an extra set of hands and a strong back for our repairs."

"We'll be fine, ma'am. If I need help, we have others in our party that should be here shortly."

She gave a stern eye to her driver. "We should welcome the help of others."

Agreeing to follow her orders, he was still very uncomfortable about the stranger. "He can help me, but he is a commoner and doesn't have permission to speak to you."

"I am speaking to him, so I have given my permission. Lower your weapon and let him approach."

Lowering his sword, he stood ready to raise it again in case he initial trust in him was misplaced.

"Come here, boy," she said with a smile.

Her soft voice and elegant wave sucked him in. Before he knew it, he was standing in front of her. His rugged leather outfit was perfect for living out in the wild but looked low class while he was standing next to her in her clean and expensive garments.

"Hi," was all he was able to get out.

"Do you think you can help my driver fix our wheel?"

Gin nodded his head and smiled.

After a few moments, she smiled back and pointed a finger in the direction of the fallen wheel. "The wheel is over there."

"Oh." He stumbled on a few potential words that came out as nonsense before turning to assist the driver. Gin had the education to understand the mechanics of wagons, but this had been the first time he would put his knowledge to practice and get his own hands dirty. In order not to look inept, he took instructions from the lady's escort and helped with the repairs.

"What takes you to Sandwell?" she asked.

"Um," Gin suddenly realized the time he had lost by helping. "The ceremony..." escaped his lips as his mind returned to his mission.

"Yes, there will be one there tonight. We're heading to it as well. Would you like to ride along?"

"Absolutely!" Standing back up, he was ready to get going.

She giggled at the naïve response. "Perhaps you could finish helping with the wheel repairs, so we can get started."

More than a little embarrassed, he turned to help the driver finish the repairs.

Before long, the wheel was back in place and the faralope had been hitched up for travel. Seeing an elegant and inviting hand reaching out from within the carriage, Gin took it and climbed aboard just as several wagons made their way up the dirt path, falling in line behind the carriage. Without any delay, the caravan of vehicles and walking men headed on its way to Sandwell, with the recently repaired carriage in the lead.

Sitting back, Gin realized how nicely the interior of the carriage had been furnished and decorated. It was rare to see such quality and beauty. Turning back to her, he realized she had been watching him with great curiosity and amusement. "Thank you for the ride," Gin said.

"Of course. You did help with the repairs. It's the least we could do."

Smiling, he nodded in agreement. "I hope we aren't late for the ceremony."

"We won't be. They won't start without us."

Gin liked that kind of attitude, especially when he was usually the one that would boast about such things. "So, the villagers know they can't start without you being present?" he asked, half-joking.

"Yes, they do." Her voice showed no signs of humor as she poured him a drink of fresh water. "I've instructed them not to start until I arrive."

"Wow. It's pretty impressive to have that kind of power." Taking the glass from her, he added, "By the way, my name is Gin."

Bowing her head slightly, she replied, "It's an honor to meet you, Gin. I am Javolo."

Chapter 6
She Speaks

Lanterns were lit down the main street and across the entire front of the temple as the sunlight began to fade from the village of Sandwell. Locals slowly made their way to the clamshell seating area of the temple and waited for someone to exit the temple and stand on the stage before them.

A procession of wagons and carriages had arrived nearly an hour earlier, and the passengers had entered the temple through one of its many side doors. Unlike a fortress, the temple was designed more like a theater with easy access for speakers and entertainers to come and go without being observed by the audience.

Pots had been filled with burning incense and placed along the perimeter of the village, giving the entire area a pungent fragrance. It also created a thin veil of smoke that hung near the ground as it wafted down the street and around the temple. The dramatic effect added to the crowd's anticipation of the upcoming event.

"He's going to miss this," Nutrix said as she waited in the forest just outside of the village. "You should have sent me with the old man."

Santorray was getting uncomfortable as well, but not because of Gin's tardiness. "He'll be fine. We have bigger issues to address." Keeping his voice as quiet as possible, he gave her instructions. "Disappear."

The brandercat had traveled with him long enough to know what that meant. Nutrix immediately changed the color of her scales across her body and disappeared the best that her aging body would allow. Fortunately, the poor lighting and heavy vegetation worked in her favor.

"Santorray?" a man's voice called out from deeper in the forest.

Searching the darkened underbrush, the blothrud finally saw the bald man from the village of Bentree step out from behind a large bush. This was followed by many more men stepping out from behind trees and undergrowth. Some had arrows cocked in their bows, while others had swords ready for battle.

"The incenses," Santorray grumbled. "You used them to block out my ability to smell your arrival."

Wittig nodded. "I've seen what you can detect with that nose of yours. Where's your feline friend, Nutrix?"

"Where's Gin?"

"Gin? The boy who can't carry out the simple mission of walking me back to Bentree?" He laughed at the idea. "He's probably lost in the woods on his way back here."

"How did you escape from him?"

"In spite of your admirable training, he not only didn't give me a fight, but he willfully freed me and sent me on my way. Fortunately for me, I stumbled upon a caravan of the king's followers who provided me with a ride back here. Once I told a few of them the story of what an Altered Creature did to my village of Bentree, they seemed very willing to assist me in capturing you and your little group of arsonists." Smiling at the blothrud he had feared yesterday, he felt very much in control today as the armed men approached the beast. "I suggest you turn around and place your hands behind your back. I've been told that Javolo led our caravan here and will be speaking tonight, so I have informed her guards that a traitor will be brought to her tonight." Smiling, he added, "You asked for my help to lead you to her, and that is exactly what I am doing."

Santorray scowled at Wittig. "I provided you the opportunity to return home unharmed. Instead, you have decided to cause yourself great pain by returning here."

"Your threats mean nothing to me anymore. And it is you that is about to feel pain." The old man chuckled. "I must tell you that I appreciate your actions, for they are providing me the opportunity to meet Javolo in person so that I can tell her all about your plans. I will be a hero and granted new rights by the Terra King, while you and your friends will be executed for your plot against our king." A devilish smile grew upon his face. "I can't thank you enough for this gift."

Various thoughts ran through the blothrud's head. He could use the darkness and forest to his advantage and win this battle. However, he was more concerned about Gin. He did not know where his student was in order to save him prior to being caught and executed.

Placing his hands behind his back, he turned to face the village. "Stay low and follow us," he said softly to Nutrix, hoping she was still nearby to hear him.

Several men approached and then grabbed the blothrud from the back and attempted to place metal cuffs on his wrists. Santorray's wrists were nearly twice the size of a human's, and ropes ended up being used before pushing him forward out of the forest and into the opening.

"Where's Nutrix?" Wittig asked.

"She ran off to find Gin a few hours ago," Santorray replied.

"I don't believe him," Wittig announced. "Take him to the stage while we search the surrounding area. Let Javolo know of his plans to dethrone the king."

Prodding him forward, Wittig's men directed him into the village and to the temple. When they approached, the seated crowd jumped up in fear of the advancing blothrud. As they backed away, a path was created for Wittig's men to guide the Altered Creature up on stage. A chain fixed to the floor was secured to the ropes around Santorray's wrists.

An uneasy crowd reclaimed their seats while staring at the beast upon their stage. Most had never seen a blothrud, and those that had knew just how dangerous they could be. Their initial fear turned to anger and hatred toward the creature. Insults and slurs began as soft comments and grew into loud angry shouts from the crowd. With little warning, they had turned into an angry mob.

Just before the locals started throwing items at the hideous beast upon the stage, several people came out of the temple and sat in the reserved front row. The Runestone design upon their white hooded robes made it obvious that they were part of the devout followers of the Terra King. There was one exception. Dressed in his old leather clothes, Gin walked out with them and slowly sat down among the followers. In doing so, he was stunned to see his mentor shackled up on stage.

Santorray was just as shocked to see his student at the gathering, especially in the front row which was reserved for the robed devotees. Regardless, he slowly shook his head, communicating to Gin to not let on that they knew each other. He was relieved to see Gin nod and relax his expression of surprise.

When all the Terra King's followers had been seated, a beautiful young lady stepped out from the front doors of the temple and onto the stage. Thin and tall, she wore a hooded robe much like the others, except hers was much more elegant and reflected the surrounding light, causing a mystical halo effect around her entire body.

The crowd stood in unison as she appeared on stage.

Taking little interest in the blothrud chained to one side of her stage, she walked forward to speak to her audience. "Praise to the Mountain King!" she said loud enough for all to hear. "For he has returned!"

The crowd repeated her words back to her. "Praise to the Mountain King, for he has returned."

Both Santorray and Gin were amazed at the level of obedience displayed by the uncultured gathering of villagers.

"He has been reborn as the Terra King to save us." She then commanded the audience to be seated with a wave of her hand. "I am Javolo, the King's Voice. I speak for him while he is keeping us safe from those who would harm us." She then slowly turned to the blothrud. "Such as the evils of the Altered Creatures and the other Fesh who reside outside of our free lands."

Santorray growled at her use of the terms against him and for painting a deceptive picture to instill fear into others.

"Perhaps some of you don't know the story of the Dovenar Civil War and how all of us were nearly destroyed by the Brothers of War and the Altered Creatures. Because of this, it is imperative that I explain to you what happened and what our Terra King is fighting for."

Gin and Santorray each stole a quick glance at each other, communicating their mutual uneasiness.

Gazing back into the crowd, she began her story. "As you know, the great Dovenar Kingdom served as a sanctuary. It was a place free from the horrors of the Altered Creatures. Peace filled the lands for hundreds of years, until several decades ago, when Ambrosius and Tarosius were born to the throne. These twin brothers differed greatly in their approaches to governing the provinces and the people within them. Ambrosius welcomed the Altered Creatures into our lands and granted them access to our crops and fresh water. Tarosius wanted to expand our lands by going to war with the Altered Creatures, forcing them farther away and opening new lands for us to prosper within. Both approaches would have cost many lives for actions we didn't want."

"Eventually the differences between them escalated as our kingdom was torn apart. These two brothers became known as the Brothers of War. The result of the increased tension was the expulsion of Tarosius and the rise to power by Ambrosius. But while Ambrosius worked on ways to join humans and Altered Creatures into one new culture, Tarosius was being trained by the Dark Oracle, Deleth. Years of training led to Tarosius becoming the most powerful E'rudite in the land, with a new name to fit his new powers: Darkmere. He then returned to take back the Dovenar Kingdom. However, Ambrosius had learned some E'rudite tricks of his own. The two clashed in a fight that led to the Dovenar Civil War and the near destruction of everything we had."

She gave a dramatic pause and watched her audience waiting to hear more. "Spells were cast to prevent armies from dying, causing slaughtered armies to continue the battle as undead warriors. The end result was horrifying. Most of our cities along the great Luthralum Tunia Lake were destroyed and the people killed. Borders were left unprotected against the Altered Creatures. Our trade lines were broken, and our resources were scarce. It was a miracle we survived."

Taking a deep breath, she continued, "As for the Brothers of War, they were shunned from our lands for the damage they had done. But they still lurk out there, waiting for the opportunity to return in order to control us. Ambrosius continues to work with the Altered Creatures, with desires to move them into our lands. Even worse is what Darkmere does on a daily basis. He takes what he wants as he goes from village to village, just like this one here where you live. After taking control, he forces the villagers to do his bidding. With each new village he defeats, he expands his regional power. This village could be his next target. Darkmere could be making plans right now to send in his army and take your goods, your family, and even your life."

The crowd was visibly shaken with fear as many called out for the Terra King to save them before it was too late.

Allowing the fear to spread like a virus among the audience, Javolo waited until there were pleas for support for the Terra King to save them. She pretended to struggle to hush the crowd with her halfhearted hand gestures. "I fully understand. I once lived in a village much like this, and we were warned about the threat of Darkmere. Unfortunately, we didn't heed the warning. When his evil army forced their way into our village and my family's home, they not only pillaged our belongings, but they also took the lives of my parents and baby sister. They took most of the men and forced them into their army before burning down our homes and killing the rest. I was one of the few that escaped with my life." She stopped and wiped away a tear before continuing. "I lost everything. Don't let this happen to you."

More pleas for help came from the locals as they screamed for protection from the monstrous Darkmere.

Taking a moment to make eye contact with many in the crowd, she continued. "This is why it's so critical for us to follow the Terra King. Several thousand years ago, when he was known as the Mountain King, he saved our people from the Notarians and their Altered Creatures. Now he has been reborn as the Terra King to save us from the Brothers of War and the Altered Creatures."

Santorray shook his large dragon-like head in disbelief at the misrepresentation of history she was touting in an effort to manipulate the villagers to serve her own agenda.

Javolo caught one of his head shakes and turned to face him. "Some feel these creatures can be tamed or even trusted. But the reality is that they are all wild and unpredictable. They may seem calm, but at the drop of a hat they can become savage and dangerous to all they are near. Because of this, we must destroy them before they destroy us. We make no plans to search them out, but once they are found within our lands, we must eradicate them before they breed like sandrats and devastate our resources. We take no pleasure in killing them, but it must be done to save ourselves and protect the future for our children."

She then nodded at the blothrud and called out to someone within the temple, "Executioner!"

"Executioner?" Santorray and Gin both said to themselves.

Stepping out from the temple was a bare-chested muscular man with a large axe. Taking a few steps forward on stage, he waited for instructions.

"Show our people what must be done to all Altered Creatures that enter our land."

The crowd stood up from their seats and cheered at the idea.

The blothrud was disappointed at how easily the locals had been manipulated and how quickly their hate grew against people they had never met. In addition, he spotted Wittig standing behind the crowd with a smug smile meant just for Santorray. The man had been busy bragging to anyone who would listen about how he outsmarted and caught the mighty blothrud warrior.

The executioner lifted his large axe to his shoulder and walked toward the creature on the stage.

Gin attempted to rush the stage to stop the unfolding events, but the crowd was forcing themselves forward as they yelled vile words at the beast. Gin was trapped in a shoulder-to-shoulder mob.

Santorray had not struggled until this point, but he had had enough of this performance, and he had no interest in being the star attraction by allowing some unknown axe-wielder to take down the mighty Santorray. "That's ENOUGH!" he yelled while pulling his hands apart and breaking the ropes that once held him. A magical spell or extremely thick chains may have been able to hold him, but Santorray had broken out of standard chains and ropes more times than these people had probably even used them.

The audience gasped at the sight of the free creature, and panic erupted amongst the crowd.

Taking an opportunity to swing his axe, the executioner made his attempt before the blothrud could escape. What he failed to anticipate was that the blothrud would be attacking him.

With a quick swing of his hand, Santorray snatched the axe out of the man's hand, knocked him down with his other hand, and then roared at the audience with such power that each villager felt like the beast was breathing down their neck.

All the villagers and Terra King loyalists screamed and ran for cover. They dispersed as quickly as possible, hiding in the temple, sheds, shops, and homes. The streets were cleared of everyone within seconds.

By the time Javolo ran upstairs and peered out the temple's window, she found the area to be empty of life, including the Altered Creature. The beast had escaped.

Chapter 7

Mentor

The normal calmness within the dark forest was disrupted by the breaking of limbs and stomping of feet as Santorray ran through the underbrush dragging a man with him. Several yards behind them, Gin kept up his pace to ensure he avoided being separated from the blothrud. Following the young man, was Nutrix, who continually peered over her shoulder to ensure they were not being followed.

This continued for several miles before the blothrud felt they had traveled enough distance from Sandwell and any villagers that might be following. Slowing to a stop in a small clearing, Santorray tossed Wittig to the ground. He had snatched the old man up on his way out of town, but now the double-crosser was on his back and defenseless. Placing a foot upon Wittig to keep him from escaping, Santorray smelled the air and listened for others.

Gin and Nutrix slowed down just as they left the tree-covered darkness and walked into the open area that was lightly coated in moonlight. They knew to keep their motion minimal as the blothrud was agitated and was surveying their location.

"We're all clear for now," the warrior said before removing his foot from Wittig's chest. "Nutrix, watch this human while Gin catches me up on the events of his day."

"Don't jump to conclusions. Listen to his side of the story. Give him the benefit of the doubt," she replied while walking over to the man lying on the ground.

"Come with me," Santorray ordered as he grabbed Gin's shirt and led him away from Wittig and into the forest before releasing him. Glaring at Gin, Santorray restrained himself from grabbing the young man by the shirt again and lifting him in the air to berate him.

Opening his palms toward Santorray, Gin hoped the gesture would help calm the tension in the air. Gin calmly said, "I can explain!"

"You better get started! My patience won't last long."

"I did as you said! I walked him back through the forest away from Sandwell. We walked for hours toward Bentree."

"It doesn't appear as though you made it all of the way."

"Well, no, I didn't. We were well over halfway before I let him walk the rest on his own."

"That wasn't our agreement."

"We didn't have an agreement. You just ordered me to take him home to prevent him from returning to Sandwell and warning others."

"Which is exactly what he did!" the blothrud yelled.

Gin's head shook as he tried to understand how Wittig made the trek back. "He's old and out of shape. He had gone without food and water. I didn't think he could even make it back to his family. It doesn't make any sense. There is no way he could have run fast enough to return before nightfall."

"Yet he was back here in time to plan our capture." Snorting and growling, he was as mad at himself for allowing this to happen as he was at his apprentice. "How did you travel back here?"

"Me?" Startled, Gin felt a bit guilty about his actions. "There was a carriage heading this way, and I took the opportunity to ride along." As soon as he heard his own words, he realized how Wittig traveled back. His eyes moved from his teacher back to where the old villager was being held by Nutrix. Embarrassed about the obvious oversight, he said with hesitation, "There was a convoy of us. Wittig must have ridden in one of the other wagons."

Santorray still was not satisfied. "It never occurred to you that Wittig would travel back the same way you did? Where was your head? What were you thinking about?"

"Javolo," Gin said softly before thinking.

"You allowed your thoughts about her to cloud your judgement and compromise the simplest of missions!"

"No, you're wrong, Santorray. I stayed focused on my task and our mission the entire time."

"Really? You never even considered the possibility that Wittig could join the same caravan that you did? Your mind was lost to her charm! Did you tell her about our undertaking as well? Does she know enough to warn the Terra King?" Santorray was furious as he stomped about the clearing. "You've compromised the entire mission!"

"No!" Gin shouted back at the beast that towered over him. "I didn't tell her anything about our goals! In fact, I used the opportunity to find out about her plans. What they are doing and what they want to accomplish!" Stepping closer, he glared straight up into the blothrud's eyes. "She doesn't realize it, but I now have an inside informant from whom I can obtain everything my father needs to stop the Terra King." Taking a breath, he looked from under his long hair that draped over his face, through the trees toward Wittig, and then back at his teacher. "If you hadn't allowed yourself to get captured by this frail old codger, I would have had the time to learn everything I needed to finish this mission and return home successful. It is your actions that caused us to fail this time."

Furious, Santorray launched his fist with great speed and power into the closest tree. The impact caused splinters to shoot out in every direction. The severed tree truck fell over, and limbs cracked as they crashed onto the earth. The loud thud of the tree shook the ground and caused the group to fall silent as small branches and leaves rained down upon them.

Santorray stood motionless with his eyes closed and his fists still clenched. "How can I trust you with major decisions when you don't follow through on the most minor of agreements?"

"Maybe I'm not trustworthy," Gin replied slowly. "Clearly I can't be like you or my father. So, who does that leave me to emulate? Nutrix? My role in life is clearly not to be a nursemaid for another. Just who am I supposed to look up to and learn from?"

Taking a deep sigh, the blothrud relaxed his voice before answering the question. "Ambrosius. He should be your mentor."

"Ambrosius? You would ask me to be like him? Surely not."

"I would never tell you to be anyone but yourself, but there are times we all need a mentor to learn from, and Ambrosius has much to teach you."

"Correct me if I'm wrong, but didn't he play a key role in destroying the Dovenar Kingdom? He's responsible for the deaths of tens of thousands."

"The Dovenar twins had radically different ideas about how to rule; this much is true from Javolo's speech. But we both know that she left out important elements to that story." Santorray shook his head slightly as he recalled her words. "I was there during the Civil War. I saw what happened. I heard the call from the Brothers of War and listened to the response from those on the front lines. You need to remember that stories of history are simplified and turned very black and white for their audience to easily understand and for them to know who to cheer for and who to fear. The truth is usually mostly gray and filled with good intentions that often end up unexpectedly hurting others in the end."

Gin lowered his guard and relaxed his strong posture. "You've spoken about Ambrosius many times. Clearly he made an impression on you."

A slight chuckle escaped Santorray's mouth before he replied. "He saved my life as well as your father's. I've been in many heated arguments with the man, but there is no one that I respect more. The decisions he's had to make, I would wish upon no one." He took but a moment to recall the memories. "You could learn a lot from the man."

"Oh, really?" It was his turn to chuckle. "Such as?"

"Responsibility, valor, integrity, and reliability to name a few."

"And what did that get him? He lost his kingdom, and now his people hate him."

Lowering his eyes for a moment, Santorray felt the opportunity was ripe for Gin to learn. "Failing to achieve a result does not mean you have been unsuccessful. Keeping the kingdom together would have been the easy thing to do, but would have also been at a great expense. The painless thing for him to do would have been to agree to turn his people into conquerors and expand his lands at the cost of all the Altered Creatures as well as tens of thousands of his own citizens. He most likely would still be in power if he had done so. But instead, he risked and then lost his power to maintain civility and compassion throughout the land."

"You want me to learn from someone who lost? I play to win. I accomplish my goals, no matter what it takes. People are stupid and should be considered expendable if they are willing to blindly follow a leader. So, the loss of their lives in a war is worth it to achieve the desired goal."

"And there lies the issue."

"What do you mean? I know you would do the same."

"No. I know I say that I expect to win every fight and those that follow me must follow my orders, but the reality is I have learned from Ambrosius to take a larger view of the world. 'Stop trying to win every battle and focus on winning the war,' he would tell me. At the time, he said that I had been focusing on every minor issue that came along instead of what truly needed my focus to achieve the desired result."

"But he lost the war. The Civil War ended with both sides losing."

Santorray grinned as he recalled Ambrosius' advice. "The objective was not winning the physical war. It was the ongoing survival of our people and communities in a civil manner that breeds a better life for each generation that follows."

"He planned to lose the war?"

"No, nor did he want to win. Hell, he didn't want the damn war in the first place. You see, a war victory wasn't the long-term expectation he wanted to see accomplished. He knew that the tragedy of war is the lives lost at the expense of those desiring change that is being resisted. A true leader fights for the betterment of his culture, and that is what he did. Initially he tried to compromise, then fought with words and ideas. But in the end, it came down to launching battles that tore the kingdom apart. He never wanted a war victory because he never wanted a war in the first place."

"How does all of this apply to me?"

"Your focus on obtaining what you want right now is so deep that you don't step back and consider the ramifications of your actions on the true goal." Taking in a deep breath, he nodded. "You have more potential than you can imagine. I simply wish you would take into consideration the approaches of the great leaders, such as Ambrosius, before acting. This would allow you to pause and not get distracted by your immediate situation. Take that moment to determine if there is a constructive action that may encourage a more long-lasting result and would favor current and future generations."

Gin stepped back as he took in his teacher's words. "Why are you working so hard to change me?"

"No, not change you. I want to help you grow into a great man. And to do that, you need to seek the wisdom and counsel of those that have come before you. Study and learn as much as you can from them."

"That's all I've been doing," Gin interrupted. "How much more do I need to learn?"

"Gin, we will never stop learning. Take what you need and leave the rest. Sometimes you won't be ready for specific lessons and they will have to be taught more than once." Santorray could see he had his student's attention, so he calmly continued. "Allow yourself to be shaped by people of integrity and compassion. Be intentional in your request for knowledge and experience. Do not rush the process. Wisdom will soon follow. Wisdom that will allow you to remain focused on your true goals without distraction. Wisdom that will allow you to take calculated risks. Wisdom that will encourage compassion for all life."

Relaxed, Santorray gazed at the young man. "You have so much potential. Use your gifts for good. Use your time to grow and expand your thoughts. Use what you have been given for the betterment of the lands."

This was one of those few times that Gin was able to have a conversation with his teacher instead of being told what to do, which inevitably turned into an argument. He felt this was the right moment to ask a sensitive question that he had been holding onto for a long time. "Are you ashamed of me?"

Tilting his head slightly, Santorray was not expecting the question. "No. Why do you ask?"

"You constantly push hard to change everything about me, and you've never told me that you're proud of me."

A slight grin returned to Santorray's muzzle. "I only have so much time with you, to train you and give you the education your father asked for. I may push harder than you would like, but I've never said I was ashamed of you."

"Yet you still haven't said you're proud of me."

"Is that so important to you?"

The young man thought for a moment. "It shouldn't be, but it would be nice to hear it from someone."

"I respect you. That is a higher compliment. Even your father has yet to say that to you."

"That's true. I haven't earned his trust, his love, or his respect. You and Nutrix are more my family than he has ever been."

Seeing the disappointment on Gin's face, Santorray wanted him to shake it off. "You will complete this mission for him. If he fails to see your value, I will invite you to come with me."

Gin's eyes lit up at the prospect of leaving home and seeing the world without having to be on tasks for his absent father.

"My service to your father will be completed, and you will have proven you are a competent adult and should be treated as such. It will be your decision to make. I will provide the opportunity, but it will be up to you to decide who you want to be with in your future, your father or me."

Gin gazed into his teacher's eyes and nodded in appreciation for the future opportunity. "Let's accomplish this mission." He then turned and walked back into the opening and spoke directly to Wittig. "You clearly have more knowledge than you've let on. Where is Javolo heading next?"

The old man laughed at the question. "As much as I would wish it, I lack the authority to have an audience with the King's Voice, Javolo."

"You said you've met her before," Gin replied.

"I've seen her in person, yes, on stage. But I have not earned the privilege to speak with her."

Seeing Santorray step into the opening, Gin felt the need to get some valuable information out of Wittig in order to prove his strength to his teacher. "I don't care if you have the authority to speak with her. I do! Now tell me where she will go next so I can finish my conversation with her."

Wittig chuckled. "It's too late. She's already on her way to Brushtower." A slightly evil grin grew as he explained the situation to them. "There is a hearty stone wall surrounding the city with guards at every entrance and even more perched across the top. They would never allow an Altered Creature in. Gin, you would be on your own, and unless you're marked as one of the king's followers, you'll have to have the proper paperwork to get past the guards."

"I'll find a way," the young man replied with a renewed motivation to prove his capabilities.

"Perhaps." Wittig's grin never left. "As doubtful as it is, let's say you make to the inside of the walls and to the Terra King's Temple. There are many layers of followers that will prevent you from having access to Javolo. The only chance you'll be able to see her is if you're in the audience while watching her perform, just as I have. You'll get no closer. I've tried. Her personal security will prevent anyone from storming the stage." His grin grew into a large malicious smile. "You had your chance in Sandwell. That was the only chance you had. You failed."

Gin thought for a moment before glancing at his teacher. "I can do this. I can talk to her if you can get me inside."

Santorray's mind was distant for a few moments as the name of the city conjured up Civil War memories for him. He then nodded at the young man. "I'll get you inside. In fact, we're all going inside."

"All of us?" Gin asked.

"Yes. If Brushtower is where we are headed, then I have some business of my own to take care of."

Wittig's grin grew even larger. "It was a pleasure meeting you before your death, Santorray."

With puzzled expressions, Nutrix, Santorray, and Gin all turned to the elderly man.

"The Terra King hasn't grown in power without thinking ahead," Wittig added. "He has posted a Knight Slayer at several of his temples, Brushtower being one of them."

Santorray's eyes grew large as he stared at the man, unsure if the truth was being told.

"What's a Knight Slayer?" Nutrix asked. It was obvious that she and Gin were in the dark on the subject.

Composing himself, Santorray's eyes thinned as he still glared at Wittig. "Long before the Civil War, a group of EverSpring Alchemists and several outcast Dovenar Knights spent years perfecting the ultimate warriors. The best fighters were combined with magical abilities to create the Wargods. Because of the magic that flows through their veins, they are stronger and faster than you can imagine." Santorray pulled his eyes from the old man and looked at Gin. "There once were over a hundred Wargods, but then they broke into two factions. One group became mercenaries for hire, and the other stayed loyal to EverSpring, the city of the Alchemists. Many of the mercenaries were hired to assassinate the remaining Dovenar Knights. They were so effective that I don't know if any of the knights are still alive. Thus, most people now call this assassin group by the name Knight Slayers."

Wittig chuckled. "You may want to rethink your journey to Brushtower."

"Santorray, surely they aren't as powerful as you," Gin said firmly, but the blothrud's hesitation gave him a truer scope of their power.

"I have had dealings with the Knight Slayers. Do not underestimate their abilities. They are unnaturally enhanced in many ways. As I've explained, they were designed and bred to be the best fighters, with skills in the art of magic. Few can compete with them."

Nutrix shook her head. "I don't want Gin in that city if one of those things is in there. I know his mission is critical to his father, but it's not worth dying for."

Santorray shook his head. "A Knight Slayer wouldn't waste his time on Gin. Their senses are typically focused on bigger threats such as an invading army or an assassination attempt on the Terra King."

"How can one sense such an action before it happens?" she asked.

"They can feel the energy of the future like ripples in the water. Their subconscious alerts them of danger before it arrives. But danger comes in many forms, and if blothruds are on the list to watch out for, then I won't have much time before the Knight Slayer will know I'm in the city."

Chapter 8
Nutrix

Once again, camp was established, and a small fire was started to cook a few freshly hunted rodents for the party. Afterward, Gin adjusted Wittig's ropes around the tree before lying down and slowly drifting off to sleep. This left Santorray and Nutrix to take shifts to keep an eye and ear open for any outsiders. The brandercat knew that Santorray always took first shift, so she started getting comfortable for the night.

Nutrix stretched her long cat body before sitting down near the blothrud as she stared at Gin through the dancing flames. "It's finally coming to an end," she said to Santorray. "Seems like just yesterday he was an infant, and I was caring for him in the nursery."

"I would think you'd be pleased. Your role as a nursemaid and caregiver for the boy is nearly complete. You'll be free from the burden."

Slightly surprised by the comment, she rolled her eyes. "I'm not in the same situation you are."

Santorray shifted his position to get more comfortable. "We all have different situations."

"You came to us and offered your services to help with Gin. My story is much different. My duties have been solely to care for the child who is becoming a man. With each lesson you teach him and each day he learns to stand alone in this world, I have one less day of being needed."

"Isn't that the goal for both of us? We want him to reach a point where he is mature and competent enough to no longer need us in his life."

"True. However, you'll simply leave afterward. I am but a slave. If I'm not seen as having value, then I am a liability. I am getting to an age where I'm too old to be taught new skills or start raising a new child. My path upon this earth is coming to an end after this mission."

Considering her words, Santorray listened to the crackling of the fire for a few moments before replying. "If you lived in the red crystal city of Ergrauth, you would know when your use is no longer needed and would surrender your body and soul to the city in order to make it a better place for future generations."

"I was born a slave, and I will die a slave. The grand events and culture of Ergrauth are not within my sight or my daughter's."

Raising an eyebrow, he nodded. "Ah, Fenia. She has a good head on her shoulders. Will she take your place as nursemaid for the upper-class families?"

"Yes. She will spend her life as I have spent mine… until she is no longer needed."

"She will be protected. She will have food and shelter. There are many who do not."

"Would you give up your freedom for these things?"

"No," Santorray replied instantly before glanced back into the fire. "If you're no longer needed, ask to leave. I can escort you to a safe location for you to live out your life."

"And leave my daughter? I think not."

"It's better than being dead and not being with her."

Nutrix sighed at the thought. "In some ways, being alive and free while knowing my daughter remains enslaved would be a daily torture that I'd rather not endure. I'd gladly give up my life for her freedom."

"Then take her with you. Buy her freedom."

"As a slave I earn no money to buy anything."

"Perhaps I can help."

Nutrix chuckled. "Don't make empty promises. You have no money either, and I don't see you getting a steady job to earn it for our freedom. Reality is, you've been edgy as of late and eager to finish your commitment to Gin and his father. Once the boy's final training is complete, you'll move to some secluded place and relax. You've been talking about hiding from the world for a long time."

He shrugged his shoulders. "I don't hide from anyone. Although I like the idea of getting away from everyone and their issues. Living off the land in isolation is one of my favorite daydreams. It sounds tempting."

"It's not your burden to bear, Santorray. My family has been slaves for many generations to many different masters. It may not be what we want, but my daughter must learn to accept it, just as I have."

"We all have our burdens to bear." Santorray glared at Gin. "I just wish he would understand his burdens and just listen to me to learn how to carry them."

"No, you don't."

"What?" He was surprised at her reply.

"Listening to you is not what you really want." She lowered her voice to make sure she didn't wake Gin. "What you want is impossible, which is why you're irritated at yourself. Unfortunately, you're taking it out on him."

Squinting, he gave her a questioning look. "And what is it that I really want?"

"I don't know why, but you want to change his moral compass." A slight smile was exposed after she said it because she knew she was right. "I've been watching and listening. Your anger is not lit when he disobeys your words or training. It's fueled by his morals being different than yours."

"Assuming he has any," he said sarcastically under his breath.

"He does. They are just not in line with yours, and for some reason that hurts you to the core."

"Why is that so unexpected? A teacher always wants their students to be in line with basic moral codes of conduct."

"Santorray, how many missions have you led into battle?"

"I don't know."

"Dozens?"

Santorray scoffed. "Hundreds."

"Did each and every one of those you commanded have your same sense of morals and beliefs?"

"Of course not. What kind of question is that?"

"Did it infuriate you and prevent you from working with them or accomplishing your mission?"

"No."

"Then why is Gin different? Why must he live to a higher standard than others?"

"Because he must!" he blurted out before thinking.

"For his sake or yours?"

"Mine! His! Both." Slightly flustered, he backed away to regain his composure.

"Why yours?"

Santorray's eyes darted about in an attempt to not make eye contact with her. After finally closing them for a moment, he opened them to see her waiting with concern. "I did something to him when he was a child that I must correct." Taking a deep gulp, he continued, "That is all I will say on the matter."

Confused, she asked, "Do you feel your action has somehow changed his morals and now you need to repair the damage?"

"I will not speak on this matter anymore!" he said in a deep commanding tone.

Nutrix had grown to know his moods, and this was not one to push, at least at this time. "We all make mistakes. We must learn from them, and in the end, we must be willing to forgive ourselves."

The only response she received was a glare that reminded her the conversation was over. Knowing they had a few long days of walking ahead of them, she accepted that.

Chapter 9

Brushtower

The early morning's thick fog blocked their view of the nearby city as they walked along a heavily used dirt road. The frequency of small thatch-roofed wooden homes and planted fields had increased as they continued toward the city's walls. Each step they took moved them closer to a darker area amidst the fog. Slowly a stone wall was discovered from within the darkness. It was so high that they could not see the top through the heavy mist. Santorray, Gin, Nutrix, and Wittig had arrived at the city of Brushtower.

Instead of following the bend in the road to the main gate, Santorray led the group off to the side and back to one of the farm homes, where they found a wheelbarrow. "Gin, grab the handles. Wittig, sit inside."

Wittig glanced at the leftover manure inside the bucket section. "No, thank you."

"It's not a request," Santorray replied in a low tone.

Gin chuckled as the old man carefully climbed into the wheelbarrow while attempting to avoid the manure. "What's the plan, Santorray?" Gin inquired.

"Wittig's job is to get you past the front gates."

"How will we keep him from alerting others of our presence?"

"We'll make sure he doesn't talk."

Wittig looked back and forth from Santorray and Gin. "Then how will I get you inside?" His smile made it clear that he felt they needed him, and therefore he was in control of the situation.

The blothrud ignored Wittig. "Gin, you'll be wheeling in a servant of the Terra King, which is obvious due to his tattooed head. Unfortunately, you found the man drunk passed out in a compost pile. You are returning him to the king's people to get cleaned up to properly represent the Terra King. Once you're inside, accidentally dump Wittig onto the ground and call for assistance. This size of city will have at least two to four guards standing within each doorway. If you can get at least two or three of them to help you, Nutrix can make her way inside without being seen. There will be lanterns, but the fog should help prevent them from seeing what she can't fully hide."

"Do your best," the brandercat told Gin. "My scales don't have the range they used to, but a momentary distraction is all I'll need to make my way inside." She then glanced back up at the blothrud. "What are your plans?"

"Don't worry about me. Use Wittig to get inside and then keep an eye on Gin. Return here and wait for me if there is trouble."

Wittig laughed at the idea. "Do you honestly believe that I plan to play along in your little charade?"

"No," the blothrud replied. "That's why you'll be unconscious."

"How do you expect that to happen?"

Santorray reached over and flicked his fingers at the back of the man's head. His powerful fingers hit with enough force to jar Wittig's head and knock him out. "Just like that."

Gin grinned at the ease of Santorray's movement. It was simple and not any more than was needed.

The blothrud grabbed Gin by the shoulders, forcing eye contact to make sure that he was paying attention to his final instructions. "Listen up. Once inside, restrain and gag Wittig so he can't alert anyone when he wakes up. Your objective is to find Javolo and gather as much information as you can from her. Try to find out how the Terra King is able to grow his territory so quickly and how he is able to make his people become so obedient. Once you know these things or have determined this information is unobtainable, you need to return to camp. We will then regroup to determine our next step. Do not put your life in danger. They will slit your throat if they discover your mission. I'd rather you return with nothing than you not return at all. We can always try again."

Gin was eager to get started and gave a quick nod to appease his teacher. "I will. I will."

Santorray was not convinced with the response. "I'm serious, Gin. We're getting close, and the stakes are getting high. I want you to end this mission with success, not in a grave."

"Trust me," Gin said with a cavalier tone to his voice.

Unsatisfied, Santorray added, "Nutrix will stay in the shadows and follow you."

"I can do this on my own," Gin argued. "I have to do this on my own to prove myself to my father."

"I know. She will only be there to assist if you request it or to help us communicate if you need to stay longer than expected. It is still your mission."

Stepping forward, the young man considered fighting the idea of having his nursemaid watch over him on this most important mission to prove his manhood, but he could tell from the blothrud's body language that it would be pointless.

"Good," Santorray said. "Now repeat the plan back to me."

Gin grabbed the handles of the wheelbarrow as he prepared to start making his way to the city's wall. "Once I'm inside, I'll find Javolo. Now understand, it might take some time to get the information I need. But when I do, I'll meet you back at camp," he said before turning toward Santorray with an inquisitive look. "I've never known you to sit at camp quietly waiting. What will you be doing?"

"I have something I need to collect before we head home, but I'll be back in time."

Shrugging his shoulders, Gin started pushing the barrow with the unconscious Wittig inside.

Shifting her scales, Nutrix moved in front of Gin to scout ahead for any potential dangers. The guards would have seen her basic shape in bright daylight, but the fog gave her enough cover to walk up within a few yards of the city entrance without being detected.

Beyond the veil of the fog, guards on the wall could not observe Gin arriving any better than he could see them. Looking down, slightly darker hues within the fog were periodically noticed and assumed to be residents going about their business. But the guards at the gate had a much better view of anyone approaching.

"What's this?" one of the two gate guards asked Gin as he made his way to the large doorway that led to the city beyond.

"Sir, I found one of the king's followers passed out and wished to return him to his people before others saw him dishonoring our faith."

Glancing at the man's head, the guard recognized the tattoos.

Gin could tell he was skeptical about letting them in. "I can leave him here," he said with a smile as he wheeled Wittig closer to the guard. "You can take him to the appropriate location to get cleaned up."

The pungent smell of manure finally wafted his way and filled his nasal cavities. "No," he replied while covering his nose and mouth. "Get him out of here and clean him up." He then waved Gin in.

Nodding, Gin picked up the handles and wheeled Wittig a few yards into the courtyard before dumping him onto the ground. "Help!" Gin called out to the guards. "Can I get some assistance here?"

Unfortunately, only one guard turned and started to walk his way. The other stayed at his post.

"He's very heavy. We'll need more support than you."

"Nonsense, I've lifted up larger men," the guard boasted. However, once he started reaching under the man, he felt the thick layer of manure on the bald man's back. Pulling his hands back, he realized the best way to pick the man up was with some help. "Get over here and help me, ya lazy fool."

As the second guard walked less than two yards from his post, Nutrix took the opportunity to enter the opening and disappear into the shadows before being seen. She then kept her distance from everyone inside the walls; while the thick fog gave her that extra advantage, she needed to move without being detected.

Gin stepped backward to give the second guard plenty of room to approach.

One guard lifted Wittig by the feet and the other by his wrists. With a few quick swings, they tossed the old man back into the wheelbarrow before heading back to their post to clean their hands.

Gin had completed his first task of helping Nutrix enter the city. His next step was to find the temple and then Javolo. Pushing the wheelbarrow into a stall within a nearby wooden structure, Gin tied up and gagged Wittig to prevent him from calling out for help once he woke. The old man was then placed out of view, behind some crates.

Once Wittig had been taken care of, Gin made his way back into the courtyard and then down the main street toward the center of the city. The farther he went, the busier it became. Shops sold everything from pottery, to hats, to fresh meat and fish, to blankets. There was more life and activity in the main part of the city than Gin had ever seen, and it made him feel excited to discover the other offerings of the city.

Without looking around, he could tell Nutrix was never far from his side. He had spent his life listening to her breathing and footsteps, so he could hear her soft noises through the crowd. "Stay hidden. I have this," he told her as he kept his head forward.

"Be careful, Gin," she pleaded, but he was swept away in the crowd without any concern for her or her words.

Watching the locals busily buying and selling items, Gin noticed several more people with shaved and tattooed heads. Not just men. There were women as well. Some were completely bald, while others had half of their heads shaved and marked with the Terra King's symbols. A few even had both sides shaved. Several of the older men who had been marked sported a long beard, some scruffy and some neatly braided.

In addition to those who had shaved their heads, many others with full heads of hair had the same tattoo on their neck or wrists. It appeared that nearly one in four people had the mark of the Terra King tattooed on their body in some location, and another quarter of the population wore the symbol on their clothes.

Nearly a third of the locals showed no symbols at all, implying they were not devoted followers of the Terra King. This gave Gin the ability to move about without looking out of place.

Gin recalled being taught lessons on history and structural designs as he made his way to the center of the city. He recognized the stone inner curtain wall that surrounded and protected the upper class in case invaders made it past the outer wall. However, the young man chuckled at the battle-damaged wall that had not been repaired as children playfully entered through large holes in the once-strong wall.

Stepping past the wall's unguarded gates, he looked upon the inner ward. Gin had learned that wards were open areas for royalty and military between the curtain walls. He also recalled that the fortified tower in the center was known as the keep. However, unlike what he had been taught, this ward was occupied by merchants and thousands and thousands of locals doing business.

His eyes panned the large open area before focusing on the central tall tower. Once the stronghold of the city, the keep tower had clearly been breached long ago and was being rebuilt with new techniques, architecture, and materials. The forebuildings that leaned up against the keep had been completely rebuilt, and damaged sections of the tower's exterior had been replaced with more expensive stone.

If Gin's training and memory served him well, then the keep would protect the ruler of this city and have a hall to hold court, and royal sleeping quarters. Kitchens, guards, weapons, and servants would be within the keep or in a forebuilding. This seemed to be the logical place for the Terra King and Javolo to be.

Feeling pretty cocky about his knowledge of a place he had never visited, he saw something his educators had never suggested. Off to one side of the mighty keep tower was a large amphitheater that could hold over a thousand people. Having seen the small temple in Sandwell, Gin was not surprised. This keep had been transformed into the Terra King's Temple.

Everything in the inner ward was covered with the Terra King's symbol. The design was comprised of five circles; one large and four small. The large outer circle had an inner circle half the size in the exact center. Then three small circles overlapped upon one another to fill the majority of the large outer circle. The design was simple and easy to recreate in most artistic medias.

The pattern had been foreign to Gin prior to seeing it tattooed on Javolo and her people, and now on the people of Brushtower. He now immediately recognized the art placed on buildings and signs as symbols for the Terra King.

In awe of the number of the Terra King's following, Gin stood near the amphitheater to assess the size of the crowd that could fill it. However, before he could finish his estimate, he was interrupted.

"Praise to the Mountain King!" an elderly lady said as she approached him. "He will protect you if you show your faith." She held out several necklaces with the king's symbol hanging from them.

Startled at first, he played along. "Oh, I'm just here to learn more. When will Javolo be speaking next?"

"Soon. She will be speaking after nightfall. But you must mark yourself with a sign of faith if you wish to partake in the service." Swishing the necklaces up a bit higher toward the boy's face, she pushed to make a quick sale. "Which one catches your eye?"

Stepping back to view them, he eventually selected one and paid her for the item before placing it around his neck and walking away. "Nutrix? Are you here?"

"I am," a voice responded from behind him. "I will stay as close as I can, but I will not be able to enter the seating area without being caught. I will have to wait for you."

"I understand," he replied. "Let's get something to eat while we wait for the service to start."

"Agreed. I hope Santorray is accomplishing his mystery task without any issues."

Chapter 10
Under the City

Following the exterior stone wall of the city through the thick fog, Santorray made his way to a waterway that entered Brushtower and then exited the city on the far end. He was pleased to see that the waterway was the same as it was so many years ago. He was also impressed that the city still existed after so many historical battles. This was one of several cities he had frequented during the Dovenar Civil War.

Stepping into the cool water, he tested the metal grate that covered the entrance to the city's lower levels. Most of the openings were just large enough for a child to climb through, so they were far too small for the rather large blothrud.

Reaching below the surface, he found branches and debris that had been trapped by the grate as well as a few damaged bars. Standing up to his waist in water, he felt an opening under the surface that had most likely been made by the ramming of the large tree trunk that was still embedded in the broken grates.

Holding his breath, he submerged his entire body and worked to dislodge the remnants of tree trunk. The heavy wood was lodged within the bars and wedged at an odd angle which had prevented it from finishing its journey through. Working against the current, Santorray pulled the trunk out and to the side before he made his way through the newly vacated hole.

Once on the far side of the grate, he found himself being pulled by the current with nothing to grab onto to slow his travels. He was quickly swept down and then dumped several stories down into a large room filled with columns, which provided supports for the roads and buildings of the city. Soft light beamed through the opening and reflected off the water in the chamber.

His body slapped hard into the water-filled room, but he quickly stood up to survey his surroundings. Cloaked by the waterfall he had fallen from, he stood ready for any potential threats. He watched, listened, and tried to sniff out any danger within the enormous room. It was filled with water, waist-high, and thick columns nearly four yards apart. Aside from where he was standing, the water was relatively calm. Once the water arrived from the outside, it dispersed in every direction except back from where it came.

With limited vision in the darkened room, Santorray began making his way underneath the city. A thick layer of sediment had coated the stone columns and walls in the underground level. It had not been maintained for over a decade, and it showed. Thick ooze slowly dripped from the ceilings, while small mounds formed high enough to breach the water's surface in several locations. It had a hideous aroma that forced him to clear out his snout several times.

As he waded through the water, he felt a deep vibration move through the water and echo within the walls. It only lasted a few moments, but it was enough to motivate him to move a bit faster as large clumps of plants and debris became wrapped around his legs. The room had collected a host of items that had been washed downstream. He found himself having to frequently remove the clinging items from his legs to minimize the drag that was slowing him down.

Vines and branches were the most common items to slow his progress. However, the thick muck that coated the floor under the water compromised his movement the most. One item he pulled up and out of his way caused him to take a second look. It was a human arm. He had seen severed arms before but did not expect to see one in the bowels of the city, especially one with a hand that was still moving.

It was at that moment that Santorray realized what waterways fed the river that had flooded the room. The battle with Kaya and her men against the undead had ended with them tossing the body parts into the river.

"Damn!" Santorray said, not sure how many of the parts had washed this far downstream.

After tossing the arm off to the side, he attempted to increase his speed through the high water. He was successful for a few steps before he felt a hand grab his leg. Ignoring it, he focused on the far end of the room, where he could see a set of stairs rising from the water.

Another hand grabbed his ankle, but this one must have been anchored to the undead soldier's body, most likely stuck in the thick muck. He had to stop and expend his energy to address the current issue. To do so, he had to submerge his body into the polluted waters to reach the offending hand that was tightly gripping him. In doing so, several more undead warriors attacked and latched onto him. After crushing the wrist of the hand on his ankle, the blothrud reemerged from the water covered with a host of body parts of the undead.

Some limbs had simply become stuck to Santorray's spikes across his back, but many skeletal jaws and hands had intentionally attached themselves to some rather inconvenient and sensitive parts of his body. Several of the Dovenar Civil War soldiers were fully intact from the waist up and put up a good fight, but they were no match for the strength and skills of an Ergrauthian Elite. In fact, the whole attack was mostly just an annoyance to the mighty blothrud.

Just when he thought the situation was under control, Santorray realized their forces were growing quickly. The undead grew from a few dozen to a few hundred as they rose from the waters and were intent on blocking his path to the stairs. He was at immediate risk of being overwhelmed by their numbers. Their combined weight alone could be enough to hold him under water until he drowned.

Committing himself to the fight, he set aside his plans to escape the room. He knew he had to snap the undead bodies into small enough pieces that could no longer hinder him. It was clear his enemy had no intention to negotiate, so he started the unsavory task of dismembering and crushing the undead to eliminate the threat.

Santorray took a deep breath as a wave of hundreds of undead broke upon him. The weight pushed the blothrud under the water's surface for a fight to the death with an enemy that could not die.

Fully submerged, he grabbed at whatever he could get a hold of in order to break it before moving onto the next. But the weight holding him down was also impeding his ability to move his arms. Even his strength had limitations, as more and more bodies were stacked upon him while he was moving, and he needed to get above the water soon to take a breath. Fighting to roll over onto his chest, he finally pushed in one violent move to lift his head above the water.

The stack of bodies still on his back, he was able to lift his head up just enough to gasp the air and see his surroundings. He was encircled by undead warriors standing around him, and hundreds more were behind them in every direction. However, in front of them all was their leader who held an old broken sword out toward the blothrud.

Korin Swiph was one of the few undead still fully intact with all of his limbs, but he stood out as the leader even among those few. "You prevented us from our revenge!" he yelled at the blothrud. "So now we will take it out on you!"

Locking his arms straight, Santorray continued to fight to keep his head above water. "I'm not your enemy!"

"You prevented us from ending our lives, so you have become our enemy!" he replied before yelling, "Tear him apart like his army did to you and your comrades!"

Santorray was close enough to the sword to see it violently shake before releasing a deep and powerful vibration in every direction. As it passed through the rest of the undead, they immediately began following Swiph's instructions, and started pulling on Santorray's legs and arms. This action caused the blothrud's arms to be pulled out in front of him and his head to fall below the water once again.

In addition to the pressure of his limbs being pulled with great force, there was still a stack of bodies resting upon his back. If he was going to do something to escape, he had to do it quickly. But even if he broke free, he would not make if far before another wave would be on him. There were just too many.

The blothrud began to twist his body one way and then the other, each time twisting further than the last. Santorray then used his twisting momentum to roll in the direction he had last seen the leader of the undead.

The pile of undead upon him began tumbling off as the blothrud's legs and arms became difficult to hold onto.

Santorray rolled until he was able to grab the legs of their leader and pull him under the water with him. It was not much of a contest of strength and the leader was easily swept down to the blothrud's side.

Korin Swiph was an undead and could not drown, so the move had little effect on him as he plunged his old sword at Santorray's chest.

Rolling over on top of him, Santorray's body prevented the attack.

Korin's body was starting to crush as his ribs began snapping. He knew he could not die, but the eternal spell they had been subjected to allowed them to feel pain. Holding the sword out he yelled from the depths, "Stop!"

Once again, the vibration emanated from the sword and the undead released the blothrud.

Not wasting any time, Santorray grabbed the broken sword from Korin's hand and pulled his head up to take a gasp of air. He then quickly stood and waited to see if they would attack him. Now that he wielded the weapon, he hoped to assume control over them. "Yield!" he ordered as he held out the sword.

To his relief, they all obeyed.

Korin stood up and watched his undead army give up the fight as they began sinking into the water to float downstream. "You have cursed us to live forever. We wanted nothing more than to end this torture that was unjustly placed upon us." He stepped back once again and lowered himself into the water. "I hope your sleep is forever filled with nightmares of the pain you have inflicted upon these people." And with that, Korin Swiph and his undead army washed away.

Chapter 11
Gin Attends Service

Gin was seated upon the long stone benches of the large amphitheater in the center of the city of Brushtower. Thousands of people were still filing in and all seats faced the stage that was built out from the ancient stone tower that had been modified into a temple. Everyone in the audience had the Terra King's symbol in one way or another, whether they wore it or had it tattooed onto their skin. No matter the mode of display, the message was clear, they were all followers of the king.

The noise increased as the excited chatter from the crowd rumored the possibility of the Terra King making an unexpected appearance at the event. The rumors continued to grow until there was an unhealthy expectation to see the king. Anything less would be a huge disappointment.

Gin was fascinated at the crowd's willingness to put so much energy into unsubstantiated gossip. He was also intrigued by the diversity of the crowd. He had hoped the event would be packed with people looking for a handout. Instead, he saw people from all walks of life and social classes. The expected segregation of classes was not to be found. Everyone seemed equal in the seating as they all waited for someone to walk out onto the stage and speak.

As the volume of gossiping voices reached its crescendo, Javolo stepped out from the ancient tower and onto the stage. As she did, several vats of oil were lit and flames exploded up into the air, adding a great degree of drama to her entrance. The flames also added extra lighting for everyone to see the events taking place on the stage.

Dressed in a beautiful white shimmering robe adorned with intricately woven symbols of the Terra King and various hexagonal symbols, Javolo commanded the attention of all. She moved effortlessly forward to the edge of the stage for all to see her. Small crystals sewn into her robes glimmered as the flames from the burning vats produced waves of moving light against her. The effect made her appear as though a glowing halo of light was emanating from her.

The crowd cheered with delight as new bursts of flames filled the area while she stood captivatingly before them. Before Gin realized it, everyone was standing, applauding, and cheering the arrival of Javolo.

Instead of joining in the loud cheering, Gin rose and stared speechlessly at her in utter amazement. She seemed bigger than reality as she stood on stage. Without saying a single word, Javolo had these people eating out of the palms of her hands. She was like a goddess to them. Gin truly felt she had the power to tell them just about anything, and they would believe it with every fiber of their being. They were ready to obey her every command. He could feel the energy and wanted to be a part of it. He wanted to learn how to obtain such power for himself. Gin was completely enthralled and found himself to be the last one still standing after everyone else had taken their seats.

Gin kept his gaze upon her as he sat down. He saw more than a beautiful young woman. He saw someone in charge with power at her disposal. Javolo had no need to utilize fear or intimidation to get them to comply with her will. He had grown up in an environment where fear was the normal motivation to obtain compliance. His father used it to get people to do his bidding and to serve his needs. However, the leaders of the Terra King's followers had something he had never witnessed. He was compelled to learn more. He needed to learn more, and he wanted to live in this environment. His father expected him to learn as much as possible to use against the Terra King's reign. The question was, could Gin do both? Was it realistic to embrace and enjoy this wonderful feeling and gathering only to help his father destroy it? He was suddenly unsure of his path forward.

Javolo began her speech much like she did in the village of Sandwell. Once she had the crowd energized she held out her hands for all to be silent. As soon as they were, she announced, "The rumors are true! We are blessed to have the Terra King himself with us tonight!"

Everyone sprang to their feet and cheered as strong and loud as they could. The noise seemed twice as loud as it was before, and there was no calming them down until they saw the man with their own eyes. Within moments they would finally lay their eyes on the elusive Terra King.

The curtains were pulled apart to reveal an extremely pale-skinned older man standing firm with his arms out wide. Tattooed symbols covered his bald white head, and the same symbols were woven into his luxurious white robe. A long white beard reached his midsection and white sandals were worn upon his feet. Aside from his skin, everything about him was without color, including his eyes. He was without an iris or pupil in either eye, making them solid white. This mighty king that was conquering the lands was completely blind.

Cheers rose from the crowd as Gin pondered how a seemingly imperfect and ancient blind man could gain so much power. The thin, old man surely could not have fought his way up to the top. He seemed to be nothing more than a cripple to Gin. The concept simply did not make sense compared to his own life experiences. He was expecting a warrior of some type, and instead saw just the opposite.

Once the crowd calmed down, an enormous black panther stepped out from behind the curtain and onto the stage. The creature was so large that a fully grown man could ride it. Its large white fangs and yellow eyes stood out in extreme contrast against its deeply black feline hair. A metal chain was around its neck, but instead of it being used to restrain the beast, it was an ornamental collar with an orange gem hanging from it.

The noise from the crowd lowered as the panther slowly stepped up to the Terra King. Exposed fangs and raised gums gave a menacing expression to the large cat's face before it nudged the king's hand with the top of its head to be petted.

The old man on stage affectionately laid his hand on the gigantic panther's ebony fur, who then regally led the blind king out to the middle of the stage. The Terra King then held up his free hand, which immediately silenced all the whisperings of the crowd. "I could not be prouder of you. You have spread my words amongst the populace in these lands. You have helped expand our following to new communities. Knowledge of my return is spreading, and we will soon experience peace across our lands. When I walked upon these lands as the Mountain King, I saved our people from the Notarians and the Altered Creatures. Now, as the Terra King, I will save you from yourselves."

A thunderous applause rose from the crowd. Everyone cheered, clapped, and stomped their feet, except Gin. He was captivated by the crowd's display of loyalty, trust, and belief in something that none of them could prove to be factual. Then again, he thought, who could disprove that he was the actual Mountain King that lived thousands of years ago?

It was an amazing scene as thousands of people paid homage to this sightless, frail, pale-skinned man who was being guided by an enormous black panther. It seemed surreal and almost supernatural, and it was something most people would never witness in their lifetime.

The crowd remained standing as the Terra King continued to work the crowd with enthusiastic rhetoric for another quarter of an hour. He then allowed the audience to sit and catch their breath so they would have the energy to cheer at the climax of his presentation.

Gin's curiosity was piqued as he realized the blind man knew when people in the audience were standing.

The king waited until it was completely quiet before starting again. Standing with one hand still resting on the back of his panther, he gave off slight emotional expressions as the panther scanned the audience. As the cat noticed specific people, the king subconsciously turned his head a bit in that direction. It was as though the blind man was seeing out of the panther's eyes.

Javolo had had her servants bring out two large hexagonal wooden displays before the king had begun to speak again. Each display was unique, but clearly based on the same basic design foundation. "These are the images of the Mountain King's

Runestones," the blind man said. "They each represent a different attribute of how we need to run our lives and our community. Today, we will discuss these two: Trust and Valor."

The entire crowd repeated his words, "Trust and Valor."

Once again, Gin was amazed at the obedience of people who were not forced or threatened to be there. They were willing participants in giving this man great power.

"These two Runestones are critical for you at this time," the king said as he and the panther panned the crowd in synchronized movements. "Like all my teachings, these have an internal and external meaning. You must learn to trust your feelings right here at this event. Does it feel right for you to be here? Do you feel good and excited? Does this gathering fill you with joy and a sense of self-worth?"

Closing their eyes, many in the crowd enthusiastically yelled out the word 'trust' as they smiled and relished the idea of believing in themselves and in the king's leadership.

"Trust is more than your belief in yourself and in me," the king said. "It is about my trust in you."

His words caught Gin by surprise. He had served his father and Santorray for years with the desire of them trusting him someday. Yet, this powerful leader was already pledging his trust and belief in him without having even met in person. Unsure about the king's motive, Gin was becoming increasingly intrigued as he continued to hang on to the speaker's every word.

"Trust must be mutual for us to be successful." The king's free hand made wide sweeping movements as he talked. "I believe in your ability to make this world a better place and free yourself of those who want to control you, whether it be a corrupt government or master who has his own agenda."

Gin felt as though the man was talking directly to him as he unknowingly started nodding his head.

"I see you as my beloved children who I will protect with my life. I will help free you from those who wish to suppress you. Those next to you are your extended family, your brothers and sisters, who will look out for you and one another and who will stand at your side in times of challenges. You can trust them, as they can trust you, as you can trust me."

The momentary pause allowed the audience to cheer quickly before he began speaking again.

The panther and the king's head scanned the crowd. "I trust all of you as I can see you all bear my symbol." It was now easy to believe that the king was seeing through the panther's eyes. "Trust is easy to say, but are you willing to demonstrate your trust with not just yourself, but also with your extended family? Are you willing to prove it when non-believers and outsiders come and try to exert their control over you? Can I trust you to fight for our belief?"

Cheers filled the amphitheater after each question. Gin even found himself getting pulled into the excitement.

"Can I trust you to help spread the word to other cities and villages?" The king's words were powerful enough to carry over the noise created by the enthusiastic congregation. "In the words of the Mountain King, we must trust each other to spread these beliefs and recruit a legion of believers. The more power we have collectively, the less they have, and the better our world becomes. The more power we have across the lands, the more power you will have as individuals."

The idea of having power and being trusted at the same time was a beautiful concept to Gin. He had always believed that those two ideas to be in opposition.

After the cheering slowed down, the king smiled at the crowd. "I am here because I trust you. But I am also here to learn who among you has valor." Again, he looked about the crowd as the panther mimicked his head movements. "Valor comes in many forms. I trust that you all have valor to uphold our faith and to help spread the word. However, today will be a fortuitous day for a few of you. I am very proud to announce that we are accepting new recruits to the rank of Grand-Fir!"

The crowd shouted even louder than before. They went wild with cries of jubilation and excitement.

"These few are special indeed. They will become my eyes and ears as they travel across these lands to help carry out my commands, which are based upon the words of the Mountain King. I will work directly with them to ensure they understand what's needed for us to be successful. Some are destined to become my closest associates, and, like the angelic Javolo, will be given authority to speak on my behalf."

Gin devoured the Terra King's words as though they were the nourishment his soul had been desperately craving. He found himself with an opportunity too good to be true. If he could become a Grand-Fir, he could learn all that was needed to complete his mission as expected by his father. Then again, he could use the skills learned from Santorray and other teachers to become the Terra King's greatest advisor. Both options held merit and tempted his ego, but for now he needed to focus his energy on being selected as a trainee.

The king smiled at the continued excitement before him. "I need to know who has the valor to take this step to ascend into the most important mission of their life." Everyone in the audience raised their hands, including Gin. "I appreciate your enthusiasm and wish I could select all of you. Unfortunately, I must be careful in my selection. I mustn't compromise our stability by choosing unwisely." Using the panther's vision, he did not see anyone sit down. "Who has the courage and wherewithal to walk away from their current environment at this very moment and never turn back?" Grudgingly, a large portion of the congregation sat back down. "There is no shame to be had here. I need to find those that are ready to take this step right here tonight. For those still standing, you must ask yourself, are you willing to break ties with your family at this very moment to come with me into my temple for a greater good?" Most of the remaining hands began to waver or drop as they also sat down. With a softer voice, the king spoke to the remaining standers, "Take a few moments to say goodbye to your parents, siblings, children, and friends. You will now give up everything you have to start a new life with me."

Gin glanced around and found himself to be one of fewer than a dozen people still standing. He truly had no fear of such a commitment for he had broken greater obligations before. This was his way in. It was also a potential way out of his current life where he received no respect or love from his uninvolved father. This was a way to start fresh and become the person he wanted to be, not what Santorray or any of his other educators or advisors were trying to make him into. He finally had the chance to become the master of his own destiny.

Unaware of what was going on within the seating area, Gin was surprised when one of the king's personal sentries grabbed him.

Knocking the sentry's hands off him, he instinctively prepared for a fight. His feet and legs shot into position for balance while his arms and hands raised with clenched fists.

The sentry stepped back with a confused look. "You had your hand up."

"Yes. So?"

"I'm here to escort you to the stage."

Gin glanced around and saw several others that had accepted the offer were also being led to the front. "Oh. Sorry. I was so excited." His attempt at making an excuse fell short, but the sentry ignored his words.

The king continued speaking. "Please celebrate these brave and valiant people for offering to become more than what they are today," he announced before stepping away from the panther and waving the beast back toward the temple.

The audience clapped as Gin and the rest made their way to the center of the amphitheater and onto the stage. Several people screamed for their loved one to come back, as the reality of loss settled into their hearts. Within seconds, all eleven volunteers stood on stage facing the crowd. The expressions on their faces revealed the wonder at their newfound popularity. Never before had they felt so important.

Javolo approached the king and led him to the first person in the line, who was a young lady. Once the king stood before her, he pulled out a small box and opened it.

The young lady looked down into the box with a perplexed expression. She was confused as to what she was seeing as a thick dark mist swirled within. Glancing up at the Terra King and then at Javolo, her view fell back to the box.

"Why are you here?" the king asked. When she started to speak, he raised a hand for her to stop talking. "Think it. Don't say it," he instructed. "Why are you willing to give up your life to serve me?"

He then mumbled a short phrase under his breath which caused a dark swirling mist to rise out of the box and move into her forehead, causing her entire body to shake in obvious pain. A thin ribbon of the mist then slowly stretched from her head and worked its way into the king's forehead.

"Ah, I can hear you clearly now," the king said out loud. "There are no secrets between my Grand-Firs and myself." He continued to nod as her thoughts filled his head. "I understand." Another soft mumble was spoken, and the dark mist left both of their heads and returned to the small box.

Javolo then led the king and the young lady to center stage. As the volunteer stood up tall and proud, many of her family members shook with emotions and pride as the scene played out before them.

The king finally announced the fate of the young lady. "She will not be chosen!"

The young lady was horrified at the news. "But I will serve you well. I will do what you ask," she pleaded, hoping he would change his mind.

"You are here for the wrong reasons," he told her before speaking back to the crowd. "She is here to escape a life of poverty and starvation. She is driven by food and shelter instead of our cause!"

Anger and disgust filled the crowd as they heard the news. Her family bowed with collective heads in shame.

"How can I trust someone who can be bought by a loaf of bread or a fresh melon?"

Yelling and screaming filled the theater. They were visibly upset at her misguided and selfish reasons to join his elite followers. How dare she dishonor herself and her family?

Desperate, she attempted to plead her case, but no one was interested in listening.

"All I asked was for a few of you to exercise a higher degree of valor, and dedication to the cause. And what is presented to me? I receive someone who lies about their intent! Did we not just speak about trust?" He waited for the crowd to get more upset before continuing. "I am troubled by the true nature of what drives this young lady. Is she a reflection of you and your community?" Again, he waited until he could hear the anger being shouted by the crowd. "Then solve your issues before they are allowed to reach out to me!" he yelled as Javolo pushed the young lady off the stage and into the crowd.

The scene was vicious, as people attacked the young lady for her attempt to deceive their king. Like piranhas attacking a bloody swimmer, some tore at her clothes and limbs. Others reached out with punches and kicks. Soon blood was seen spraying from the scene as sharp objects were used to cut into her arms, legs, and face.

By the time her family reached the mob, they found her unconscious, nearly naked, and bleeding. In their attempts to cover her and carry her out, the family was pushed and taunted to ensure they also felt some pain before exiting the amphitheater.

Once they left, the Terra King took control again. "I hope no one else up on this stage has less than pure motives."

The remaining ten people stood silently as they shivered from the threat of being tossed into the audience for a wrong thought or misunderstood desire.

Gin was not immune to this. Hundreds of thoughts crossed his mind as he worked out potential escape plans as well as fighting his way out if the king should find him not worthy, or worse, on a mission to destroy the king's power. He was the last in line which gave him plenty of time to watch the mystical vapor penetrate the minds of others and reveal their dark secrets.

Sweat began to form on his face and hands as he watched a third of the volunteers being tossed back into the crowd for severe punishment. He was beginning to doubt his half-baked plan, and he knew that, this time, Santorray would not be around to bail him out.

Chapter 12
Santorray & Wittig

At one-point, Brushtower had been a great fortress, but many of its towers had been destroyed in the Dovenar Civil War. Since then, new growth had filled its streets, but the underground tunnels had mostly been forgotten and ignored.

Dark and murky passageways were filled with thick moist air that left a heavy dew on the first few floors below the streets. Beams of sunlight and lantern light were able to shine down through drainage grates into these underground corridors, but they extended no further. The lower levels were in complete darkness and a thick layer of sediment had coated the walls and steps. In this region, the sound of dripping water was overpowered by a river flowing directly under the city.

It was at these depths, within a half-sunken chamber far beneath the streets, that the water stirred in the underbelly of the city from the motions of a beast. Rising from the dark and dirty fluid, Santorray slowly made his way through the chamber and to a staircase, after he had survived his battle with the undead. He was exhausted.

Taking his first steps out of the waist-high water, he plucked a disembodied skeletal hand that had been impaled on one of his shoulder spikes and tossed it to the side. But to his disappointment, the steps were anything but dry. Instead, they had a thick coat of organic material that squished out with each step he took.

The sloshing of the blothrud's steps continued up the stairs until he was on a floor that provided him with glimpses of light from the street above. After taking a moment to rest, he moved down the tunnels just a level below Brushtower's streets. and headed toward the center of the city. Santorray began his journey through the labyrinth of passageways.

***

Back up on the open streets of the city, chores were being performed before the locals took their midday meals. Cleaning and preparing for the afternoon activities comprised of a series of mundane tasks that had to be completed before the locking of doors of many businesses.

A boy, not more than nine years old, was making his way to clean the last stall in one of the many city kennels. However, he stopped in his tracks as he heard a muffled moaning coming from behind several crates. Upon investigating, he discovered an old man lying on the ground, bound and gagged, and covered in manure. The boy stood motionless at the unexpected encounter.

The gagged old man's eyes grew large as he attempted to yell, only to snort and mumble, while snot ran down his face.

Unsure what to do in such a situation, the boy turned and ran from the scene without thinking twice.

Wittig cursed the boy for leaving as he continued to attempt to work on freeing his hands. Not as limber as he was in his youth, nor trained in the art of escape, he struggled to make any headway. The only thing he had going for him was that he was now awake, so he had a chance to get some help. Then again, his potential rescuer just ran off, leaving him to fend for himself.

Wiggling his body back and forth across the dirt and hay-covered floor, Wittig wormed his way over to the front door of the building and flopped his way out onto the dirt-covered open area with a loud thud.

Waiting for the wall guards to rush over to help him, he was disappointed that only a few guards even looked his way. One chuckled at the sight while the other gave a sigh before walking over to investigate.

"Hitting the sauce a bit too much, mate?" the man asked as he approached. However, each step he took allowed him to understand the urgency of the situation. The man had holy symbols tattooed on his bald head. One of the king's followers had been tied and gagged. "What in the blazes happened to you?"

Once the gag had been removed, Wittig unleashed his story in cryptic partial sentences. "They're here. Protect the king! They're spies. One is a blothrud!"

Stopping his assistance, the guard yelled out orders to his companions, "Intruder alert! We have a blothrud in the city! Protect the king! Alert the Knight Slayer!"

A horn blew and people ran to spread the news. It would not take long for the entire city to be in lockdown.

After removing the rest of the ropes, the guard helped Wittig to his feet. "Tell me what you know!"

"There are three of them. A blothrud, a brandercat, and a young man with long brown hair. They're after the king. They mean to take him down."

"They plan to kill him?"

"I don't know. They could be. I just know they're here to find him and remove him from power!"

"Come with me!" The guard pushed Wittig up into a wagon before jumping into the driver's seat. "The Altereds should be easy for our people to see, but you will need to point out the young man. He snapped the reins, and the two-legged faralope leaped into action and bolted forward, nearly knocking Wittig out of the back of the wagon.

Racing under a large archway that separated the gate courtyard area from the main city street, the guard yelled at the locals to get out of the way. Unfortunately, the city's loud warning bells caused people to file out of their doorways into the street to see what all the commotion was about. This of course was the opposite of what they should have done, and the wagon had to slow down to avoid running over the masses that filled the street all the way to the king's temple.

"Get out of the way!" the guard yelled in frustration, though with very little success.

Chapter 13
Gin's Fate

Gin stood nervously as the Terra King finished questioning the woman next to him. The dark vapor had reached out into her head as the king demanded that she stop fighting his will to find out her secrets. Unable to uncover the truth he was looking for, the king ordered the mist to cut off her breathing until she succumbed to his will. Splitting in two, half of the vapor lowered into her chest and squeezed her lungs.

The woman wished to be a Grand-Fir with all of her heart. She had no ulterior motives, but felt she had to hide one part of her life that she wanted no one to be aware of. At a young age, she had been raped by an uncle. The dishonor of that event getting out would destroy her family and label her as an unworthy option for the pure and innocent who were personally trained by the king. Because of this, she resisted. The pain was unbearable. She attempted to scream, but no sound escaped her mouth. She was desperate to prevent him from finding out her deepest thoughts.

"If you won't allow me to know your hidden secrets, then you shall no longer know them either," the king said in disappointment. "Remove all of her memories," he ordered the vapor.

Releasing the hold on her lungs, the vapor focused all of its energy on her head. The wisp of a creature went to work extracting all treasured moments as well as those she wished to forget. As it did, her expression faded to a lifeless stare. Within a few moments, she no longer knew anyone, not even herself. Dazed and confused, she was escorted off the stage to start her life over again and create all new memories. She was now an adult with the mind of an infant.

Stepping up to Gin, the blind king held out the small box before him. It was his turn to see if he was worthy of being one of the king's Grand-Firs.

Javolo was very pleased to see Gin again, but she restrained herself from greeting him in front of the king during the ceremony. Instead, she smiled and gave him a quick wink.

Hiding his nerves, Gin attempted a smile at her before gazing down at the box being opened once more. He had to control his thoughts and convince the king he was a faithful follower and free of deception. This would be a monumental task for him. He had lived his life only caring for himself and saying whatever was needed to get what he wanted. Then again, if he blocked too much of his past, he'd risk becoming a vegetable, like the previous candidate. He had to control his thoughts and guide the vapor to only access the thoughts needed to assure his selection. He had to be in control of his mind and emotions, as Santorray had taught him.

The king opened the lid of the small box, allowing the dark mist to once again escape and rise to eye level before moving forward. It easily entered through Gin's forehead and began to latch onto his thoughts and memories.

Gin attempted to focus on peaceful thoughts instead of his constant conflicts with Santorray.

The king frowned at the first images that were sent to him through the dark mist. "A blothrud?"

Gin's thoughts had already betrayed him.

Javolo's eyes grew. "Yes, I saw him as well. He was the one who destroyed our venue in Sandwell. This young man was there at the time. The creature was quite violent."

Gin's thoughts jumped from memory to memory as the mist was accessing his thoughts and playing them out. Knowing the danger of the king learning his plans, Gin attempted to control what memories would surface.

The king shook his head slightly. "There is more about this blothrud than that event." Despite his blindness, the king's solid white eyes glared at Gin. "That creature is planning something that involves me."

Gin began to shake with pain as the mist forced its way past the young man's attempt to block it.

"Wait, I see something," the king announced. "That blothrud is here at this very city."

It was then that the local bells rang out, alerting the public of danger. Normally this was a sign of an attack by an army, but the Terra King knew better. Pulling the vapor away from Gin and back into his little box, he quickly tucked it away before addressing the crowd. "There is a blothrud within our walls! He is intent on destroying our way of life. He wishes to create chaos by removing me from power. Now is the time to exercise your valor! Form a circle around our temple and protect me from this dreadful creature! Let no one enter unless I approve it."

The king's words caused his flock to rush out of the amphitheater and surround the complex, which included the temple and several recently built structures for his high level followers.

Beyond the Terra King's Temple area, the clanging warning bells filled the city's residents with anxiety of not knowing the source of the danger threatening their city. It was assumed they were under attack, but they had no idea from what army or from what direction.

Javolo escorted the king and those who remained on stage into the King's Temple, where they were safe from the eyes of anyone wishing to do them harm. Several of the original stone walls had been rebuilt on the outer walls as well as the innermost chamber. Helping the blind man onto his throne, she looked over at Gin with concern. "What do you know of this?"

Gin's mind filled with options for fabricating a story that not only allowed him to live but could enable him to get closer to the king. "Yes, I was there at Sandwell. The blothrud broke free from the stage and captured a few of us before escaping into the forest."

The giant panther approached and lay down next to the throne to protect the king from his enemies, as well as to attack and kill anyone if ordered.

It was more than a bit intimidating to be developing a story on the fly, knowing that if it did not work, his life would surely be at an end. "The insane beast eventually stopped and tied us against a few trees. I could tell he was an arrogant beast, so I questioned him about himself. His pride eventually got the best of him and before long he boasted that he was hunting the Terra King."

"Why would he want to kill the king?" asked Javolo.

Gin tried to control his eyes from looking away from her as he continued to pull together his story that would play on their fears and goals. "The usual reasons; power and money. He was promised these by Darkmere."

Javolo studied his expression and body language before speaking to the king. "I believe him. We are the only real threat to Darkmere in these lands. We knew he would eventually try to stop us."

Nodding, the king agreed with her as he still faced the young man. "What did he want with you?"

Gin was starting to feel more comfortable with his story and welcomed the opportunity to tell more. "I was just in the wrong place at the wrong time. He grabbed two of us in hopes of gathering information. Neither of us were able to provide him your whereabouts, so the beast began satisfying his hunger. He was so engrossed in eating the other man, I was able to escape."

"You left the other to be killed?" Javolo asked.

Gin put on his best attempt at a sad face before continuing. "I am but a young man with no weapons or training. The beast is twice my height." Gin could tell they disapproved of his lack of valor. "It was then that I had to make a choice. I could risk my life to save a man who was most likely going to die anyway due to his limbs already being devoured, or I could race here to warn you of the plans of this blothrud assassin."

The Terra King sat back and took a deep breath as he considered the story.

Kneeling before the blind king, Gin took a deep breath before speaking. "I give you my life, worthy king, to do as you may. I can die with honor knowing that I have made difficult choices to bring you this warning that could save your life. It was between his life and yours, and I chose the Terra King." Gin was all in. It would now be up to someone else to determine his fate. It was a position he hated to be in, one he felt he was in most of his life, but he seemed to have no other option.

"Javolo," the king said, "Take this young man to the Grand-Fir preparation chamber. Burn his foul-smelling clothes, shave his head, and brand him with my mark. We will want to keep an eye on this one. He has great potential."

"As you desire, my king," she said with a slight bow of her head. She then reached down to help Gin stand and led him out of the temple's central room.

Gin did his best to not show any signs of relief. In fact, he was very pleased with himself for being accepted and having access to the real workings within the Terra King's world. This was more than he had planned to accomplish, and it surely was more than his father or Santorray had assumed he could pull off. He beamed with pride on the inside as he considered how much smarter he was than everyone else. Hiding a grin, he followed Javolo to a structure built against the original stone tower. Within it was a long hall lined with doors on both sides, and a central large open area filled with tables. The building appeared to be living quarters for the king's followers.

Walking to the far side, it became clear to Gin that the main entrance to the building was on the opposite side from the temple. They had entered from an internal access, causing the staff to look up in surprise at seeing a young man with long dirty hair and filthy attire within the temple. Only the king's selected followers were allowed in there and he most certainly didn't look the part.

Javolo snapped her fingers to get everyone's attention. There were only six elderly women working at the time, all wearing the same style of robes as Javolo. Of course, Javolo's clothes were far superior and extravagant. "Our king wishes for this young man to be fully processed and marked. Return him to my side once you are complete." They all acknowledged in unison with a slight nod of their head. Satisfied, Javolo turned and briskly headed down the hall from which they came.

Watching her leave, Gin was once again mesmerized by the soft approach with which she commanded the attention and action of all. And again, he desired to possess such command.

By the time he turned away from Javolo, he was shocked to find the elderly women approaching him and grabbing at his clothes. "What are you doing?"

"These rags you're wearing must be burned," one lady said. "Then you must be scrubbed down and cleansed before being allowed to be in the king's presence."

Before he realized it, they had backed him through a doorway that led to a large tub of water at its center. As some pulled off his clothes, another grabbed soap while one pulled scissors from a shelf. As the door slammed, the normally cocky Gin could be heard screaming for help in a most undignified way.

Chapter 14
Chameleon

Fighting their way through the city of Brushtower as the bells continued to ring, Wittig and the guard had abandoned their wagon and made their way on foot. The dense population of confused locals in the streets made the trip toward the center of the city painfully slow.

"What's your name?" the guard asked.

"Wittig. Yours?"

"Edwar," he called back over the noise of the crowd. "We're almost there. Tell me what the young man looks like so we can both be looking for him."

"He's about as tall as my shoulders, wears dirty brown leather, and has long greasy brown hair that hangs over in his eyes and past his shoulders. Just look for your typical, dirty, low-life pickpocket."

"Any markings, such as the king's symbol tattooed on his body?"

"No. He's not a follower. He's an anarchist with a hot temper that can be set off without warning."

"Understood," Edwar said while pushing his way out of the main street into the open area that surrounded the King's Temple. "Make your way around to the right, and I'll go left. After notifying my superiors I'll meet up with you on the far side."

With a nod, Wittig was off on his mission to find the miscreant that beat him up in a tavern, burned down his village, covered him in manure, and tied him up in a stable. He was seeking more than a little revenge.

The central court of the city was not nearly as packed as the streets. However, there was a ring of the king's followers surrounding the temple and the attached complexes. It appeared their objective was to protect the temple's occupants from any threat. Wittig was concerned that they didn't know what this threat looked like.

The old man from Bentree felt it was his duty to alert them, so he approached the line of followers protecting the temple. "What are you protecting the king from?"

"There is a blothrud in the city," one man replied.

Slightly surprised that they were already aware of the threat, he nodded. "True, but there is also a brandercat and a young man that are a serious threat. I must alert the king of a potential assassination attempt."

Placing a hand out in front of him, the man stopped Wittig in his tracks. "No one is to enter this area without the Terra King's approval."

"How can he approve my entry if he isn't aware I'm here to warn him about this serious issue?"

"Sorry. No one enters until we are notified otherwise."

"Will you at least relay the message to him?"

"The Terra King is safe as long as we hold our line."

"Can you not pass on my warning?"

"Sir, please go about your business before we have someone remove you from the area."

Frustrated, Wittig grumbled and finally walked away, following the circle of followers around the public venue. His eyes darted from the people creating the protective barrier to the locals wandering the open area. He had to find that young man before it was too late. He would walk the streets for days if he had to in order to bring that lad to justice.

Clean and in fresh robes, Gin sat quietly in a chair as the last bit of his hair was shaved off. He was now bald and ready to be marked. For that, they had him lie down as they tattooed the king's symbols onto his head. The pain was terrible, but he knew the benefits would be worth it. Besides, once his hair grew back out, no one would ever see the markings again.

Once completed, he looked at himself in a mirror. He had never imagined seeing himself bald, let along with tattooed symbols on his head. He found it fascinating and intriguing; he had been transformed into someone he barely recognized. The game was becoming devilishly fun, and he looked forward to seeing Santorray's face once he realized how much better than expected he was at deception and infiltration.

Now that Gin was presentable, he was escorted out of the living quarters and into the main courtyard on the way to another structure that leaned up against the King's Temple. The construction was much stronger and more decorative than the quarters he had just left.

Halfway across the open area and just inside the protective line for followers, they met Javolo, who was standing tall with her silky robes flowing in the light breeze. She was a sight to behold. Searching the streets beyond the circle of followers around the temple area, she waited to see or hear some news of the threat. Taking a slight glance to the side, she had to take a second look to believe her eyes. "Gin?"

A smile grew on his face as he approached. "In the flesh."

She was shocked at the transformation from his thick hair covering his face and his heavy leather garments to a clean-shaved head with lightweight flowing robes. "It's good to actually see your face for a change."

He rolled his eyes at the lighthearted dig. "What's the next step, now that I'm an official follower? When do I get to strategize with the king?"

She gave a slight chuckle. "You may look the part, but you have so much to learn before you are granted such an opportunity."

"Learn? I've been studying my entire life. When do I get to start using this knowledge?"

"We are never too old to learn more," she replied.

Showing a bit of frustration with a roll of his eyes, he responded without thinking. "I've heard that enough times."

"Really? By whom?"

Gin had to think fast. He surely could not tell her that he'd been trained by Santorray. His name was too well known as the most powerful blothrud in the lands. "My father."

"Oh. Sounds like an intelligent man. Why are you not with him? Surely, he would not send his offspring out into the wild without protection."

"No, of course not. He died from injuries he received from a blothrud." Gin continued to weave his story together on the fly. "That is why I don't like blothruds. In fact, it could be the same blothrud that I escaped from."

"The one who is here to assassinate the king?"

"Yes. It very well could be. I don't know. I'd have to look again. It was dark."

"Do you understand the nature of the threat the king is to people such as Darkmere?"

"Darkmere wants to prevent the king from expanding his following across the land. With each village and town that becomes faithful, he becomes more powerful and more of a threat to others that do not understand the peace and stability that the king provides us." His nerves caused his eye to twitch as he waited for her to accept his story.

She stared at the young man for a bit too long, making him uncomfortable. "You seem to know a lot about what's going on in the events of our land."

A slow swallow allowed him to think of his reply. "Yes. Well, like I said, I've been studying my entire life, and I've learned more about these issues than you may think."

They walked slowly toward the new building while she continued the conversation. "Clearly you are beginning your Grand-Fir training with more knowledge than most. Perhaps we could expedite the process for you. I'll give it some thought."

Pleased with how things were unfolding, Gin glanced out past the line of protective followers and saw Wittig just a few dozen yards from him. The man was staring directly at him. Unsure how to react, he played the part of his new role and gave Wittig a slight respectful bow of his head.

To Gin's surprise, and relief, Wittig nodded back before continuing his search for Gin. The changes to his appearance were enough to fool the old man. This gave Gin an added sense of confidence with his subterfuge. His goal to learn more about the king's weaknesses for his father was changing to learning how to exploit his position best serve his own interests. New seeds of greed and desire began to grow within him as he accompanied Javolo to the living quarters of the king and the higher-ranked followers. It was exactly where he wanted to be.

Stopping at the nicer quarters, Javolo instructed Gin to stay outside until she received approval for him to enter. After seeing his polite nod, she entered the building and left him to wait.

Taking advantage of the quiet moment, Gin plotted his next move. The thought of deceiving these people evoked an unfamiliar feeling within him: a feeling of control over others. It was intoxicating, and was much more enjoyable than expected. He thrived on the excitement of conning others into believing his lies. "People are so stupid," he mumbled to himself with a wicked laugh.

"Don't confuse trust with being stupid," Nutrix said from nearby.

Twisting around toward where the voice came from, he could barely make out her faint outline. "Perhaps I should have said people are naïve fools who believe whatever you tell them if it fits with their beliefs or agenda."

"Gin, you're getting in way over your head. We need to find an exit strategy for you."

"Leave? I'm at the door of discovery. I'm at the eve of learning everything I need to know."

"You have made it this far with a blend of skills and fortune on your side. But you're getting careless, and your luck is bound to run out."

"Nonsense! Everything is working as planned. They don't have a clue."

Nutrix moved a bit closer. "They will if they see you talking to me. Now turn back to your waiting position and talk to me with a bit more subtlety."

Caught making such an obvious mistake, he turned and gritted his teeth. "Leave. I don't need your help. I can do this on my own."

Sighing as she recognized the wall he was building between them, she attempted to calm him. "I'll always be here to help you, because I love you."

"I am not a child any longer," he said with frustration. "I am an adult now."

"You're growing up so fast that it's easy to want to prove yourself before you're ready. I need you to slow down and think this through. One bad decision could change your life forever, and not necessarily for the better."

"No." His answer was short and stern. Her arrival had squashed his feeling of independence and cleverness over the king's people. He felt as though she was taking that away from him. Turning his head toward her, he scowled at her. "I am no longer the child you raised. I don't want to be treated as one, nor do I have the use for a nursemaid in my life anymore. I can make my own decisions. I don't need you."

Nutrix was crushed by his words. She knew he lashed out like this when he was upset. He was young and she understood he was trying to prove his independence. But that didn't take away the pain from his words and actions. She could feel the muscles around her heart tighten as tears began to form in her eyes. Gin was right about not needing her anymore. She had just hoped his youthful bond would have lasted a bit longer and their relationship would end with his appreciation of her unconditional love instead of his clear frustration at her interference. She was not his biological mother, but she never experienced such pain as her daughter grew to be an adult. She wondered if it was a phenomenon unique to mothers and sons.

Gin slowly turned his back to her to resume his wait for Javolo's to return.

"I will find Santorray, and we will meet you back at camp once you have accomplished what you came for, as you agreed to." Nutrix waited for a response but never received one, not even a nod of his head. "I will always love you, Gin, no matter how much you push me away." Waiting once again for his acknowledgement, she eventually gave up and left to find Santorray.

Gin stood quietly as he watched the crowds of people continue to protect an old blind man, who was not actually in any danger. He was obsessed with learning the secrets to creating such a loyal following. He had to learn how to obtain such power in order to control his own future.

The door Javolo had disappeared behind eventually opened, and she once again stood in the doorway. Seeing the distant look in Gin's eyes, she asked, "What's on your mind?"

Snapping out of his trance, he smiled at her. "I just feel so fortunate to be here and to have this opportunity."

Feeling he was leaving something out, she still nodded in agreement. "We all are. I've talked to the king, but with the current security threat, he has several meetings with local leaders. He will, however, be able to fit you in after our evening meal. Meet me back here as soon as you're dismissed from the table."

He agreed, but hid the frustration he felt at having to wait yet again for someone else's schedule to free up for him.

Chapter 15
Treasure

Tunnel after tunnel looked the same. Most were pitch black with the rare glimpses of the sun's rays making their way in from the streets above to breach the darkness below. Lacking a torch or lantern, the only way to navigate the lower levels of the city was to follow the walls to know when they turned. It was a slow and arduous journey.

A low frustrated growl escaped Santorray's muzzle. He felt lost and disorientated. In his mind, this was a sign of weakness which he had to overcome. He had never been one for hiding his presence, but the sloshing of his footsteps gave away his location to anything or anyone that was down there, assuming anyone was. The chance was low, but he was not in the mood to attract anyone looking to stop him from his task. He hoped Nutrix and Gin were having better luck on their venture.

Never one to give up, he continued forward, one step after another while dragging his hands along the walls. His efforts allowed progress, but not without running face-first into a few objects and tripping over unidentifiable objects in his path. He felt more productive fighting an army of undead than he did walking aimlessly through the dark. As far as he knew, he had been walking in circles for hours.

"How does a proven war hero, such as myself, end up scampering about in the sewer levels of a city?" he asked himself. Visualizing himself scampering caused him to let out a soft chuckle which eased his stress a bit. "You're losing it, Santorray. Pull it together," he told himself.

Continuing forward, his ability to see in low lighting was not helping much as he was often in pitch black. However, he did have the ability to smell changes in the air. Slight changes warned him of approaching walls and notified him to widening walkways. A small alteration in air direction was quickly recognized and helped guide him through the underground.

It was this sense of smell that alerted him of a drastic change in his surroundings. The tunnel had opened on both sides of him as well as above him. Coming to a complete stop, he listened closely as he sniffed the less stale air. Pulling a remaining undead hand off his back spike, he tossed it out in front of him. He heard it hit the floor, but the expected sound of it rolling to a stop never arrived. Moments later, he heard it crash upon rocks far below him before splashing into water.

Making a few more observations, he was able to determine that he was standing at the edge of a chasm with a bridge directly in front of him. He didn't know how wide the chasm or the bridge was, but he estimated the fall was enough to potentially kill him.

Sliding his foot out in front of him, he searched for the edge of the ledge. Not finding any for over a yard, he turned sideways to do the same thing again. This time he did not have to go far before his foot fell beyond the ledge. Pulling it back in, he turned around and conducted the same experiment only to find a ledge there as well. It was now clear that he was standing on a bridge that was less than a yard-wide which crossed the chasm of an unknown depth.

The bridge was in no better shape than the corridors he had traveled through. The same thick mixture of mucus-like material coated the surface. Wet and slippery, the bridge was not to be crossed easily, especially without any light available. Regardless, he was going to continue. He was almost to the room he was searching for.

Slowly shuffling his feet across the unseen bridge was an image Santorray he was glad no one would see. His father would have ridiculed him ruthlessly for looking so vulnerable. Then again, he rarely lived up to his father's expectations.

Santorray found himself nearly slipping off the bridge more than once, despite his cautious speed. Slow and steady, he achieved his goal, but it did nothing to boost his pride.

Reaching the opposite wall, Santorray found a carved-out opening with two large wooden doors that had been warped by the moisture and jammed into their closed position. Santorray smiled at the opportunity to rip something apart or bust something down. It played on his strengths and subconsciously filled his mind with praise from his estranged father.

After busting one of the doors off its hinges, he walked into the dry and dusty room. "So, you've been cut off from the rest of the underground all these years," he said to the room as the smells reminded him of the last time he had been there. Memories of the Civil War rose and fell in his mind as momentary flashbacks of faces and events made him stop and recall the layout of the location he now stood within. "Let's see if you are still hiding that precious treasure you held all those years ago."

The area had once been a hidden throne room filled with statues, tables, chairs, and a host of beautiful art, none of which Santorray could see now. But he did recall the basic floor plan and worked his way over to the throne chair. Once there, he lifted the massive chair over his head and then smashed it onto the ground. Thick wood splinters sprayed across the room as metal trim and buttons spun across the floor. The once luxurious chair was no more. But it was not the chair that was important. A small hidden compartment within the chair had broken apart and released the treasure Santorray had come for.

Lowering himself to the ground, he started sifting his hands through the broken chair rubble until he found what he was looking for. "Ah! You've been waiting for me." Pulling at a necklace chain, he lifted it up until he found a large crystal hanging from it. This was the prize he was seeking.

Placing the crystal in his palm, he used his other hand to brush away the debris. It was then that he saw a vision of a man approaching him from behind and stabbing him in the side with a magical dagger, cutting deep into his body. Santorray fell to his knees, watching blood pour out of his body as the acid from the blade ate away at his flesh. He screamed in pain, but then the vision ended as suddenly as it had started. The blothrud found himself on the floor clutching the crystal with one hand and his side with the other. To his surprise, there was no wound. It had not really happened.

With a sigh of relief, he noticed the crystal was giving off a warm yellow glow which helped him see a few yards. After checking his side for a wound one more time, he slipped the chain over his neck and attributed the incident to being hit one too many times by the undead.

He quickly extended his interest past the crystal and onto the room now that there was light. A layer of dust coated all the furniture and art, and they were casting shadows on the decorative walls. Some of the shadows from the statues were not what he expected. In a way the dark silhouetted shadows created their own artistic flair.

As he took one last glance about, he thought he saw one of the shadows move. Upon a second look, he realized that the shadow was not coming from any of the art, nor anything else around him. There was nothing in the room to create the shadowed image before him, let alone one that was moving.

The dark image upon the wall moved once again, and it was now obvious that it was a shadow of a man; however, Santorray still could not see the person who was casting the shadow.

Regardless, he leaped forward to make a grab for the invisible man that was casting a shadow. Santorray's attack resulted in grabbing nothing but air. He instantly spun around and called out into the room, "Knight Slayer! I know you're here! Face me like a real warrior!"

A crushing blow against the blothrud's jaw took him by surprise, causing him to stumble. Santorray regained his balance and launched another attack of his own. Once again, he came up empty handed, but he was rewarded with a kick to the back of his knees which took him down. It was obvious that his enemy was not only invisible but was also able to see in the dark.

Rolling back onto his feet, the blothrud grabbed the crystal to control the light. It would not help him see his enemy, but he would use the shadow to gauge his location. Before he could respond to the moving shadow, he was slashed across the chest with a sharp object.

Despite the pain, he reached out to grab whatever was attacking him. His opponent was too fast and had the advantage. However, if he could get him into a corridor, then his opponent could only attack from one direction, which would give Santorray a better chance to retaliate.

He dove for the doorway of the large open room. Once there, he knew he had to cross the slippery bridge over the chasm to take his fight with the Knight Slayer into the tunnels.

A blunt blow cracked Santorray across the lower back, knocking him forward onto his knees. It was then that his previous vision played out as the Knight Slayer became visible long enough to stab his magical acid-covered dagger into the blothrud's side.

Screaming in pain, Santorray fell forward onto the slippery bridge. The burning pain continued to eat at him as the dagger stayed lodged in his body, held firm by his opponent. Turning to swing back at the invisible warrior, the blothrud struggled to not slide off into the chasm. Missing again, he was able to knock the dagger from his enemy's hand as it popped out of his side and tumbled down below the bridge. In great distress, he stood up and started working his way backward across the chasm.

Nearly halfway across, Santorray heard the sloshing of his opponent's feet upon the slushy bridge. Finally, the blothrud knew the exact location of the Knight Slayer. Not letting on to his awareness of the approaching footsteps, Santorray continued to walk backward across the bridge until the Knight Slayer was close enough to attack.

Stepping forward, the blothrud used his sharp spikes attached to the back of his hands to stab the unseen man. He felt an impact, and the faint yellow light gave him a view of spraying blood. His method worked; his opponent was finally injured.

Unfortunately, the powerful swing of his arm caused him to lose his balance, and he began to fall. He reached out to grab the warrior to take him down with him. With a bit of luck on his side, he latched onto the Knight Slayer and pulled him forward. As they both slipped, they fought to use the leverage of the other to push and pull themselves in the opposite direction. Before either realized it, they had fallen on opposing sides and had both grabbed onto the slippery bridge.

Santorray took no more than a single breath before he started pulling himself up. As he did, he felt a hard kick from his rival who hung onto the far side. Thinking quickly, the blothrud used his legs to lock onto the Knight Slayer in order to pull him under the bridge and then release him. The plan began to work before Santorray's grip on the slimy stone bridge gave way, causing him to fall instead of his adversary.

Still clenching his legs onto his opponent, Santorray hung upside down while the Knight Slayer struggled to sustain his grip with the additional weight. It was obvious that they both were going to fall to an unknown fate. At least it was obvious to the blothrud until he heard the man's voice.

The invisible warrior began speaking in an ancient tongue that echoed within the chamber. As he spoke, a light blue glow surrounded one of his hands before the stone from the bridge began to soften and extend around his wrist. Within seconds, there was a stone ring attached to the bridge holding the Knight Slayer from falling, even if he released his grip.

Once his magic spell had been completed and the blue glow faded, he let go of the bridge and used his free hand to grab another dagger from his belt. He then buried it into Santorray's leg that was intertwined with his own.

Still hanging upside down, Santorray yelled again but refused to release the tension of his legs on his enemy.

A second and third stabbing with the blade caused deep wounds that bled down Santorray's legs and torso, and then onto his face.

Santorray attempted to lean up to grab the man, but the blothrud's wounded side muscles were no longer strong enough. His leg muscles continued to spasm until they finally gave up. The great Ergrauthian Elite fell from the Knight Slayer into the chasm.

Slapping the rocks with the back of his neck and shoulders, Santorray bounced off several boulders before splashing into the flowing water at the bottom of the chasm. He was not dead, but he was severely compromised. To keep fighting was out of the question. His only hope was to float his way out of the city and then climb out of the river and return to camp to mend his wounds.

Chapter 16
Recovering

Santorray limped his way back into camp before falling to his knees to rest. He had lost a lot of blood and his cut leg muscles were shaking from overuse. But they would heal. He was not so sure about the deep gash in his side from the magical dagger. The river had washed away the acid, but the magic was preventing his body from healing itself in its normal fashion.

"Santorray!" Nutrix called out as she returned to camp after gathering wood for their fire. "What happened?"

"I had a little run-in. I'll be fine."

"That's more than a little run-in. It looks like you're lucky to be alive." She immediately started cleaning the wounds to see the extent of the damage. What she found was not good. "If these were any deeper you would have bled to death. As it is, it wasn't wise to be walking with these gashes. You've no doubt caused further damage."

"I'll heal."

"I know you will. Your body heals faster than any creature I've ever met. But that doesn't mean you're invincible."

"I'm pretty sure I was taught that earlier today."

"Then stop taking unneeded risks!" Continuing to mend his wounds, she was noticeably more emotional than normal.

"What's wrong with you?"

She refused to make eye contact as she worked on him. "Why did you have to go in there? What was so important that you would risk your life? What were you trying to prove? Why are you always being so darn stubborn? What are you trying to prove?"

"I wasn't trying to prove anything." His voice was softer than normal as he reflected upon her uncharacteristic tirade.

Seeing the yellow crystal hanging from around his neck, her emotional state became tenser. "You risked your life for treasure? I may never have seen you again, all because you wanted a shiny object to hang from your neck! When are you going to start thinking about the rest of us?"

"The rest of us? You and Gin?"

"I know this is our last mission together and we'll never see each other again after this, but you could at least have the respect to pretend to care about us until it's over."

"Nutrix, what the hell happened to you? Why are you acting like this?"

The brandercat's scales shifted to various colors as she struggled to regain control of her emotions. Finally, she turned to hide her crying. "Gin."

Santorray sat up straight with tightened fists, although his side wounds caused him to wince. "What has he done to you?"

"No. it's not like that. He just…" She took a moment to control herself, "… expressed that he no longer needs me. And he's correct. He doesn't need me anymore. He's too old for a nursemaid. I can't teach him anything more."

"You could teach him respect. He still has a long way to go in that area," Santorray said firmly before wiping tears from her eyes. "You still have so much to teach him, but he has to be willing to learn. That's just not where he is right now in life. He feels he knows everything and everyone else is an idiot, including us. He feels we're holding him back." He smiled as she nodded her head. "We can only hope that he gets past this stage, realizes he still has much more to be taught, and becomes open to learning from others."

Wiping her final tear onto the bandages she had wrapped around his leg, she nodded in agreement.

"Is that why you were upset with me? You feel everyone is leaving you and no one needs you?"

"I know it's petty, but all I've ever wanted to do was be helpful to others. I foresee that coming to an end."

Santorray pulled the chain necklace over his head and held it out in front of him. "While in the underbelly of the city I found the Du'Kor Crystal." Watching her expression, he could tell the name meant nothing to her. "Trust me, it's worth a fortune."

"How did you know it was in that city?"

"That's a long story which I will gladly tell you after this mission is completed."

Her eyes saddened. "Are you're saving the story to be our final conversation before you leave."

"Close. I'm saving it for our final conversation before we both leave." He could see the confusion in her face, which he expected.

"You risked your life to find a treasure. For what purpose?" she asked.

"To buy the freedom of someone who has given her entire life to care for others."

It took a moment to sink in. "Santorray, no. You can't do this."

"I already have done this, and I have new scars to show for it," he said with a slight laugh. "This is my payment for you and your daughter's release from slavery."

"This is not your responsibility. You should use this for yourself and your future."

The blothrud laughed. "I have no need for money. I could live off the land by myself and never get tired of it. You, on the other hand, deserve freedom, and this crystal can buy that for you."

She was in shock and still could not believe what she was hearing. "What would I do? Where would I go?"

Santorray smiled. "What wonderful questions to explore. I can't wait to find out what you do with your life once you're free to live it. Once our mission has been completed, you can do whatever you want." Checking the dressings on his leg, he was pleased that the argument was over, and they would soon be heading back to Gin's home. "Where is Gin?"

Nutrix's face became a bit more rigid. "He has been accepted as one of the Terra King's key followers. They have shaved & tattooed his head and dressed him in their robes. You wouldn't recognize him."

"Did he find the information he was looking for? Will he be ready to leave soon?"

"No. I think he's going to stay with them for a while."

"What's a while?"

"Until he is ready."

Now it was Santorray's time to show some pent-up frustrations. "Is he expecting us to just sit here at camp for days or weeks until he decides to return, assuming he does return at all?"

"That is my concern. I am not sure what his plans are. He might be staying with them until…"

"Until when?"

"I get the impression he means to stay until he can gain some power within the Terra King's ranks."

Furious, Santorray smashed his fist upon the ground. "That is not the objective! I need to see him. Show me where he is!"

"No! You're not going anywhere. First off, you need to heal that gash in your side. Second, he's in the center of that city and protected by the city walls, the city guards, and the Terra King's followers." Seeing that he was considering an option to fight his way in, she took charge and notified him of the plan. "You will stay here while I go back in. I have been able to get past the guards when they aren't paying attention or by simply catching a ride on the back of a wagon. I can come and go with little risk of being seen. I will contact Gin again and then return to you with his decision to return with us or join his new master, the Terra King. If he wishes to be an adult, then it is time for him to make some hard decisions."

Intrigued by her more forceful manner, he had to ask the obvious question. "What's changed?"

"What do you mean?"

"You've never been willing to let him go. You've coddled him and forgiven every inappropriate thing he's ever done."

"I still love the boy. I still think of him as my own child," she said softly. "But there must come a time when I allow him to push away from my shores to sail out into the water without me." Her eyes lowered. "If I have done my job correctly, he should not need me anymore. So, I should be pleased that he pushed me away."

Santorray grimaced at the image of Gin sending Nutrix away, especially after everything she had done for him. "I don't give a sandrat's ass what his youthful infatuations and inexperienced yearnings are. He may push us away, but it is our responsibility to bring him home regardless of his desires. He can do what he wishes after the mission is complete."

Chapter 17
Control

Hours had passed since the warning bells had stopped, for no one could find any danger within the city's walls. As the residents started going back to their normal routines, Wittig was taken for questioning about his warning of danger that never came to fruition.

Meanwhile, Javolo led Gin into the high chambers. Unlike the repaired keep tower, which was a mixture of old and new stone blocks, the high chamber building had been recently built with all new materials at great expense. Marble floors shone clean and grand columns reached up to the high-arched, thick wooden ceiling. Carvings decorated the wooden beams while stone sculptures of giant Runestones filled the walls to make the inside feel like a completely different world than what was seen from the outside.

Gin's head spun as he was mesmerized by the grand feeling and the amount of money it must have taken to create such a place. He unconsciously smiled as he realized the wealth accumulated by the Terra King in his efforts to grow his flock across the lands.

At the far end of the room was the giant panther that had accompanied the Terra King on the stage. It was now sprawled out behind a stone throne filled with plush pillows. The cat's solid black hair was in stark contrast with the white marble flooring and columns, and the creature's size was hard to accept as real. The feline's white teeth, yellow eyes, and orange gem on its collar appeared to shine against the darkness of its body. It was a daunting scene of magnificence and danger.

The large cat glared at all who approached the king as he sat on the throne. If the intent was to intimidate everyone who wished to speak to the king, then it had accomplished its mission.

Javolo placed Gin in the line to speak to the king before she walked up to the opposite side of the throne from the cat's head. With a soft touch to his shoulder, she alerted the king that she had returned, and they could continue meeting with the locals. Dozens of people stood along the side and back walls as they waited to be granted the right to step forward and enter the line behind Gin.

"My king," Javolo said with a slight bow of her head, "the mayor of Brushtower is here to see you."

A slight nod from the blind king was all she needed to proceed. Turning to the mayor, she gave him permission to advance forward. "Mayor Galia, you may now speak to the Terra King."

Short and skinny, the mayor nervously stepped toward the throne while eyeing the enormous panther. "Thank you," he said with a high-pitched cracking voice as his long, thin mustache quivered.

The feline could sense his fear, and its body began to stiffen while the hair on its back began to rise. Long dangerous claws began to extend from its paws as it prepared to pounce on the mouse of a man that squeaked forth.

Sweating and shaking from head to toe, the mayor nearly hyperventilated as he stepped forward to speak to the king. His eyes darted back and forth from the king out of respect and the panther out of fear. "My king, thank you for gracing our city with your presence." A heavy swallow interrupted his speech. "Our people are so honored to have your support in these difficult times. I know you have already given us so very much, so it is difficult for me to ask you for anything else."

There was a long pause as the king waited for the man to enlighten him as to the purpose of his visit. "Speak your mind. We have no secrets here."

"Thank you, my king," he replied with another nod. "Again, we are so grateful. But the cost of this new temple has pulled critical resources from our city. Food and supplies are becoming scarce. Our coffers have all but dried up."

A low growl from the panther shook the man to his core and he immediately stopped talking and froze in place.

"I am confused," the king replied. "Have I not given your people the Mountain King's words to live by? Have these words not reduced crime in your streets? Have my followers not followed our rules and made this city an icon of peace for all the land to envy?"

Nodding to the comments, the mayor agreed. "Yes, to all of those, my king."

"Good; I want to make sure I have done my part. However, it sounds as though you are having issues with your economy."

"Yes. We are struggling."

"I see," said the blind man. "I will help you get through this."

Dropping to his knees, the mayor was pleased at the answer and thankful for not being punished for bringing the bad news.

"I will transfer funds to this city to ensure it stays strong. We will make sure we have a robust military to keep non-believers in line and that they pay higher taxes for living in our city of peace. Businesses will become part of our flock so we can control what's being sold, for there is no reason to sell items that do not support our cause. I will be adding my people to your staff to control the coffers to ensure you won't need to make this uncomfortable request ever again."

The mayor's nodding had slowly turned to shaking as he listened to his city fall under the king's rule. "Thank you, my king. However, the root of our financial issues stems from the efforts of building this beautiful temple. If you could simply assist in paying for this, we would have a chance to resolve the other challenges."

The king smiled and gave a slight laugh. "When I first arrived here, many years ago, this city was still in ruins from the Dovenar Civil War and your people were angry and refused to work together. You made a commitment to me to pay for my temple if I helped bring peace and unity to your broken-down city. I have carried out my part. Surely, you aren't going to go back on your word, are you?"

Mayor Galia realized the hole he had dug himself into, and his feeling of being trapped was obvious from his body language. "I would not go back on my word, my king, but you are asking so much more than originally expected. The price of your temple continues to increase faster than we can support it. You have left me with the option to either halt the construction or hand over the city to you, which will take away the free will of our people."

The room fell silent after the comment. Rarely did anyone have the nerve to speak so openly to the king. The uneasiness was interrupted by a low growl from the panther, who exposed its teeth to the man kneeling before the king as it prepared to spring forward and attack.

However, before the feline could leap forward, Gin noticed that the king gently covered one of his rings with the palm of his other hand. In doing so, the orange gem on the panther's collar sparkled for a moment and the giant animal relaxed and settled back down near the throne.

Gin tried to hide his slight smile as he realized how the king was controlling the black panther while everyone else was focused on Mayor Galia or the feline. Perhaps they had never seen magical rings, necklaces, and other such devices. The young man realized how fortunate he had been to have been schooled in the functions and capabilities of many magical items. Unfortunately, he lacked the powers to create any on his own. Yet being able to spot them gave him an advantage over most.

Now that Gin had an idea of how the king was controlling his personal protector, he needed to know how he was utilizing the mist in the box. It was a frightening advantage to have such power that could force others to tell the truth. The idea of gaining such capability caused Gin's grin to grow larger than he had realized.

Mayor Galia knew he had crossed a dangerous line with his statement to the king. It was his last chance at keeping the people of his city free to run their own businesses and lives. He had hoped to do this without it costing his imprisonment or potential death. Unsure of his fate, he kneeled silently and waited for his judgment to be called.

Standing up, the Terra King adjusted his thick robes so they would flow evenly around his feet. Once presentable, he pulled one arm out slightly so that Javolo could reach around it and escort him to the mayor. With each slow step he took, the tension in the room grew.

Unlike most in the room, Gin remained unaffected. If anything, he was anxious to see what was next. He was enjoying the drama and studying how the king was exerting his control over his subjects. It was like watching a master thespian at work as the young man studied the craft of timing and movement.

Reaching the mayor, Javolo had the king stop less than a foot before him. She then motioned for the mayor to stand up to face the ruler eye to eye.

Doing as instructed, Mayor Galia stared into the white eyes of the blind man, waiting to hear the reply to his request for financial support without the deliverance of a complete regime change.

"I don't believe this is about money," the king said to the mayor. "I think there is an ulterior motive to your statements. What drives you to make such a request, my dear faithful follower?" Placing his hand on the mayor's shoulder, he waited for an answer.

Shaking uncontrollably with fear, perspiration trickled down the city leader's face. "There is no hidden agenda, my king. The cost of the temple and its supporting buildings are draining our city of much needed funds. All I ask is that we use our money for our city until we have enough to put toward the temple once again."

Shaking his head in disappointment, the king replied, "It saddens me that you can't tell me the entire truth."

"But it is the entire truth. It goes no deeper than that issue."

Reaching inside his robes, the king pulled a small wooden box from a pocket and lifted it up near his chest.

The mayor's knees began to wobble, and his hands became fists with the anticipation of the oncoming pain.

Filled with excitement, Gin watched intently in order to learn how the wisp of darkness was controlled. He recalled the king softly saying a command before controlling the shadowy vapor when they were on stage. But at the time, Gin was too concerned about how he was going to control his own thoughts to pay attention to the command words used. This time, he leaned forward and listened intently.

"Rise, Civej, at my behest," the king said softly while opening the little box.

A controlled stream of mist fluidly snaked its way out of the box and in front of the mayor's face, where it waited for the king's orders.

"No! Please!" the mayor pleaded, for he had seen the damage the mist had done to others in the city.

Ignoring the pleas, the king proceeded as planned. "Find out the true reason why the mayor wishes to stop building my temple. Has he lost faith?"

Gracefully flowing forward, the mist pushed up against the man's forehead and then into it. No cuts or openings were visible, but it was obvious that the stream of dark vapors had penetrated his skull, as it began searching the man's mind.

Attempting to scream, the mayor let out a series of gasps while fighting off the pain as his eyes rolled back into his head. He no longer had any concept of his surroundings. Instead, he was alone with the mist that was raping him of his thoughts and raising havoc with his nervous system.

Cupping the small box with both hands, the king closed his eyes and bowed his head in concentration. "No, not that," he said softly to the mist several times. "Ah, there. Show me what that is." Nodding, he continued to give instructions to his mystical servant at the expense of the mayor's pain.

"I see the issue," the king finally said as he raised his head. "You're afraid." Tapping the side of the box, he whispered, "Yield, Civej," to the dark wisp, causing it to pull out of the man's head and slither back into its home.

Mayor Galia collapsed upon the marble floor in a heap of exhausted flesh and bones. His breathing was labored, and his body shook with spasms for a few moments before he began to regain his bearings.

"I understand your dilemma," the king said softly. "You are filled with fear over this change. You feel as though you are losing control, when the truth is just the opposite: as our followers grow in numbers, we have more control. Completing this temple is more than a financial challenge. It is a symbol of our faith in the Mountain King's words; in my words."

"The people must be free," the short and scrawny man said as he rose from the floor onto his knees. He was not willing to give up yet.

"Absolutely!" the king said with pride. "We want free will to flourish. But we want to do it safely so that chaos does not reign over our lands. To accomplish this, we will guide them with a set of rules that will provide peace and prosperity to everyone."

"What will you do to those who choose not to follow you?"

The blind man gave a warm smile. "I bear no ill will toward the choices they make. I will never fully understand the mental challenges or lack of intellect that would cause people to want chaos over harmony and order. Perhaps there is a sense of evil and barbarianism that lurks in some people that prevents them from understanding what we have to offer. In those cases, we must ensure they do not infect our followers. We must protect our followers from this threat. It's our duty as leaders to keep them safe from the non-believers."

"What becomes of them?" the mayor asked again. "Will they be executed?"

"If they choose a path of chaos, we must encourage our people to do whatever is necessary to prevent them from polluting our way of life with their misguided ways."

The mayor closed his eyes as he focused on lifting himself back up to his feet. Once there, he stood only inches away from the king. "You would ask our people to attack non-followers and run them out of town?"

"No, my son." The king said with a grin. "That would only push the issue off on others. We don't want that to happen. It's best if these lost souls are sent to Della Estovia where they can do no more harm."

"You want our people to kill their fellow man because they don't follow you?"

"We can't save everyone. Some people are simply too far gone to help."

Mayor Galia was furious. "I won't allow you to do this to my people!"

Nodding, the king tapped his ring as he replied softly into the man's ear, "And there lies the issue. They are no longer your people."

Grabbing an ornamental blade from his belt, the mayor moved to stab the old man who had taken everything from him. However, before Galia could thrust it forward, a giant set of claws raked across his arm, severing it from his body. In absolute shock, the mayor turned to see the black panther's open mouth envelope his head before biting it completely off. His headless body then fell to the ground.

Javolo had pulled the king back a few steps to minimize the blood splatter upon his robes as the growing pool of blood moved across the floor. It was a hideous scene that she had become accustomed to.

Guests gasped at the sight while the sound of cracking bones from within the panther's mouth echoed within the hall. Several people fainted while others simply turned their head. A few ran from the room in fear or to find some place more appropriate to vomit.

Javolo reached down and picked up the mayor's beautiful short dagger as though she was shopping for a gift. "There's no reason for this to go to waste," she said as she tucked it into her belt.

It was obvious that neither the king nor Javolo were shaken by the gruesome event, for they had experienced such events before in other cities. What did seem a bit odd was that Gin's stance was unchanged. He studiously observed every action of the king, Javolo, the panther, and the mayor. His response was unnatural, as though he too was immune from the horrors of the last few minutes.

"Gin, are you alright?" Javolo asked.

Gin nodded with a smile. "Very entertaining."

That was not the answer she expected. "This isn't a show. We are dealing with life and death here."

"Oh, I understand that. But all actions taken by leaders are made for a purpose to obtain something."

"And what is it you feel the king has obtained?"

Feeling a bit superior to the others in the room, he carried a slight attitude in his voice. "The king has shown publicly that he will not tolerate those who are not fully committed to his ways. He has demonstrated that defiance is not heroic, but instead is a death sentence. Only a fool would stand up to him." Taking a slight tilt to his head, he added some additional thoughts. "The people in this room were also able to learn that those who deny his gifts of peace will be identified and eliminated. Word will get out and his flock will carry out these actions without him ever having to command them to do so. Peer pressure will keep everyone in line."

Before he could continue with his analysis of the events, the king raised his hand to stop the young man from speaking any further. "And where do you stand?"

Javolo's eyebrows raised as she waited to see just how cockily he would respond as the giant panther continued eating the mayor just a few yards from them both.

"I understand your motives and am intrigued by your ability to grow such a loyal flock. I would be honored to stand at your side and assist you."

"You?" The king found the idea amusing. "The tenor in your voice sounds like you're still a teenager, your words and reasoning resonate like an advisor, and your attitude and confidence are that of a warrior. How is this possible? Perhaps it is you who is performing."

Nodding at the thought, Gin kicked the mayor's severed arm out of his way before taking a few steps forward. Ignoring the growling of the massing feline, he stopped and answered the question posed to him. "I have been taught by the finest educators on the historical events of our lands and the military tactics they have used for quest and conquering. I know what has been successful and what has failed and why. I have also been trained by the greatest of fighters and know how to handle myself around any threat, regardless of the environment I'm in. I may still be very young to you, but I have spent every day of my life learning to better myself. I didn't waste time playing like others my age. Instead, I focused on becoming a useful resource to myself and all of mankind. I am a powerful tool at your beck and call. Utilize me to reach your goals."

The king stayed quiet as he contemplated Gin's comments and considered the next move. "You have come to my home and made yourself known. You have convinced Javolo to grant you this audience with me. What is it you want?"

"Want?" Gin asked. "I want nothing."

"Now I know you're lying. Everyone wants something. That's why they come here to speak to me."

"I can't argue with that logic, my King," Gin said as sincerely as he could play his voice. "What I want is to offer you something."

"What do you offer, and what are you expecting in return?"

"I offer my knowledge of historic leaders, their tactics, and strategies. I offer my experience as a fighter and traveler. In short, I offer you my life to help you become the greatest leader of all time."

"Are you suggesting I'm not already on this path without you?" The king smiled. "Are you suggesting that I need you?"

"Not at all. However, you have many obstacles in your path to growth. With the kingdom fractured, this is a prime time for Ergrauth to pull his Altered Creatures together and wipe us all out. We have Darkmere building his empire and Ambrosius attempting to unite all the leaders to create a collective power. In addition, these lands have many regional leaders that have strongholds and fortresses too strong to overpower. There are many threats that still lie ahead of you which I can help you resolve, for I have studied their cultures and their leaders."

With his smile long gone, the king stared out from his blind white eyes. "And what is it you want?"

Gin took another step forward. "I want to be a part of your success. I want to see the mighty arrogant fall from their self-imposed thrones. I want to be at your side when their unstructured ways of controlling their people collapse in disarray. I want to see those leaders bow down to you."

Clearly intrigued, the king had to know more. "Why do you wish to see them fail?"

"Because they are pompous and believe they are smarter than the rest of us while they continue to implement the same overused ideas that have failed our people time and time again," Gin spoke spitefully before adjusting his tone. "What you're doing is based on the original Mountain King's words and teachings. It's the only culture that has survived for thousands of years. It's the only one that will continue. These words, your words, this is the way of life that must prevail."

The king stood quietly before turning and walking back to his throne with the assistance of Javolo. Once there, he faced the young man in deep thought. "I will consider your words and notify you of my answer."

"Thank you, my king." Gin bowed in deference to the king before winking at Javolo.

Chapter 18
Broken Bonds

Santorray's body was able to heal itself much faster than most creatures, including those of the same species. It was a unique quality he had, but healing was not instantaneous. A wound that would normally take a few months to scar over for most blothruds was at the same point within several days for him. Likewise, the gash from the magical dagger should take years to mend, if at all. But with Santorray, it was healing at a faster pace and would take around a month.

Pulling the bandages from the injuries inflicted by the Knight Slayer, the blothrud examined the progression of healing. He was never pleased with having to wait for his body to repair itself. To speed things up, he often used the mucus from snails and slugs, which seemed to reduce the time a little bit.

While hobbling around the woods hunting for snails, he heard Gin's voice; the young man and Nutrix had returned. "Good. You're done," Santorray presumed. "How did your final mission go?" Limping back into the camp, he could tell immediately that the brandercat was upset about something. "What happened?"

"It's not over," she told him.

"Why?"

Gin stepped in before Nutrix could reply. "Santorray, I have them eating out of my hands!"

"Who's eating and what are they eating?"

Gin was nearly bubbly with excitement about his news. "I played them, Santorray! I wish you were there to see it. I stood with courage, faced the king, and convinced him that he needed me!" he shouted. "I'm in!"

Confused, the blothrud was still trying to catch up. "The Terra King is here?"

"Yes! And I used my skills of persuasion to get the ear of the king."

"Gin, are you saying that they slipped up and you overheard something of value?"

"No," Gin replied to such a strange suggestion. "These people are idiots. I simply talked my way in. They believe everything I say. It's like fishing in a bucket!"

Santorray was trying to visualize the events. "You talked your way in; what did you learn?"

"Well, for one, I learned how he controls that giant black panther of his."

"He has a panther?"

"Huge panther. His back is as high as my head."

"How will that help your father?"

"I don't know yet, but I also know how he controls that dark wisp."

"Dark wisp?" Santorray was trying to understand the situation, but it was getting more confusing.

"Yes! He opens this box, and this mist reaches out and sucks your thoughts out of your head!"

"Is this how he controls his people? Is this how his power is spreading across the land so fast?"

"No. Well, it's part of it."

Santorray was getting a bit frustrated. "What have you learned that will meet the objective of this mission?"

"He seized the Mountain King faith and passed it off as his own. He is promoting that his followers become judge, jury, and executioner for those that do not follow his way. In a sense, they all are doing his bidding for him by holding their family, friends, and neighbors accountable to the king's rules. The fear of being caught not following the rules forces them to comply, or at least pretend to, in order to live. The Terra King can grow his control in every direction without him having to drive it. It's all through peer pressure based on his rules. It's brilliant!"

Santorray considered the implications for a moment. "This will be an excellent place for your father to start his planning to prevent the Terra King from expanding into your lands." Nodding with a bit of pride, he grinned at Gin. "You have succeeded. You have completed your mission."

Shaking his head, Gin clearly disagreed. "No. Not yet. The king will be making a decision on allowing me to stand at his side and help him with his strategies going forward."

"We will be a long way away from here before he calls for you."

"I need to go back. I want to be there when he agrees to this."

Nutrix stepped in with the issue she had been struggling with. "And what if he says no? What if he realized that you're an imposter or a threat to his sovereignty? What if he uses that black mist on you and finds out that you were sent here to find out his secrets?"

"He won't. I already have him where I want him. This is my game. I'm in control of it."

"No, you're not," Santorray said with a commanding voice. "I am in control of your game until I get you back home."

"I'm not ready to return! I have a chance to understand what his plans are and his ultimate goal. We will never get a chance like this again."

Nutrix shook her head. "It's too dangerous."

"I agree with Nutrix. You have met the expectation of the mission, and we shall return home victorious."

Gin was livid. "You're a coward!"

Santorray instinctively lifted an arm to backhand the young man for such an insult but stopped himself.

Gin stood strong, waiting for the attack. "I used to want to be like you, but no more. I finally have a chance to do something that could change our world, and you don't want me to take any risks. You, Santorray, are now teaching me to not take any risks? What happened to you? You used to be so brave. You used to do whatever it took! You were once able to teacher me, but no more. I can't learn from a weak-backed Fesh of a creature."

"Gin!" Nutrix yelled to get him to stop. However, in silencing the young man, she only achieved a moment of quiet before Santorray replied.

"Mboy! I have taken more risks in my life than you could ever hope to count. So much so, that I know the difference between knowing what risks are worth taking and which ones are a fool's errand. You think you're so much smarter than everyone else, and that is what's going to bite you in the ass. But I'll be damned if I'll let it be while you're still under my watch. Yes, you're intelligent, but intelligence and wisdom are two completely different things. You are ridiculously weak when it comes to the latter. You make terrible decisions that cause havoc and hurt anyone in your path."

"Santorray!" Nutrix yelled to get him to stop before he regretted what he said.

Unfortunately, there was no stopping Santorray. "Even if the king agreed to let you in, you soon would reveal your major deficiencies in wisdom and morals. You wouldn't last a week before he'd behead you for your actions. Hell, I'm surprised Nutrix is still alive after being around you! You cause nothing but problems for everyone around you! I don't know why I thought I could help you. You're hopeless!"

"I'm not hopeless! I can do this! I'll show you I can finish this mission better than you!"

"If you go back there, you'll die! Get this through your head: you aren't as good as you think you are!"

And there it was. There was no taking back anything he had said, nor any way for Gin not to recall those words for the rest of his life. Nutrix knew it had created a rift that may never be fixed.

Gin's fists shook in rage as tears ran down his face from his teacher's words. He did not know what to do or say. He was furious as he turned and walked out of camp with a scream filled with rage.

"You pushed too far." Nutrix turned to go after Gin but was stopped by Santorray.

"Don't go to him. He's no longer a boy. It's time he realizes that his temper tantrums won't be fixed by cuddling with his nursemaid. Give him some time to think, then we'll all head home." Upset with his student and with himself, he plopped back down to the ground to reduce the pain from his still all-too-fresh wounds.

Nutrix watched Gin sulk as he slowly walked away from the camp. Once he was out of earshot, she turned and glared at the blothrud. "How dare you!"

Santorray looked away from her. He was already angry; he did not need an additional reason. "Let it go."

"No," she growled. "I will not let it go. Have you lost your mind? This is not one of your soldiers. He's a young man trying to find his way. He needs a role model that he can aspire to, not a drill sergeant."

"I gave that boy three years of my life to learn from me. If he hasn't grasped my teachings yet, he never will."

"Raising a boy to be a man is not a mission with a time limit on it. You can't just place a start and end date on this event!"

"We've had this conversation many times. I didn't set the timeline for his training."

"But you agreed to it!" Nutrix made sure he understood that this was his choice.

"Only because I knew that was my only opportunity to train him."

Nutrix watched the blothrud's intense focus. "I've asked you this many times, but you've never told me the answer. I demand to know the answer this time. What did he promise you?"

"Who?"

"Gin's father. You've given up years of your life to train his son, yet you've never been willing to share with me your reasoning. You don't value money, and you don't crave power over others. You expect him to grow to have high integrity and values, but not to follow in your footsteps. So, what did he promise you?"

A slow shallow sigh was released as Santorray turned to look at the nursemaid. "He promised to freely release one from under his rule, without any backlash toward them if they chose to leave with me."

Nutrix was shocked to hear he had given up so much of his life to save another. "Who? Who did you ask for him to release?"

"I didn't say. Yet he agreed. He must have felt my training of his son was worth the life of anyone under his control."

Her eyes grew large at the realization that came to her. "That has been your desire all along. You have been risking your life to train Gin with the purpose of having him freed from his father's control."

Santorray gave a low growl before responding. "He shouldn't have been under your master's control in the first place."

She backed up a few steps as his words continued to sink in. "You've spent all this time trying to brainwash him into your way of thinking so when you ask for the boy's freedom Gin will choose you over his father." Her eyes tightened her stare at him. "Why are you attempting to steal this young man from his home?"

"It's not like that. You don't understand all the facts."

The scales across her back turned various reds, and her stance grew more aggressive. "I have been Gin's nursemaid since he was an infant. It is my charter to protect him from any threats, and right now this could include you."

A small smile grew upon his face as he thought about her statement. "Do you recall the first time you saw Gin?"

Hesitating at first, she did not like the fact that he was changing the subject, but her demeanor eventually relaxed a bit as she remembered. "Yes, he was such a helpless thing."

"How did he come to your care?"

"My master ordered me to watch over him with my life."

"Where was his mother?"

"She had died in childbirth."

"Ah, so he had just been born when you took over?"

A perplexed expression crossed her face as her scales turned back to their normal light brown. "No, he was not a newborn. Someone had saved him and taken care of him for a short time before bringing him to us."

"I see. He was brought to you. From where?"

She nodded at his statement. "His mother was attacked while traveling, causing her to give birth early. Gin was then brought back in secret to prevent any further attempts on his life."

"I see. Who brought him back?"

"I didn't meet them, but it was my understanding that it was one of the master's loyal servants."

A relaxed grin filled Santorray's muzzle. "That was I."

The idea was not hard to grasp, but still took her by surprise. "You saved Gin?" Her mind quickly switched from the past to the present. "Now you wish to take him away? Why the change of heart?"

A heavy sigh escaped the blothrud's mouth before he replied. "I have my reasons. Circumstances change."

Her mind raced to put all the pieces of his past together. "What did you do to the boy so many years ago that has forced you to believe he needs saving from his father and home?"

Santorray shook his head. "That is a conversation I wish to have with you after we return from our mission. What's important now is that I can teach him values that will give him a better life."

Growling, she clearly did not approve of his answer. "We've also had this discussion. You can't change someone's moral compass. The same boiling water that softens the potato hardens the egg. You can't get the same results from him with the techniques that you've used on others. He'll crack!"

"You may be correct, but I have to keep trying."

Nutrix was still upset from the hurtful words that had been exchanged. She had a deep desire to help resolve the issues and bring them back together before leaving for home. Her chest tightened at the idea of walking all that way without anyone speaking to each other for the final days of them being together. "I'm going to check on Gin." Seeing Santorray raise a hand to stop her, she was quicker on the draw. "This is not negotiable."

Santorray lowered his hand as he watched her walk out of camp and into the woods. He was amazed at how strong she had become in the few years he had known her. She had grown into so much more than just a nursemaid. She was a voice of reason and sanity when he and Gin struggled to cooperate. She was like a mother to them both as she made sure neither of them went too far. And when one did, she would scold the one and console the other. "I wouldn't have lasted a year with Gin without you," he said softly to her distant ears.

Adjusting his position, he realized he was bleeding again. His leaping to his feet earlier in order to yell at Gin had caused his wounds to reopen. "Damn," he mumbled as he removed the bandage to see how bad it was.

"Santorray!" Nutrix yelled as she flew back into camp. "Gin is gone! He must have gone back to the city!"

"I've had enough! I'll bring him back once and for all." Attempting to stand, he collapsed back to the ground in pain.

"You're not going anywhere," the brandercat ordered. "Stay here and mend your wounds. I'll find him." With that, she sprinted off into the forest.

"Wait!" the blothrud yelled before attempting to get up once again, only to make it a few yards before grabbing onto a tree for support. He knew there was no way he could reach the city before Gin. Nutrix was their only hope.

Chapter 19
Impatiently Waiting

Hour after hour passed as Santorray impatiently waited for Nutrix to return with Gin. Each moment that slipped away added to his stress as he wondered what had happened and what he could have done to prevent it. He was helpless to assist them, which was one of his most detested situations. But even if he were completely healthy, his options would be limited. He had no idea where to start searching for them. As a blothrud, he could not walk the streets, even at night, without causing the city's entire military to assault him. And if he did leave to find them, he could easily miss them while they returned to camp. Worse yet, he could place them in danger if they came looking for him within the city. It was a terribly frustrating predicament.

His nerves were shot, and his senses were on high alert, resulting in several false alarms. Noises in the woods sounded as though someone was approaching. But each time he checked to see who was coming, he was unable to find anyone. The smell of humans wafted his way without any evidence to back it up. He wondered if the Knight Slayer's poisoned dagger was causing him to sense danger where none existed. Whatever it was, he knew he had to remain in control of his emotions to keep the panic at bay or he would miss potential indications of any real danger heading his way.

Every few hours his frustration would build, and he would toy with the idea of storming the city walls. He was fed up after an entire day had gone by without any knowledge of his companions' fate. Enough was enough. He had to make his trek to the city to at least try to find them. Perhaps he could enter the underground rooms once again and then try to make his way up to the surface at night. It was a terrible plan that had little chance of success, but he simply refused to sit by and wait any longer.

Gathering his gear for the trip, he heard some rustling in the woods. Something or someone was making its way toward him. Perhaps the Knight Slayer had finally tracked him down to finish his fight. Just in case it was him, Santorray grabbed a thick branch to clobber the intruder before he had the opportunity to strike first.

Bushes and small tree saplings were pushed aside as the unknown intruder approached. Squinting, the blothrud was unable to see anything that was coming his way; therefore, it had to be the Knight Slayer. Pulling his weapon back to strike, he swung with all his might just as the branches near the camp were pushed apart. Missing his target, Santorray's weapon crashed against a tree and shattered into hundreds of pieces that sprayed into the woods.

Catching himself against the same tree, he turned to see his opponent. There he watched a brandercat change from nearly invisible to a brownish red. Nutrix had raced into camp and slid to a halt before running into Santorray's weapon. Out of breath, it was obvious to him that she had been running for a quite some time.

"They left," she said, panting.

Relieved, he regained his bearings and immediately wanted to know more. "Who left? Gin?"

"Yes. He left with the king," she replied with a heavy breath. "They are traveling to one of the larger cities."

"Did you talk to him?"

"No. I tried, but I couldn't get close enough."

"How do you know where they are going?"

After a few more deep breaths, she was able to talk a bit clearer. "I was able to get close enough to overhear them talking. The king has accepted Gin into his high chambers. They are taking him to the king's main temple for additional training and to work with the king's advisors on new strategies to expedite his conquest of these lands."

"When did they leave?"

"I raced here just after they headed downstream. We have the fortune of already being on the right side of the city, but we'll never catch up to them with your wounds."

Straightening himself up, he demonstrated to her that he was mobile and had strength to walk. "My side is still healing slowly, but my legs will carry me for as long as we need. We may not be able to head them off, but we should be able to catch up with them once they stop for the evening. It's a few days' journey to the next city. We'll have to reach them during their trek if we want any chance of finding Gin."

"What do you propose we do if we find him?"

Santorray stopped himself from blurting out his initial thoughts about teaching Gin a lesson. Instead, he simply said, "We need to offer him one last chance to return home. If he declines, he needs to know that his father will never extend the offer again and he will be shunned from his home."

"Do you have the authority to speak on behalf of our master?"

"I have spent enough years with him to know what he expects of me and his son."

Giving him a nod of agreement, they left the camp and headed toward the river road in the hopes of catching up with the Terra King's traveling procession.

The camp fell quiet. The fire was out, and the red ashes had turned to shades of gray. The camp returned to being just a small opening within the forest until the footfalls of an unexpected intruder broke the stillness. Wittig had made his way out of the city after being humiliated for making false claims of a planned attack on the king's life. He had returned to the site to discover what he could with the goal of proving himself worthy once again. Staying downwind of Santorray's powerful nose, he was able to see the blothrud and brandercat together. However, he was unable to overhear their conversation, so he would have to follow them to find out more. He desperately hoped they would lead to the young man as well.

Chapter 20

Betrayal

Several faralopes had been unhitched from their wagons and tied up to eat and sleep for the night. Provisions were taken out, and the fragrance of a hot meal carried across the river's shoreline. Tents were being erected and lanterns were being lit while the sky turned an array of oranges and reds as the sun drifted behind the clouds.

Within the largest of the tents, Gin had carried in a handful of moss and placed it on top of a map that was sprawled across a table. He had already added rocks and other items to the map before the Terra King was escorted in.

Javolo's eyes grew as she saw what he had done. "This is not a child's play area!" Clearly upset at seeing the mess upon the table, she was decidedly disappointed in the lack of responsibility with this newest recruit.

Raising his hands to calm her, he smiled. "I think our king should see what I've done before we place judgement on my actions."

"I am the eyes of our king, and I don't like what I see."

"I know, but this isn't for you. I made this for him." Gin waved his hands toward the table in an effort for her to lead the elderly blind man to it. Once she had done so, he respectfully requested, "My king, reach out with your hands and feel the map before you."

The Terra King was skeptical at what he was about to feel, but knew he was surrounded by Javolo and his personal guards. He was safe to reach out, and once he did, he was surprised at what he discovered.

Gin smiled at the reaction. "I assume without your sight you've never been able to truly understand how your lands contrasted with the lands you desire to add to your kingdom. If my assumption is correct, you've been dependent on others to advise you on geographical strategies without fully comprehending what lies before you. I've taken this bold move to give you the opportunity to see your lands and their beauty as well as explore what is still out there waiting for you."

The king began to softly run his hands across the map.

"There, under your left hand is a carriage bolt which represents the city of Brushtower," Gin said. "I dripped streams of candle wax for rivers and shorelines. The wax near the bolt you are touching is the river road we have been traveling. The walnuts that you will feel are the villages currently under your power, while the grapes are the villages waiting for your words to free them." Pleased with the king's response to his work, Gin continued to follow the king's hand as he explained what each item represented. "There, those rocks are the Guardian Mountains, the area covered in flour is the O'Sid Fields, the sand you feel is the Kiri Dunes, and I have placed moss for the Lakewood Forest."

After several moments of touching the geography upon the paper map, the king stood up with slight tears in his eyes. "Can you show me more?"

Ecstatic, Gin clapped his hands together and began to rub them. "Absolutely! I can gather more items and place them on other maps."

"No," the king interrupted as he continued to discover the map in front of him. "When we reach the city, I want a room dedicated to these types of maps. You will receive access to improved materials to make these more accurate and long-lasting. I want to see how far these lands go and how much work is yet to be done."

"I would be honored, my king!"

The old man nodded. "Good. Now, go find something that shows me our borders and where our enemies reside."

Winking at Javolo on his way out of the tent, he knew he had once again moved a step closer to the top. With each step he felt more confident in his abilities and his relationship with Javolo.

Impressing them with his intelligence would surely achieve what he wanted.

Once outside, he had a bit of a bounce in his step, which was noticeable by anyone watching him. In this case it was Javolo, who had followed him outside. "Very impressive," she said with her hands on her hips.

Gin stopped and composed himself. "Thanks! Anything I can do to help our king."

Javolo walked up to him so she could lower her voice while they talked. "You're not the same boy I met a few days ago. You've become much more confident."

"Thank you," he replied with a bit of cockiness.

"Perhaps a little too confident."

Gin was surprised by her negative reply. "Why do you say that?"

"Something is different about you. Your expressions of excitement and fear seemed more natural when we first met. Now all signs of fear or doubt have been lost and you've quickly adopted a superior air about you. What's changed?"

Gin had hardly planned for the conversation and took a moment to compile his thoughts. "I was in awe when I first met you and then the king. But now that I understand what you are doing, I know I can help with your cause. I'm filled with confidence because I feel safe with you and the king being at my side."

One eyebrow raised upon her face. "The king is feared or followed without question. I have never met anyone so eager to help him without an agenda for themselves."

"Javolo, I don't think you understand. I grew up being trained to protect myself from any who wished to kill me. My father's dealings placed a mark on my head to be assassinated. Can you image how I felt being told as a child that someone would want to murder me? I was scared every day of my life. I woke up every morning wondering if this would be my final day." Gin pulled elements from his real life to make the story more authentic. "Then I met you and the king, and I knew if I used my knowledge to help you, you would keep me safe. Now, for the first time in my life I wake up without being afraid and with a direction in my life."

Javolo studied his face for any signs of deception but could not find any. "That's a fine story. I hope it's true, because if I find out you have other plans, I will have the king's Knight Slayer slice you in half before you have time to explain yourself."

Gin was interested in changing the subject, and she had given him an excellent segue. "Speaking of the Knight Slayer, he doesn't talk much, does he?"

Javolo glanced over her shoulder at one of the other tents. "No. It's best to leave him alone."

"I'm curious about his skills."

"Don't be," she instructed. "Few know what he's capable of, and it's usually during their own demise that they find out."

The more mystery that surrounded the assassin, the more intrigued Gin grew. "Surely, he has to communicate with someone to see that his needs are met. Someone must have learned something about him."

"Yes, I have worked directly with him from time to time. He has alerted us to threats on occasion while other times he has simply reacted to his unique senses and hunted down those that he feels are our enemy."

"How does he sense who your enemies are? Does he have incredible hearing or ability to smell odors of different creatures? Or is it more of a magical sensation that warns him of pending danger?"

"Why are you so curious about his skills?"

"I'm surprised you and the king aren't. Don't you want to make sure you know who you're consorting with? What if a rift develops in the relationship or someone else offers to pay a higher price for his services? I think it's in the king's best interest to know how we can defend our king from the Knight Slayer if it becomes necessary. One never knows when loyalties will change."

Shaking her head, she gave off a bit of a grin. "You are definitely different than anyone else I've ever met."

Taking it as a compliment, he smiled back at her. "In what way?"

"I met you in the forest and you were a scraggly dirty peasant with nothing to your name. Now you're a clean and head-shaven young man in noble robes with the ear of the king and a head full of ideas of how to make our lives better. My head is still spinning from your transformation and how fast it occurred."

"Impressed?" he asked with a cheesy swagger.

"Let's just say that I'm on the fence between being impressed and suspicious."

"Suspicious? Of me?"

"Face it, Gin. You are an unknown. You have the ability and courage to get what you want, but we don't truly know you well enough to say we are all working towards the same goal."

His smile fell from his face. "I have done whatever you and the king have asked. What must I do to remove the doubt from your mind?"

"Nothing at the moment, but the time will come when you will need to prove to us your loyalty, and we will be watching to see your reaction."

"I look forward to that time to prove myself."

Gin's words held enough sincerity for her to drop the subject. She could see that the cook was ready to serve the meal. "I need to prepare a plate for the king. You should gather yourself one as well."

Glancing to his side, he asked, "How about the Knight Slayer? Will he be joining us?"

Shaking her head about his curiously, she answered, "No. We'll have someone make a plate for him and bring it to him. He's not much of a social creature."

"I'll do it."

"What? No. We have others who can perform that task."

"It's okay. I don't mind."

Javolo couldn't think of a strong argument to refuse his offer, so she gave in. "Just drop off the food. Don't engage him. He doesn't want to be bothered."

Nodding with excitement, he followed her to the food and made a plate similar to what Javolo was making for the king. From there they parted ways.

Nearing the Knight Slayer's tent, Gin stopped and took a deep breath as he prepared to play the game of being naïve in front of the assassin. After a slow exhale, he pushed the fabric aside and walked in. "Mealtime!" he announced as he nearly plowed into the man standing near the entrance.

The man within the tent was dressed in thick dark leather with red lines and symbols embedded into it. Several blades were set in various leather pockets throughout his outfit, each having a different shape for a different purpose. Small vials of colored liquid were tucked into secure loops, and a few metal flasks hung in leather pouches. He was prepared for battle.

With his arms crossed, the Knight Slayer glared at Gin without saying a word. His pupils were filled with miniature flickering lights like those sees in the night sky. Damaged skin from severe burns covered most of his face and neck, and his nose had been broken and never repaired. A jawless skull of an ape-like creature was used as a helmet, and the man looked out from the helmet's empty eye sockets.

Expecting to see a typical warrior, Gin was unprepared to encounter such an intimidating image. He nearly dropped the plate of food upon seeing the powerful-looking man. It was one of the few times in his life that he was speechless.

The man snatched the plate out of Gin's hands in a blink of the eye and then pushed Gin out of the tent.

Flying backward, the young man rolled upon the ground before coming to a stop. The last time he had been stunned at such a sight was the first time he recalled meeting Santorray. They were both in a class far beyond Gin's reach when it came to a strong, alarming physical appearance.

Gin considered a reattempt but wisely decided not to press his luck. He would have more opportunities to learn about the Knight Slayer in the future. A soft smile crossed his lips at the idea of having such a warrior under his command. "Someday…"

"Gin," came a voice from the edge of camp. It was barely audible over the sounds from the camp.

Unsure what he heard, he turned to see a faint outline of a brandercat. "Nutrix?" Getting back up on his feet, he walked toward the image as it disappeared into the trees and undergrowth.

Knowing he had to control the situation to prevent his cover being blown, he slowly made his way out of camp without being spotted. Once he was out of sight and earshot of the king's entourage, he subtly called out, "Nutrix?"

"I am here," she answered from only a few yards away before changing her scales back to normal, allowing him to see her in the faint moonlight. "Follow me."

"No. I am not going with you."

"Gin, this is not the time to discuss this."

"It's the only time to discuss this. If I follow you, Santorray will force me to go home."

"We'll talk about it before a decision is made."

"You know that won't change anything. He'll never listen to me or consider my ideas. You heard what he said, I make terrible decisions that cause havoc." The memory of that argument was etched deep in his mind. "When I'm with these people I have a voice. They listen to me. They respect me. Here I have control over my life. If I return with you, I am at someone else's command."

Nutrix was hurt by his perspective. "Do you honestly believe that you are safer with the Terra King and his followers? All it will take is one mistake and they will turn on you."

"Then I'll just have to make sure I don't make any mistakes."

"You're making one right now!" a deep voice said from the darkness as Santorray entered the area wearing a crystal on a chain around his neck. "You're coming with us!"

"No! I refuse!"

"Don't be a spoiled little brat!" Santorray reached over and grabbed Gin, pulling him in and lifting him up under one arm. "You're coming with us even if I have to carry you the entire way!"

Gin thrashed about; kicking and punching seemed to have no effect on the blothrud, who was still wounded. "Leave me alone!" Seeing the blood-soaked bandage on Santorray's side, he firmly punched the injury.

Santorray yelled in pain, dropped Gin, and clutched onto his own side. "Mboy! I'm going to…" Stopping mid-sentence, he could tell that others were approaching. Unfortunately, the distraction with Gin had prevented him from noticing the impending danger.

Before he had the time to get up, Gin spun his head to see what had pulled the blothrud's attention away.

Javolo was the first to arrive as she assessed the three. She shook her head in disappointment at Gin before glaring at the elderly brandercat, who didn't look to be a threat. A blothrud, on the other hand, was always a risk, so she took the time to assess him. Fortunately, he had no weapons, but he wore a necklace that could have powers or value. "Take them back to camp. I'll take that necklace," she said, pointing to the gem hanging at the Altered's chest.

Before Santorray could reply, the Knight Slayer stepped into the area wielding a long shiny blade. They were both ready for battle.

Growling, Santorray removed his hand from the injury on his side and tried to stand up tall to intimidate his enemy. "I see you finally have the guts to face me without hiding behind some invisibility spell."

The two warriors assessed each other and squared off before the battle could start. However, there was more danger than just the Knight Slayer. Several of the king's men arrived and surrounded them.

Stepping up near the Knight Slayer, Javolo gave Gin a disappointed look. "Come with me!"

Gin eyes darted back and forth from Nutrix to Santorray, as both waited to see where his alliances were. Standing up, he dusted himself off and turned to Javolo with a nod to follow her lead.

Javolo placed her hand upon the back of his neck to guide him over to the tents. She was just leaving the area when an old man crashed his way through the forest undergrowth to reach them.

"See! I was right! That blothrud is here!" Wittig said proudly as he stumbled into the center, directly between Santorray and the Knight Slayer. Gasping for air, he pointed at the beast as though he found him first.

Javolo acknowledged his words. "You were correct, and now we have him. The king is grateful." With a patronizing nod of dismissal, she started marching Gin out of the area. Calling back over her shoulder to her guards, she said, "Bring the blothrud and brandercat to the king!"

With spears pointed at him and the Knight Slayer standing before him, Santorray knew that a fight would only end with many more deaths. Even with his injury, he felt he could survive such a battle, but he could not predict the same for Nutrix and Gin. Nodding to the brandercat, he indicated it was time to do as they were told.

Wittig had a bounce in his step as he stepped up to Santorray to taunt him. "I did it! I outsmarted you! You can't shove me around anymore, can you? You're nothing but a low life Fesh!"

Santorray shoved the old man out of his way, sending him staggering into the Knight Slayer.

Before Wittig could complain, the Knight Slayer pushed the little man off to the side and into the forest where he tumbled to a stop. Neither of the two warriors had any time for the Bentree villager, as they continued to glare at one another to size up their opponent.

Chapter 21
Captured

An ornate wooden chair awaited the king. The traveling throne was intricately carved with images of the Mountain King's hexagonal Runestones and adorned with a soft pillow. The chair was truly fitting of a great leader.

The giant black panther rested near the throne awaiting her master. Her black fur made it nearly invisible in the dark of the night. Light from the campfire and surrounding lanterns reflected off the panther's large eyes, causing an illusion of free-floating eyeballs.

Guards and servants stood in rows on each side of the throne, anticipating the king's arrival. Also waiting for the Terra King were Gin, followed by Santorray and then Nutrix along with their less-than-friendly escorts. The blothrud was secured with thick chains and metal bands that restricted his head, arms and legs. The brandercat was restrained with a neck collar fitted with two chains that were being held by a guard on each side of the aisle.

At the opposite end of the aisle from the king's chair stood the Knight Slayer, providing added assurance for everyone's safety. Silent, as usual, he was ready for the order to kill.

Wittig stood off to the side as he enjoyed watching the events unfold. He felt vindicated for what they had done to him, and his village of Bentree. After searching through a pile of gear that had been taken from Santorray, he was disappointed that the only item which appeared valuable had already been taken by Javolo.

The low mumbling of discussions amongst the guards faded away as Javolo escorted the Terra King into the area and led him to his wooden throne. She was wearing the necklace with the yellow crystal as a trophy of her deeds. Once the king was comfortable, she stepped to his side and announced, "Praise to the Mountain King, for he has been reborn as the Terra King!"

All but one of his followers repeated the line. The Knight Slayer stood quiet and focused on the blothrud.

"We are saddened to have found a threat to our king," Javolo said in her theatrical stage voice. "The idea that anyone would wish him harm is surely a sign of an illness or a disorder of the mind." She then focused on Gin. "Why have you brought these Altered Creatures here?"

Gin stepped forward and stood up straight and tall. "I didn't bring them here. I was trying to escape from them." Glancing over his shoulder at the tall blothrud, he shook his head. "I told you to leave me alone! I told you I had found my calling where I felt appreciated! Yet you tracked me down and have now put my life in jeopardy."

"How long have you known these creatures?" Javolo asked.

"Too long," the young man replied with a spit to the ground. "This is the legendary Santorray; the leader of the Ergrauthian Elite and the supposed greatest warrior of the lands," he announced while pointing at the blothrud. "He came here to capture me, not the king. He wishes to take me home to live a life I do not wish to continue."

Nutrix bowed her head in shame at Gin's betrayal of his former teacher, while Santorray stood like a statue without expression as metal bands and chains weighed him down.

Gin turned back to Javolo. "What I told you was the truth. I am exhausted of living my life in fear of being assassinated for actions by my father. I don't want to live in the shadows of those that can't say they are proud of me, never measuring up to their standards, and being disrespected every time I attempt something on my own. I'm tired of being completely unappreciated. Now that I've found you and the king, I don't want to go back to it. I'd rather die than return. For the first time in my life, I feel respected for who I am and valued for what I can do."

Turning around to face the blothrud again, Gin was furious at the creature. "You browbeat me every chance you had. Nothing

I did was ever good enough for you! Every time I stepped up to face a challenge, you knocked me back down!" Tears ran down his angry, red-flushed face. "I spent years trying to meet your expectations only to be convinced that I was worthless and juvenile! In your own words, I'm nothing but a spoiled little brat!"

The brandercat's head sunk a bit lower as she recalled the most recent incident between the two she loved. She knew Santorray had pushed Gin too far and he was beyond the point of reason. The child she had raised was now lost, snapped from the pressure of the last few days.

Facing the king, Gin took a few steps toward him before falling to his knees. "I will serve you and do as you ask, my king. Please do not allow these Del'Unday to take me back to a life of torment."

Javolo had only heard the end of Gin's argument with the blothrud when they were discovered in the forest, and his words of refusing to be taken away matched his current story. As bad as it appeared, she once again felt he was telling the truth. "My king, I suggest you allow Civej to explore the blothrud's mind to expose the truth of the relationship."

Raising his silvery gray eyebrows, the king turned his head slightly her way. "Why not the boy?"

"The physical threat right now is the blothrud. With Civej's powers we can keep the beast under control while we find out the truth. If Gin has lied to us, we can easily end his time here. I think it would be safer than focusing on the boy while a blothrud stands in our camp."

The king seemed a bit confused. "I hear chains rattling. Are they not placed upon the creature's arms and legs?"

"They are, my king. But this is the legendary Santorray; the leader of the Ergrauthian Elite and the greatest warrior of the lands." Repeating Gin's earlier statement was meant to mock the blothrud as well as to justify the true threat before them.

Pulling his hands together in front of him, the king played with his ring which caused the orange gem upon the panther's collar to glow. "There is more than one way to keep our blothrud guest under control."

A loud roar billowed out of the giant panther on cue to remind everyone that the king was in full control.

Smiling at the power felt by the feline behind him, the Terra King laid his other hand upon the ring to douse the gem's light and calm the cat. "I think Shrii would enjoy the taste of the beast's flesh."

Javolo nodded in agreement. "I'm sure she would, but let's first have Civej find out why he is truly here." Once the king consented, she gave instructions to the hostages. "Stand aside, Gin. The king wishes to determine the validity of the blothrud's intent." Waving him to the side, she could tell she had not yet attracted the beast's attention. "Santorray, step forward and kneel before the king!" she commanded.

She waited for several moments before nodding to the Knight Slayer to prod the Altered Creature into place.

The Knight Slayer drew his long sword and stepped forward, placing the tip against the wound on Santorray's side.

With a bit of pressure, Santorray gave up his stone face and moved slightly forward. His steps were small due to the chains that linked his ankles, but he made them, nonetheless.

Pressing the blade tip into the prisoner's skin when needed, the Knight Slayer prodded his enemy forward until he was standing before the king. He then forced the blothrud to kneel by kicking him behind his knees. Sliding his sword up against Santorray's neck, the Knight Slayer took a position behind the blothrud, ready to slit his throat should the beast try to attack the king.

Growling, Santorray glared at Gin for his actions. "I thought of you as my son."

"You treated me as your enemy," Gin fired back.

As the two stared at each other, Javolo directed the Terra King near to the end of the blothrud's muzzle. Pulling out a small wooden box from his robe, the king gave his soft commend as he opened it, "Rise, Civej, at my behest."

Santorray watched as wisps of dark smoke moved around the exterior of his muzzle with a mind of their own. Reconnecting, the ribbon of smoke moved across his snout, between his eyes, and then hovered near his forehead.

With his eyelids closed and his hands cupped around the box, the king nodded approval for Civej to enter the beast.

Obeying its master's command, the dark vapor entered the thick skin and skull of the blothrud.

Santorray clenched his jaw, and his head naturally snapped back from the pain. His eyes tightened and his fist shook as he fought to stay in control. His chains moaned from the stress he was placing upon them.

The king nodded and appeared to be looking around inside his prisoner's mind. "Tell me, beast. Why did you come here?" Waiting for an answer, he pushed his servant to dig deeper to find the truth. "Destroy any memories that are in your way. Tell me what his plans were."

After a relentless attack of his mind, Santorray's eyelids began to flutter as his eyes rolled back into his head. He was losing the battle for his mind as he pulled on the chains between his wrists, stretching the links into elongated shapes, but not enough to break any of them. His attempt to break free seemed futile.

The Knight Slayer adjusted his sword to prepare for any escape attempt, while at the same time he was forced to help the blothrud stay upright.

"There!" the king shouted. "Show me that memory." He studied what he had found, while his victim shook uncontrollably. "You did come here for the boy. You came to take him by force to return him to his home."

A sigh of relief escaped Gin as his story was now validated. Glancing at Javolo, he could see she was just as relieved.

She looked directly at the Knight Slayer and gave him a clear order, "Prepare to kill the beast after Civej has released him. Be sure to strike before the blothrud can recover."

The Knight Slayer nodded and tightened his grip on him.

"No!" Gin said to everyone's surprise. "I would like to request the honor of killing him. I suffered the most from this blothrud. I will live with the scars of his torment for the rest of my years. I deserve the right to put my enemy down!"

A smile graced Javolo's face as she pulled the Brushtower mayor's dagger from her belt. "The honor is yours," she said with pride. "Wait until Civej has left his mind before you kill him, otherwise Civej could be killed as well."

"Understood." Taking the dagger, he moved closer to his former teacher. He then stood ready with the blade.

As the king was starting to pull Civej back, he hesitated. "What's that there?" he asked. "They were working together on a mission to dethrone me?"

Before anyone could react, Gin quickly sliced the sharp blade down, cutting off several of the king's fingers.

Screaming, the king dropped the wooden box and grabbed his injured hand as he fell to the ground.

Leaping forward, Gin grabbed the box and yelled, "Yield, Civej!" before kicking the blothrud in the chest to break the mind link.

The wisp popped out of Santorray's head, as the young man kicked the blothrud, causing him to flop backward. In doing so, he landed heavily on top of the Knight Slayer. The spikes across Santorray's back cut deep into the Slayer's chest, locking the two warriors together.

Nutrix immediately adjusted her scales to become as invisible as possible. Unfortunately, the guards on both sides of her still held the chain that wrapped around her neck. As hard as she tried, she could not break free.

It was only a matter of seconds before three guards jumped upon Gin to beat him into submission.

With considerable effort, Santorray disconnected himself from the Knight Slayer's body by rolling off him. The blothrud was desperately trying to return to his normal state of mind as quickly as possible. Civej had played havoc with his memories, but nothing had been permanently destroyed, just scrambled a bit. Even in his fuzzy state, he was still able to jump at the first guard he saw. Unfortunately, his ankles and wrists were still bound, so his attack only resulted in knocking the guard off his feet, making them both crash to the ground.

Sparks and smoke rose from the front of the Knight Slayer. The blothrud's spikes had not only pierced his armor and skin, but they had broken flasks and containers of magical components which were now eating away his clothes as they worked their way to his chest. Rolling away from the fight, he unbuckled and removed his vest and shirt, exposing his burnt and scarred torso.

An act of unexpected luck fell upon Nutrix, for the guard that Santorray had knocked over dropped one end of her chain. She turned and leaped up at the other guard, clawing at his body until he ran from the nearly invisible predator. Once she was free, she surged forward with all her might onto the men holding Gin down. The momentum of her flying body knocked them off and they all rolled off to one side, with her being injured in the process. She had inadvertently landed on one of the men's weapons.

Finding himself free for a few moments, Gin grabbed the king's severed fingers. Finding the finger with the ring he needed, he removed the ring and placed it on his own finger. As he was pummeled by another wave of guards, he tapped the ring instead of fighting back. It was a poor decision short-term as several body blows knocked the air out of him, but the long-term effect was what he needed.

The giant panther immediately became connected with Gin and attacked the guards to protect him. It began shredding some men with its enormous claws and biting some of them in half. Shrii was now fully under Gin's control.

Shaking his head to clear the disorientation, Santorray began to reconnect with his surroundings. With excellent timing and a bit of luck, he pushed his shackled feet toward the long sword the Knight Slayer had thrust in his direction. The blade crashed into the stretched links of the chain and snapped it into pieces. Now the blothrud was able to freely move his feet and legs. The Knight Slayer's unfair advantage was eliminated by the Slayer himself.

The Knight Slayer swung his mighty blade again at the fallen blothrud. He showed signs of being injured himself, as a consequence of when Santorray fell backward onto him. Several puncture marks through his leather armor and into his chest were visible and the open wounds bled out, running down his body.

However, he appeared more savage than he did before as he began screaming with each attack.

Wittig grabbed a fallen blade from one of the dead guards and raced toward the young man who had caused him so much grief since their first meeting in the Bentree tavern. With the sword raised over his head, he screamed at Gin, "You'll pay for this, you little piece of—!"

Just as the villager reached Gin, the giant panther pounced upon the old man and quickly ripped off his legs before returning to the rest of the guards. Tossed to the side, Wittig's screams of horror did not last long before he died from the extreme injuries. The only fortunate part of his fate was that he did not actually have a wife and children to mourn his death. Apparently, no one could trust the man, even in Bentree.

As Shrii dealt with the majority of the king's men, Gin looked for the king, only to see Javolo rush him away into the Knight Slayer's tent. Without thinking twice, he raced after them.

Santorray rolled away from another strike of the Knight Slayer's longsword. Wincing from the pain of his prior injuries caused by the Slayer and Civej, he quickly got back up on his feet to finish their fight that started under Brushtower.

Chains continued to hang from the blothrud's body as he let out a massive roar. His wrists were still bound together, but the sight of the towering angry beast would provoke fear into any sane person.

Leaning forward to pounce on his enemy, he realized the Knight Slayer had once again used his magic and turned himself invisible. "Show yourself!" Santorray called out as he stumbled a bit while still pulling his mind and body back under control.

An attack from behind pushed Santorray into one of the campfires, face-first. Burning logs scattered everywhere as his hands landed deep into the red-hot ashes. Yelling from the burning of his own flesh, he rolled off the campfire. His body was covered with flaming embers.

With the mayor's dagger still in hand, Gin flung the front cover of the tent to the side to expose Javolo as she finished helping the king into a chair. "I'm not after you," he told her. "I am here for the king."

"Why are you doing this?" Randomly grabbing one of the vials of liquid from the Knight Slayer's supplies, she stepped forward and held it up as a weapon to throw at him should he approach.

"I came here to learn how the king expands his lands and influences people to do his bidding. It's impressive how he uses an ancient religion to draw them in and then convince them to demonize all those that don't believe in the Mountain King ways. Clearly there is much more to learn, and I intend to. Now that I know how to control his personal servants, I will use Civej on the king to obtain all the knowledge I desire from his own memories."

"No! Absolutely not!" She was appalled at the idea. "How dare you come into our lives to cause destruction and mayhem. Especially after we have brought peace and harmony to these chaotic lands."

Gin laughed. "Peace and harmony? What you have obtained is obedience through peer pressure, which appears to be a successful model of ruling." Gin's true appreciation of their success was obvious. "Javolo, you know all of the details of expanding a ruler's grasp. Come with me, and we can do the same on a larger scale. With my intellect and your loyalty to the cause, we could be invincible."

Appalled at the suggestion, she stepped back to the king. "You think you're so much smarter than the rest of us."

"I know I am." His cocky tone was enough to infuriate her even further.

Leaning over to protect the king, she used her free hand to palm the yellow crystal so it would not swing out and hit the old man. As her finger wrapped around it, a vision flashed through her head of the Terra King screaming in pain as Gin used the dark mist to torture the blind man. The image was so real that she launched the vial at the young man to prevent her vision from coming true.

Gin's training with Santorray kicked in, and without even thinking, he swatted the vial back at her.

She attempted to block it with her arm. But the vial smashed upon the bracelets on her wrists, shattered, and the acid inside sprayed across Javolo's arms and face.

Shrieking, she rushed out of the tent toward the river to douse her head before it was too late. This left Gin alone with the king, who was cowering as he held his fingerless hand to stop the bleeding.

Pulling out Civej's wooden box from his pocket, Gin smiled as he opened it up. "Rise, Civej, at my behest."

Meanwhile, the battle raged on within the camp.

Cracking Santorray upside the head with his weapon, the invisible Knight Slayer was giving the blothrud a major beating. Even with his injuries, which caused him to move slower than normal, the Slayer was able to evade most of the blothrud's retaliations.

Santorray searched the camp for signs of his enemy. Aside from the giant panther feasting on the guards and servants, the camp appeared empty; however, the periodic attacks by his unseen assailant told him otherwise. "Know your opponent," he mumbled to himself. "He's invisible and well trained. He's also injured." Searching the ground for blood droplets, he spotted a fresh one near him.

Swinging his arms to one side, Santorray collided with the Knight Slayer, knocking the man backward. "Know your capability and your surroundings," he mumbled to himself again. "I'm injured and my wrists are chained together. The campfire light isn't casting strong enough shadows to help me see." He needed something more. There had to be more resources available to him, but where?

Seeing a pile of his gear near one of the tents, he had an idea. It was a longshot, but he was running out of options. Before he could take any actions, he was stabbed in the side from a rear attacker. Falling forward, he crashed onto the ground once again. By the time he rolled over, he could see the Knight Slayer standing over him, ready for his final strike into Santorray's chest. He also saw a faint outline of a brandercat limping up behind the man.

Striking out with one of his legs, Santorray kicked the man, who then tripped over the unseen brandercat.

Landing with a thud, the Knight Slayer dropped his longsword, which skidded a few yards from him. Reaching for another weapon, he pulled out a circular blade and threw it at the object he tripped over.

Nutrix yipped as his sharp blade sliced across her shoulder. With her focus lost, her scales shifted, giving the Knight Slayer a full view of the brandercat.

Swinging his weapon at her neck, the Knight Slayer felt the entire weight of Santorray pounce upon him. Several of the Knight Slayer's ribs cracked from the crushing impact before the man rolled away and vanished from sight again.

"Nutrix!" Santorray yelled.

"I'll live!" she yelled back. "End this battle!"

Unaware, of where his opponent went or how long before he would return, Santorray had to make a difficult decision. He pulled upon whatever strength he had left and jumped forward, grabbing a sword from his gear before he raced out of the camp.

Still on the ground with several injuries, Nutrix watched her friend run away into the darkness, only to also see a trail of blood from the invisible warrior following him.

By the time the Knight Slayer reached his adversary, he was no longer invisible. His own injuries were taking their toll on him as he slowly walked out onto the rock-filled shores of the river. Coated with moonlight, he reached down and collected a handful of small rocks. He then placed them in a leather bag along with a few magical components he had from pouches that hung from his belt. Once he tied off the bag, he looked back up to stare at his foe.

Santorray had crawled up onto the far shoreline with what little strength that remained. Soaked from his trek across the river, it was still easy to see blood pouring down his body from his wounds. He was running out of strength as he used a nearby tree to help him stand.

They both took a moment to size each other up and plan for their final fight. The only noise for several moments was the river lapping up against the rocks as it passed by.

The Knight Slayer broke the tension by starting his walk across the river. "I can't fight you in a fair hand-to-hand combat and expect to win," he yelled across to his rival.

"I know," Santorray replied without any arrogance in his voice.

Walking in waist-high waters in the center of the river, he made sure the small leather bag stayed clear of getting wet. "I have killed many blothruds, but you are greater than the others I have faced."

"I know," he replied again as he leaned his back against the tree.

"You have been a worthy opponent, but it is now time I use the remaining magic resources I have at my disposal to end this."

Soaking wet and exhausted, Santorray could not wait for this fight to be over. With his wrists still bound, he raised his sword and pointed it at the Knight Slayer. "I have resources as well."

A slight smile on the man's face gave him a menacing look as he rose from the deeper waters and came closer to Santorray's shore. "You clearly don't understand the power of magic," he said as he tossed the leather bag forward.

Landing at Santorray's feet, the rocks inside smashed together and ignited the magical components. The bag exploded with electrical sparks, which engulfed the blothrud and the tree he was bracing himself against. The blue flashes lit up the shoreline and the trees nearby.

Santorray's muscles twitched and shook as the ongoing electricity surged from the remains of the burning leather bag. Most of the water and blood vibrated and evaporated off his skin, while the remaining liquid only helped carry the intense energy across his body. Nearly immobilized, he could only make small movements. He stood vulnerable before his enemy.

The Knight Slayer moved a bit farther toward shore but stopped at knee-high water, keeping his distance from the small lightning bolts flashing out a few yards in all directions.

Santorray was frozen in place with his sword still out in front of him, pointing at the man. A layer of sparks covered his skin as he worked to speak through his clenched teeth. "I know more about magic than you may think."

It was not the reply that the Knight Slayer had expected. Standing before the blothrud, he searched one last time for any risks before he approached for the final kill. The blothrud looked immobile. He was definitely injured. Aside from the spikes on his back and arms, the only weapon he had was an old broken sword. He did not see any danger in and finishing him off.

"Attack!" Santorray said as strongly as he could.

Upon his words, the ancient broken sword gave off a deep vibration that caused the shoreline and river to shake.

Confused, the Knight Slayer scanned his surroundings as he felt the power that emanated from the weapon. Not seeing anything happen, he eventually turned back to the blothrud. "Less than impressive."

Santorray took a deep breath. "It was worth a shot."

Feeling comfortable that the vibration had passed, and nothing had come of it, the Knight Slayer said, "It's time to take care of you before my magic ends." Stepping forward, he found some resistance on his leg. Reaching down to remove the weeds or whatever it was from his leg, he was shocked to pull a flesh-covered bony hand and arm. With a confused expression, the Knight Slayer glanced up at his rival.

Still frozen from the electrical shocks, Santorray gave him grin of his own.

Before the man knew what was happening, he was being attacked by the undead that had washed downstream from the city of Brushtower. Bony arms from every direction latched onto him, preventing him from moving. As he fought them off, full-bodied undead soldiers rose from the waters and attacked. One after another crowded up against him to the point that he could not swing a weapon or even move his arms.

The Knight Slayer continued to fight them off the best he could, but the weight of dozens upon dozens of the undead began pushing him under the water.

Santorray watched the man sink under the surface as the mound of bones and flesh continued to increase for several more minutes. He stood restrained by the electrical magic as the Knight Slayer drowned a few yards away and his soul faded off to the land of Della Estovia.

About the time the Knight Slayer's magic wore off, the undead began to disperse from the man and approach the shoreline.

Santorray fell from exhaustion and landed on the rocks as he still leaned up against the tree, which was now smoking from being electrocuted. He watched as the undead made their way to him. Those that still had full bodies walked out of the river, one of them being the undead leader he had met twice before, Korin Swiph.

Stopping a few feet before the blothrud, the leader bowed his head, and the rest of the undead with heads did the same. "You wield the sword that commands us. You are now our master."

Santorray gazed upon the army of undead and the parts of bodies that clung to the shoreline. He knew exactly what to do as he raised the ancient broken sword. "I am not your master," he said to the group before directly addressing the undead leader. "The Dovenar Civil War took you from your families and robbed you of everything you had, including death. No one should control your paths but you." He then turned the sword around, so the blade pointed at himself. "Take it," he instructed the leader. "Take it and do what you must until you find a way to end your suffering."

There was a moment of silence before the undead leader reached forward and grabbed the weathered grip upon the sword's hilt. Once Santorray lowered his arm, the leader was left standing with the sword pointing at the wearied blothrud.

Santorray was not sure what the leader would do with the sword, but he still felt he had taken the right action, even if it meant his own end.

Korin Swiph gave his troops their instructions. "We do not take, but we are willing to trade. Bring him an exchange."

Santorray was unsure what they possessed that he would want. Regardless, he would take it as a symbolic gesture.

Moments later he noticed a few more full-bodied undead rise from the waters, but this time they were dragging out a human body. It was difficult to know who it was, even in the moonlight, until they reached the shore and tossed the body down. The facial skin and hair had been burned off with acid, leaving a grotesque sight before them.

"Not one of ours. Must be yours."

Santorray nodded at the exchange, as he recognized the clothes. It was clearly the King's Voice, Javolo, although he had no idea how she ended up in this state.

Lifting the sword over his head, the leader of the undead pointed downstream. "Continue our search for death."

Before they could leave, Santorray gave some advice to the leader. "Seek out Captain Dare. He is a trader of unique items. If anyone has something that can end this curse upon you, it would be him."

And with a final nod of appreciation, Korin and his army slowly went back into the river and under the surface of the water.

Santorray watched them leave and then noticed that Javolo was wearing the chain and crystal he had taken from the depths of Brushtower. The sight pleased him as he realized it would be back in his possession, but then a moment of panic filled his body as he recalled Nutrix being injured.

Grabbing the crystal, he stood and made his way back across the river. Still in great pain as he entered the camp, Santorray found half-eaten human limbs scattered about. There, among the devastation, a brandercat was resting near one of the campfires.

"Are you okay, Nutrix?" he asked while running to her side.

Her cuts were deep, but not enough to prevent her from walking. However, it had damaged the scales on her shoulder enough that they would never change colors again. "I am not a fighter, my friend. This battle was too much for me."

"I know. I should have never let you be exposed to it. How severe are your wounds?

"I'll live. Are you injured?"

"Always," he said sarcastically. "Nothing that won't mend over time."

Taking a moment to look around camp, she asked, "Where's Gin?"

"I was a little busy to keep an eye on him," said Santorray as he assisted Nutrix to her feet.

As the two began to search for Gin among the dead bodies that littered the forest campsite, they heard a low growl. Turning, they saw the giant panther moving toward them. Blood dripped from Shrii's mouth and coated her paws. With all the guards dismembered, disemboweled, or eaten, she was now looking to hunt the only other things alive in camp: Santorray and Nutrix.

Hurt and slightly hunched over, Santorray turned to face the enormous feline. "Nutrix, find Gin! I'll hold off this oversized rat-catcher."

Nutrix limped away as quickly as possible, but the panther had its eyes on her.

Watching the wounded brandercat attempt to leave, Shrii lunged for the easy kill.

Nutrix turned to see the massive panther fly toward her. She knew her body simply didn't have the energy or ability to escape before Shrii's large paws would grab her.

In the panther's mid-flight, Santorray slammed his own body into its side, knocking the giant feline to the ground, and allowing Nutrix time to escape to find Gin.

Rolling across the camp and through a few tents, they stopped near one of the wagons. Santorray was on his back, while Shrii was standing over him.

They both growled at each other before the panther opened her gigantic mouth and leaned forward to bite off the blothrud's head.

Santorray grabbed and held Shrii's mouth open, as it straddled both sides of his face. His wrists still in chains, so he was not able to pull them far enough apart to break the panther's jaw. With each passing second that he held her jaw from snapping shut, he could feel the panther's teeth cut deeper into his hands.

Shrii used her weight to press down on the blothrud, forcing her mouth around his muzzle as his head slowly entered the cat's mouth. The feline's tongue licked his face as it prepared to eat him.

Santorray searched for options, but only came up with one. He chomped down on Shrii's tongue.

The panther wrenched her head up in pain, blood shotting out of her mouth and spraying his face. In doing so, she left herself vulnerable, and received a hard kick onto her stomach from the blothrud.

Rolling back up onto his feet, Santorray spit out a chunk of the cat's tongue. Then, with bent knees and arms out in front of him, he was ready to continue his fight with the panther.

"Gin!" Nutrix called out while peeking into several tents until she found the right one. Upon entering, she saw Gin holding a small wooden box with a dark vapor stretching out of it that led to the blind Terra King's forehead. The king was shaking uncontrollably with spasms throughout his body. "Gin!" she shouted. "Stop!"

Closing his eyes, he nodded. "That will be enough for now. Yield, Civej." His voice was calm, and he waited for the wisp of a servant to return to the box before he addressed his nursemaid. "The king is no longer a threat. I have taken away his powers."

"Perhaps some, but that panther is still out there, hunting down Santorray!"

The young man had completely forgotten about Shrii. Placing a gentle hand over the ring, he mumbled, "Relax."

Sounds of Santorray and the cat fighting immediately drifted to a halt. Their battle was over.

Gin smiled at Nutrix with a new level of confidence in himself. "You'll find that yellow crystal necklace around Javolo's neck. She ran toward the river, but I doubt she made it that far." His dispassionate voice over the loss of someone he knew was unnerving.

"What has happened to you?"

He smiled as though he was teaching a child of his own. "I've grown up. The child you raised has become a man of power. You should be proud of what you've helped create."

Nutrix felt uneasy about his first full taste of power without controls set upon him or the wisdom to harness it.

The tent flap behind the brandercat ripped open, exposing Santorray. "Mboy!" he growled. "I should knock you on your ass for getting us into this mess!"

Gin's instincts caused him to back away for a moment before he regained his newly found confidence. "We would have been slaughtered out in the forest where they found us. My agreement to come with them and pretend I was on their side was our best hope of survival," he said strongly. "We have completed our mission, and now I am ready to return home. I have proven to my father that I am a man, and I should be given respect and treated with dignity."

As mad as he was at Gin, it was hard for Santorray to disagree with him. The mission was now complete, and it was time to start the trek home. After a long growl, he finally said, "Grab your items so the three of us can get out of here."

Gin shook his head. "We will be taking others back with us."

"Others?" Santorray did not like the sound of that.

"Yes. Shrii and Civej are now my servants. I've earned them as my reward, and I know how to control them. They will be returning with us."

"You don't know how to control yourself half the time, let alone these strange creatures."

"I'm not leaving without them. They are mine to keep," he said confidently.

Seeing that the blothrud was ready to argue, Nutrix stepped in and addressed Santorray. "It will be Gin's father's decision whether he can keep them permanently. You only have to deal with them on the way back home."

Baring his teeth, he showed his disliked for the idea. "Keep that panther out of my way, or I'll break its neck. And if I see you use that dark vapor on anything, I'll crush that little box in my palm."

"I'm taking the Terra King as well."

"What?! Why? For what purpose?"

"He's coming with us as my trophy which I intend to give to my father."

"Trophy? We have witnessed the destruction here and can vouch for the end of the king's power. We don't need to bring him."

"He's coming with so my father can question him."

"He'll slow us down to a snail's pace!"

Gin thought about it for a moment before answering. "No, he won't. He'll be strapped onto the panther's back. Now that I have control over the creature, I can ensure this happens without issue."

Gin and Santorray stared at each other until the young man gave him a cavalier smile. "You have to admit, Santorray, I succeeded in my mission. I have met and exceeded the challenge and am returning home victorious."

Taking a deep breath, the blothrud nodded. "You may have not met the intent of what I was trying to teach you, but you have met the goal of this mission. Although, you were reckless in how you did it."

Gin smiled. "The stories I've heard about you lead me to believe you have taken that path a few times yourself."

"Perhaps." Calming down, he realized that his student had landed on his feet even though he went against orders. He was still dangerous, but perhaps Gin could become responsible with additional training. "Gather some food and supplies. I want to leave before sunrise."

Chapter 22
Truth be Told

After a full day of travel with little to no discussion between them, the group found a place to spend the night. They were heading to the fortress where they would end their travels together. In doing so, their relationships could not be the same once they went their separate ways. Nutrix would no longer be Gin's caregiver and Santorray would no longer be his instructor. Words simply could not convey the emotions between them, so the silence would have to suffice.

The mission had not only been completed, but Gin had exceeded the original expectations. Instead of discovering the weaknesses of the Terra King to plot a way to overthrow him, the Terra King had been captured and was unable to create any further danger. To top it off, Gin now had control over the creatures that had served the king to keep him safe. In Gin's eyes, this was the best possible outcome scenario.

After tying the pale, weak, dethroned king up against a tree, Gin gave the rope an extra tug to ensure the rope was secure. He ignored the blind man's complaints just as his companions were doing. They simply became background noise.

It had been a long journey, and everyone was clearly exhausted. Santorray and Nutrix performed their duties to get the campsite in order, but at a slower pace due to their injuries. Gin ensured Civej had been hidden away and that the giant panther was calmed for the night. What seemed like a time to rejoice for their victory was instead a time of reflection and an ending to their journey.

"Thank you," Gin said to Santorray as he tossed a few broken limbs into the fire.

Santorray was surprised to hear the words from the young man. It had been the first time he had used them sincerely. "For what?"

"For taking the time."

"It was my job to train you."

"No, I mean taking the time to be with me. You could have trained me without caring about me, but you didn't. You were genuinely concerned about my well being, which caused you more grief than you had signed up for."

"I knew what I was getting into and was willing to make the sacrifice," he said with a hint of a smile.

Gin stared at the flames for a moment before looking up at his mentor. "That is more than my father ever has done. To be honest, you've been more of a father to me than he ever was." His eyes stayed locked in place, because he wanted the blothrud to fully understand the sincerity of his meaning. "I was serious when I said I don't want to go back to being under my father's power. I have tasted freedom, and I want more of it."

"Freedom is a double-edged sword, Gin. Be careful what you wish for."

"I'm not wishing any longer. When I return, I plan to leave my father, his trade, and his reach. I'm going to disown him."

One of the blothrud's eyebrows raised in interest. "Where will you go? How will you feed yourself?"

"I will learn from the best. I'll take you as my surrogate father to teach me how to survive on my own." Pausing, he looked his teacher firmly in the eyes. "That is, if you would have me."

Santorray was not expecting the speech and stood slightly shocked by the request. "I am not a good father figure. You will find someone much more worthy on your journey."

"No, I have chosen you. Who else would put their life on the line for me the way you have?"

The blothrud bit his lip as he attempted to hold back his thoughts, but he no longer could. "Gin, you're now old enough to know the truth."

"About what?"

"Your father."

"I don't want to talk about him. He's had his chance."

"No, not him. Your real father."

Unsure what he meant, Gin stood there puzzled. "Real father?"

Santorray nodded. "The story you know of your birth and arrival is not completely true."

"What do you mean?"

"I was the one who brought you as an infant to your home where Nutrix raised you."

"It was you who saved me? Were you there when my mother died from my birth?"

"Yes, I was there when she died, but it was not due to your birth."

Confused, Gin's knowledge of his own life was starting to unravel.

"She was at full term when they raided her caravan." Santorray's eyes quivered a bit as he recalled the scene playing out in his memory. "We couldn't keep up with them. We were outnumbered."

"Who? Why? What happened to her?"

"By the time I reached her, they had slit her throat and lodged a sword through her stomach and the unborn child."

Gin staggered back. The stunning tale made no sense to him. "How did I survive?"

"Her child did not live. I had been hired to bring her and her child back safely, and I had failed."

"But I'm here! I'm of flesh and alive! You recall the story wrong. Civej must have damaged your memory."

"I wish that were true. Unfortunately, it is not."

Gin was starting to get agitated with the blothrud. "I don't like this game. Is this another test? If so, stop playing it!"

"I was hired to protect her and the unborn, and I had failed. However, there was too much at risk to not bring the infant back. It had to be done, and the infant had to be alive." He gritted his teeth at the choice he made. "It was then that I took actions that will haunt me for the rest of my days."

Shaking his head in denial, Gin did not want to hear any more of the story.

Santorray continued despite the protest. "I knew of another human who would be in labor soon, so I went to her." The blothrud's eyes filled with tears as the vision came back to him. "She had twins. Two boys." A deep swallow interrupted his thoughts. "I broke in and took one of her infants from her. It was that child who was brought back and then grew into the young man I see before me."

"No! That's not true! Why are you doing this?"

"I need you to understand who your real father is."

"Damn you! Why have you lied to me about this?"

"Because your true father is Ambrosius."

There were an uncomfortable few moments of silence. Gin was horrified to hear about his mother's death and who his father truly was. His life had just been uprooted, and he began questioning everything he had been told over the years.

The young man spun his head over to look into Nutrix's eyes. "Did you know about this?"

Bowing her head slightly, she replied, "I suspected as much. Your scent and essence were different than that of my master."

"Yet you never thought to bring that to my attention?"

"What value would it bring to tell you of my speculation? It would have simply driven a greater divide between you and your father… my master."

"According to Santorray, your master is not my father!" he yelled in frustration. "You promised to protect me, but instead you kept secrets and misled me. You've encouraged me to listen and to honor the wishes of a man that wasn't truly my father." By this point, Gin was shaking with anger. "I've wasted all these years preparing for a curse that was meant for a child who was never born!"

Santorray continued to stand firm as he watched the outburst. "No. The curse was for you, not for the child who died."

"What? How is that possible?"

"The curse is based on a prophecy that foretold of the sons of the Brothers of War. The two sons would fight to the death, for only one would survive. Ambrosius' wife had twins. Ericc was raised by Ambrosius as his only son. You, Bredgin, were raised by Darkmere as his adopted son. The two fathers were twins of the royal family and caused the civil war that destroyed the kingdom. Now their sons are poised to fight to the death in the near future."

"Adopted? Are you suggesting my father knows that I'm not his true son?"

"I am."

"Then why would he not slay me for being of Ambrosius' lineage?"

"Would it not give him greater pleasure to see Ambrosius' sons fight each other to the death? Darkmere has trained you to win this battle and return to his side to defeat his brother once and for all."

"I can't trust anyone!" Gin yelled into the night air.

"You can trust me with your life," Nutrix said strongly as she approached him to calm his nerves. "I have protected you with my life on more than one occasion."

Grabbing a stick out from the fire, he held it out to keep her at a distance. "No. Protecting me shouldn't include lying to me! You have been raising me all these years to watch me fight to the death for your master's amusement."

"You know that's not true," Santorray said from behind him. "Nutrix has given her life to raise you to be the best that you were capable of being."

Swiveling about, Gin turned the flaming stick on the blothrud. "You came back after a decade to train me in order to make sure it would be an outstanding battle between Ericc and I."

"No, I came back to see if I could find the core values of Ambrosius within you. If so, I had planned to take you to him so that you could reunite with your true father and brother." He took on a cleansing breath before continuing. "My goal has been, and continues to be, to undo what I did when you were an infant. I want to get rid of this wretched curse of a prophecy by preventing you and your brother from fighting to the death. My goal was to save you both."

Considering his words, Gin shook his head. "No. No! Your goal was to clear your own guilt for taking me away from my mother in the first place. That's what you truly care about! It was never about me. I'm simply an object in your story that you stole and regretted afterward."

"Gin, you're more than that to me," Santorray raised his voice to give his words strength.

"Liar!" Gin pointed at the blothrud and then the brandercat. "Both of you are dead to me! I refuse to hear another word from you. You've poisoned me to the core. My heart aches at the thoughts of the betrayals you have played out at my expense." He grabbed his chest with one arm as the emotion caused his body to hurt deep from within. His life was collapsing around him, and his view of the world became narrow as he focused on himself and his own pain.

"Gin," Nutrix stepped up behind him to comfort the boy she had raised.

Startled by her approach, Gin turned quickly and clobbered the brandercat upside the head with his stick. As unintentional as it was, rage had filled his body with so much anger that he was oblivious to what he had done. Instead, he screamed into the air with hopes that everyone and everything would disappear.

Upon his strike, sparks and wooden shards flew in the air as Nutrix fell backward to the ground. A large piece of wood had broken off and impaled her deep into one of her eye sockets, and blood filled the area. Nutrix yelled and rolled in pain as she attempted to get the large wooden splinter out of her skull.

"No!" Santorray yelled as he backhanded Gin out of the way while rushing to Nutrix's aid.

Flying across camp, Gin landed near the giant panther. Overflowing with the energy of a battle, he took his blade from his boot sheath and rolled to his feet before charging at the blothrud. The young man had lost all sense of reason and gone mad in his emotional revenge.

Seeing the young man leap at him, Santorray took another swipe of his arm at Gin. This time the young man was tossed over the giant panther and into one of the large trees beyond.

Cracking his head against the tree trunk, Gin fell to the ground. Disorientated and still filled with adrenaline, he crawled forward and began releasing the giant panther. "They have betrayed me! Stop them!" he said as he tapped his new ring.

Still tied to a nearby tree, the Terra King had seen everything. "You're insane! Shrii will kill us all if you set her free!"

Hearing orders from anyone at this point made Gin even more furious. "Shut up, old man!" he yelled as he stepped away from the panther to the blind man.

The king refused to stay silent. "She must be controlled, or she'll kill everything in sight!"

"Then you will all die!" Gin screamed as he swiped his blade across the man's neck. "My soul has just been murdered by those who swore to keep me safe. You can all go to Della Estovia and meet Bakalor, for all I care." Watching the king bleed out, he finished untying the panther with a sadistic smile. "Kill."

The panther sprang forward, landing on top of the unsuspecting blothrud who was tending to his brandercat friend. The strong spikes across Santorray's back stabbed into the panther's underside, but the sheer weight of the giant feline caused Santorray to be knocked away from Nutrix.

Rolling across the camp, Santorray smashed into two thick trees before coming to a stop. Shaking off the unexpected attack, his blurred vision caught the panther picking Nutrix up in her jaws and shaking her in the air. "STOP!" he shouted while getting back to his feet. Unfortunately, by the time he was able to reach the panther, it had released Nutrix and sent her soaring into a nearby tree.

Plowing into the side of the panther, the blothrud knocked the cat over onto her side. He then pressed the spikes on the backs of his elbows into the giant creature's stomach.

The giant panther panicked from the pain and kicked Santorray before leaping away from the fight to regroup. It had been a lucky strike to the blothrud's forehead.

Santorray's head snapped back further than it normally should, and his neck cracked. His spine locked up and he fell backward into the campfire. The hot coals began burning his skin and cooking his flesh before he rolled off to safety. But even then, he was immobile. He had been paralyzed from the neck down.

Unable to move, the blothrud lay helpless next to the campfire. He could hear and see, but his body had failed him.

Santorray heard footsteps approach as Gin's boots came into view. "Don't do this," the blothrud forced out.

Stopping with his boots just shy of touching the blothrud's muzzle, Gin took a moment to look down at his former trainer. "I am dead on the inside, and it is you who has killed me. And for this, you are dead to me."

"Gin. It doesn't have to end like this. We need to talk about this."

"No, we don't. I'm no longer answering to you. I will no longer play your games and try to meet your expectations. Not only will I not meet with Ambrosius and Ericc, but I will have my father train me in the ways of the E'rudite so I can hunt down and kill Ericc."

"Ericc has done nothing to you!"

"The prophecy says one of us will kill the other, and I refuse to let it be me. Besides, his death will live upon your shoulders for taking the raw clay of the boy Gin and making him into the skilled warrior of Lord Bredgin. You shall live with the fact that you could have prevented all of this from happening in the first place. That is why I will allow you to live, so you will see the suffering you have caused your friend, Ambrosius."

"NO!"

The young man stepped away and could be heard talking to the giant panther. After a few minutes they left the campsite. Gin knew Santorray would eventually regain the use of his arms and legs, but he would be long gone before that happened.

Santorray stared at the dark forest for hours as the sun slowly began to glow in the horizon. Parts of his body slowly began to function again. The snap to his neck should have paralyzed him for life, but once again, the blessing of self-healing presented itself. However, in this case it was a curse as he watched Nutrix suffer by herself from across the campsite.

As his functions returned, he began crawling his way over to Nutrix. He started off very slowly, but by the time he reached her he had the use of most of his upper body.

"Nutrix!" he called out, hoping there was some way she had survived the attack. Unfortunately, the injuries looked too severe. The wood shard still lodged in her eye socket had prevented her from bleeding to death. Her mangled legs made it apparent that she would never walk again. Not apparent was how extensive her internal injuries were.

Crawling up next to her, Santorray brushed debris away as he stroked her face and ears. "Stay with me, Nutrix" he said softly as he gently ran his hands over her scales.

The labored opening of her remaining eye allowed her to finally catch sight of her friend. "Santorray."

"I'm here. You're not in danger any longer."

She struggled to give a slight smile at the thought. "You tried," she coughed out.

"Yes, but I failed." After grumbling, he continued. "I failed Gin, Ambrosius, and you."

Coughing up blood, Nutrix forced herself to ask the burning question. "Why did you do it?" Before he could speak, she clarified her question. "Why did you take Gin from his true mother?"

Santorray's eyes lowered. He had never spoken of the subject, and it was difficult to start now. However, it was a dying request of a dear friend, and he felt obligated to answer. "Darkmere had lost the civil war and was at a point of no return. He was prepared to destroy all life and had the means to do it. The only thing that stopped him was word that his wife was carrying his child. It was this small glimmer of hope that ignited enough compassion in him to abort his plan to unleash a plague intended to kill all of us." The blothrud took a quick moment to recall the details. "Years earlier, Darkmere had saved my life, which is how I became one of his personal guards for a short time. I volunteered to escort his wife out of hiding to rejoin Darkmere. Unfortunately, we were attacked along the way and everyone was killed… except for me. If I returned without his child, Darkmere would have unleashed his painful horrors across the land. I took one of Ambrosius' twins to prevent the death of all Unday, humans, and Polenums."

With great effort, Nutrix managed a slight smile for her friend. "It must be difficult for you to live with your decisions," she said in a raspy voice. "But you will always have my respect and love."

He leaned forward and placed his forehead against hers. "I don't deserve it."

"Learn…" her gruff voice became weaker, "… to forgive yourself." She could tell it would be difficult for him to heed her advice, so she gave him some of his own. "You were right when you said, 'sometimes hanging on does more damage than letting go'. So, let go of your guilt and find what brings you peace. Perhaps that remote forest you keep talking about. Start fresh and learn to be content with your life."

"I will," he promised as her body started to go limp within his arms. Closing his eyes, tears ran down his face and onto hers. By the time he opened them, the life within her had faded away.

Chapter 23

Home

It was late and the sun had set many hours prior to Gin's arrival at his father's fortress. Lanterns lined both sides of the drawbridge that allowed for safe travel over the fast-flowing river across the front of the stronghold. The light was strong enough for the guards to see clearly for about a dozen yards past the bridge, but not much farther, which is why they became quite unnerved when they spotted the glow of two large yellow cat eyes floating toward them.

Pulling their weapons forward, they watched intently as the eyes grew closer, and eventually the outline of a giant cat emerged with a human controlling the feline mount.

Riding upon his giant black panther, a young bald man carried the decapitated head of the Terra King under his arm as a trophy. Gin sat up proud and determined. He had left his home as a boy and was returning as a man of power.

Several of the guards stepped forward to stop the outsider's approach until they realized who it was. They then returned to their post and opened the doors for Darkmere's son.

The panther slowly entered the main gate, where she was met by a tall and thin man with long mahogany hair and a beard that had grown past his chest.

Stopping his ride, Gin dismounted and approached the man. "Father."

Standing rigid like a statue, he replied. "Son."

"I have a gift for you, Darkmere," he said as he handed the severed head to the older man. "The Terra King won't be giving you any more territorial problems."

Darkmere took a moment to study the tattoos upon the king's extremely pale bald head. "It would appear you did more than simply find out his weaknesses for me so that I could overthrow him."

"Clearly," he replied with a bit of an attitude.

Looking up from the king's head, he noticed the similar tattoos on his own son's now shaven skull. "Just how much information did you acquire on his following and his plans before you removed his ability to tell us more?"

"Considerable. I became one of his faithful followers and students." He then patted the side of his giant panther. "The king used this Fesh as his personal bodyguard and the legend of the Mountain King for his religion. I watched him perform on stage, and thousands of followers were spellbound to follow him on anything he ordered. They were loyal to a fault."

"Interesting." He stroked his long beard for a moment. "You said they were loyal. Are they not anymore?"

A confused look grew upon the young man's face. "They may stay loyal, but to whose orders? Once they realize he's dead, his power over them should fade."

"Was it a public execution?"

"No, and we left no witnesses."

A devious look grew upon his father's face. "What if they don't find out about his death?" Darkmere pulled the severed head up to eye level and studied the dead man's face. Within seconds, Darkmere's facial features began to change. The hair on his head began to disappear as tattoos blossomed upon his skin. Within a few moments, Darkmere had used his E'rudite powers to transform himself into the exact image of the Terra King. "Perhaps I could fill in for the poor king in order to help his followers find their way."

Gin took a quick study of his father's new face and nodded with approval. "That's him. What do you plan to do with his power?"

"I plan to take back the kingdom that is rightfully mine."

There was no surprise on Gin's face. "What becomes of me?"

"You?" Darkmere replied with a large smile. "First of all, you will teach me what you have learned about the Terra King.

Then you will accompany me back to his throne so we can start controlling his people to benefit our future."

Considering the idea, he was not against it, but it did not excite him either. "And what is it that I get for doing this for you?"

Darkmere tilted his head in surprise. It had been far and few times that his orders were challenged with an expectation of reward. "Are you looking for land of your own? If so, I grant it. You are now Lord Bredgin over my eastern mountain range."

"No, I have no interest in the daily decision-making of land management."

"Well, what is it then? You clearly have something in mind."

"You have hired the finest instructors to educate me on academics, survival, and fighting."

"I have. Are there other lessons you wish to learn?"

The thinning of his eyes was accompanied with a slight nod. "It is time for me to learn the techniques of the mighty E'rudites."

Darkmere stood without expression as he studied the young man who had returned victorious. "What do you plan to do with such powers?"

Stepping up to him, he kept his demeanor calm and firm. "I shall hunt down and kill Ambrosius and his son, Ericc."

An overwhelming pleasure filled Darkmere as he realized the boy, Gin, had finally grown into the man he had always wanted. "I am in partial agreement with you. I wish to see Ambrosius suffer before his death, but Ericc is all yours." Seeing Gin's expression that he wasn't getting what he requested, his father added a bit more. "You have exceeded my expectations. I am proud of you."

And with that, Gin knew he made the right choice.

Chapter 24
Full Circle

*D*ays later, Santorray made his way to Darkmere's fortress. He had fully recovered, with the exception of a few new scars upon his body, which blended in with the collection he had acquired over decades of fights.

A wide range of emotions tugged at him as he made the long walk. He was relieved his commitment to train Gin was over. He was disappointed in himself for not being able to change Gin into the son he wanted to present to Ambrosius. He felt guilty for taking the boy from his true family in the first place. But most of all, he was furious over the pointless killing of his dear friend, Nutrix.

The large metal doors were open, as they normally were during the day. Several guards stood ready to grant or deny access inside. Additional forces were only a whistle away from rushing in to help, should they determine any problems.

Santorray had crossed the drawbridge many times in the past few years, when he returned with Gin and Nutrix after various training sessions. But this time he was alone. He recognized the guards, and they all knew him well enough to stay out of his way. So, it came as a surprise when one of the guards sent a signal for reinforcement.

"They'll need more than a few dozen guards today," the blothrud grumbled to himself.

"Halt!" one of the guards called out.

"I'm not in the mood, Pax," Santorray barked back as he continued to march forward.

Ten more guards came to support the original four who stood at the entrance. In addition, up above, several more stood ready with their bows and spears. Any rational person would take the hint and stop approaching. Unfortunately for the guards, Santorray was not a person, nor was he in a rational mood.

"Pax, tell your forces to get out of my way before they get hurt! I have business to finish here."

The captain of the guards arrived and stepped forward. Kaya was clearly not pleased about the situation. "I'm sorry, Santorray, but we've been ordered to escort you to Master Darkmere, if you arrived."

Not missing a step, the blothrud continued to march forward. "Escort me if you must. Just stay out of my way."

The guards were several feet shorter than the creature, and despite having the numbers, the guards still felt at a disadvantage. Nervous hands changed grasps of weapons while the guards stood their ground as Santorray continued toward them. They knew him well enough to know they were all in danger if the blothrud chose not to comply.

Just prior to the outsider walking into her guards, Kaya gave her men and women their orders. "Escort Santorray to the master." Her words caused a sigh of relief among the guards as they stepped to the sides and began leading the blothrud to the great hall.

"We're under strict orders," Kaya said as she fearlessly walked alongside the blothrud twice her height.

"I don't care."

She marched with him for a bit before saying her piece. "This will most likely be the last time we talk, so I will make it brief." Waiting for a response, she did not receive any. "I want you to understand that my guards and I have a great respect for you."

The unexpected comment made him stop and look down to see what game she was playing.

She took advantage of the moment and explained her thoughts. "We know your training of Gin is complete and the master no longer has you at his calling. What we don't know is what he has planned for you or what he may order us to do to you. I have yet to see anyone leave from under his control."

Lifting the skin across his dragon-like muzzle, he exposed his teeth as he gave a low growl. "What are you trying to tell me?"

She showed no signs of being intimidated. "I want you to know that no matter what happens, we have learned a lot from you. You gave us your time and guidance between Gin's missions, and it has helped us. You have made my guards better fighters, and you have made me a better leader. You have earned our respect. We would be honored to fight at your side if you should ever call upon us."

Santorray could see the seriousness in her eyes. As he stood there, the other guards bowed their heads in admiration for the creature who had spent countless hours training them over the years. "You serve Darkmere."

"We do. But if you should need us, we will be there for you."

"I have no need for an army or a following."

She nodded a single time to acknowledge his response. "Regardless, I wanted to make sure you understood that we would follow you to Della Estovia and back if asked."

Uneasy with the sentiment, he shook off the conversation and looked forward. With less bitterness in his tone, he replied, "Let's get this over with."

Calling to her men and women, Kaya ordered them to continue to escort the mighty blothrud, and within minutes they arrived at the great hall.

The decorative doors were immediately opened by the guards, exposing a long hall designed for large gatherings. Santorray was quite familiar with the room and had always admired the structure. The details within the floors, walls, and ceiling were superior to anywhere else in the fortress. Today the extravagance of the great hall was muted by the dim lighting throughout. The last time the blothrud had been in the hall, he was hanging a chuttlebeast skull on the wall and there were bright lights and festivities. He found it unfortunate how much it had changed in his absence.

The long tables and chairs had been replaced with a large royal desk and chair at the far end. They were illuminated by a few oil lanterns, and it was the only well-lit area. Sitting at the desk was Darkmere, while Gin stood to his side. They both looked up from the table once Santorray and his escorts entered from the far side.

Santorray never changed his posture as he marched across the marble floors with the guards in tow. He was here to terminate their business dealing one way or another.

As he approached, he could see several maps and documents spread out upon the desk. It was obvious they were reviewing their potential land grab now that the Terra King was dead.

"Welcome," Darkmere said casually to the advancing blothrud.

"I don't feel welcomed," he replied as he glanced to the guards around him. "Why the escort?"

With little concern, the man moved his attention back to his maps. "It is my understanding that you and my son parted ways on difficult terms."

"If you mean he became an unhinged and ruthless murderer, then yes."

Glancing at Gin, Darkmere could see the young man wanted to retaliate, so he intervened. "Is it not true that his anger stemmed from your poor choices? I find it hard to blame Bredgin for your deceit. I think you realize that at some level. You know, deep down in your heart, he had the right to retaliate after your betrayal."

Grinding his teeth, Santorray felt the stabbing pain of his words. "I'll take the blame for my deception and lies. Those I will own. However, the murder of Nutrix is upon your son's shoulders."

Darkmere found the comment odd. "The nursemaid? You feel there is weight to her life? She was at the end of her usefulness anyway. Why would I care how her life ended?"

His lack of respect for his dear friend infuriated the blothrud. "She gave all of herself to care and raise the boy, and he pays her back by taking her life?"

A subtle shrug of Darkmere's shoulders showed a complete lack of sorrow for the loss of his loyal servant. "We have more nursemaids. Shall I toss one your way? You appear a little stressed and in need of emotional support to get you through these challenging times."

It took every bit of self-control to keep Santorray from launching an attack on the man. However, he was well aware of Darkmere's E'rudite powers. With a thought and a touch, Darkmere could change Santorray's skin to salt and his bones to rocks. A head-on attack was futile and most likely would result in him becoming a marble statue within the man's gallery of prior victims.

Realizing he had the blothrud under his control, the master of the fortress asked, "Whether you realize it or not, I have been keeping my eye on you for many years now." Eyeing the blothrud from head to toe, he nodded at his own thoughts. "You have a lot of potential, Santorray. You could stay and become a great leader of my army. As your master, I could provide you with more opportunity than you have ever had."

"I have served a master before, and I will never do so again."

"We are on the edge of a great new empire that will take over all of these lands. You could be a part of this new world. Simply do as I command, and you will enjoy a life filled with all the battles, victories, companionship, food, and drink you could ever want. You can have as many nursemaids as you see fit."

Nothing he said was of interest to Santorray. "I will never serve a master again."

"I see. How unfortunate." Darkmere was not going to beg, so his interest in the blothrud was over. "If you are firm in your conviction to not work for me, do we have any further business here?"

Growling at the situation, he replied, "My training of Gin has finished."

"Ah, yes. And you have done an amazing job. Stellar performance on his last mission, which has expedited my plans to rebuild the Dovenar Kingdom." He waved his hand over the maps on the table. "I simply couldn't have expected such an advantageous outcome. I gave him to you when he had nothing to offer, and you have returned him to me as a solid warrior with the ability to accomplish his mission and the spirit to succeed no matter what the cost." Nodding to his son, he received a respectful nod back. "I can't thank you enough. Bredgin will be the key to my success, all because of you."

The future that the blothrud had put in motion was the opposite of what he wanted. As he stared into the eyes of his former student, he could see no remorse reflecting back to him. Gin's core values had hardened before Santorray could fully help in their formation. "Then our business deal has come to an end."

Ending a deal with a handshake was rare for Darkmere. "That seems to be the case. How do you see us parting ways?"

"I gave you the service you requested. Now you give me what I asked for in exchange."

For the life of him, the E'rudite failed to recall what that was. It had been several years, and he never assumed he would have to pay for it. It would be a unique event for him. "Please, refresh my memory."

"You agreed to free one from your control." Santorray glanced at Gin with regret. The blothrud recalled his original plan to free him from Darkmere and return him to Ambrosius.

Darkmere followed his gaze at his son and chuckled. "Absolutely. I will honor this arrangement and free one from under my control." Leaning forward toward the blothrud, he added to his thoughts. "Just because I do does not mean he will go with you."

For years, Santorray had worked to put an end to this chapter of his life. His desire to right his wrong was so close. Yet he knew that Gin would not go with him, nor would he give Ambrosius a chance. Santorray had failed and he struggled to see how any good could come of asking Gin to leave with him.

"Go on," Darkmere said. "Ask for his release, and I will grant it. Then you can be on your way empty handed."

Still glaring at Gin, he bit his lip until a few droplets of blood dripped from his mouth. "I will ask for the release, but it will not be Gin."

Both Gin and Darkmere were caught off guard.

"To fulfill our agreement, I will take you up on your offer to free one of your nursemaids. I request the release of the one called Fenia."

Thinking it was a joke at first, Darkmere asked, "Perhaps one of my chefs to keep your belly full would be a better selection than a servant to clean up after you."

"Are you going back on our agreement?" Santorray's voice boomed out loudly, letting all know he was serious.

The power behind the blothrud's commanding voice caused Darkmere to take a moment to regroup his thoughts. "If that is who you wish to free, then take her, and we will end our agreement on good terms."

"Then make it so," Santorray demanded.

With a nod to Kaya, Darkmere signaled for her to fetch Fenia. Once she left, Darkmere walked around the table and stood before the towering blothrud. "I will offer this one last time. You could stay. I could use a powerful leader such as yourself."

"To conquer lands and force villagers into following you?"

"Oh, dear no. I've changed my ways," he said while waving away the idea. "We have a better way to take back my lands." Using his E'rudite powers, he morphed his physical features to appear as the Terra King. "I'm done fighting, I now plan on using the people's own ancient beliefs against them. Why fight the people when I can simply manipulate their culture to meet my objectives?"

"They'll figure it out and eventually turn on you."

"You would be great at shepherding my flock into submission."

Santorray grinned at the wording. "That's where you're wrong, I'm not good at being within anyone's flock. I work best alone. It's safer for everyone that way."

Frustrated, Darkmere waved his hand to end the discussion and accept the blothrud's decision. "Normally, I would not allow anyone to leave, but I have a feeling you'll be back. At some point, you'll work on my behalf again." And with that, Darkmere walked off and left the great hall.

Still surrounded by several guards, Santorray waited for the door to shut behind the man before turning to the master's son. "Gin."

"Lord Bredgin," the young man corrected the blothrud before he could continue.

The trivial nature of the boy's name did not faze him. "Do you feel any remorse for Nutrix's death?"

Stunned by the words, Bredgin quickly answered, "Absolutely not. Her death was your fault. I'm the victim here. You let me live a lie for your own selfish motives. You played me for a fool, and for that I can never forgive you."

"If that is truly how you feel, then it is I who failed to adequately train you to become a great warrior. A great warrior would never claim to be a victim of the events in their life, nor do they use such events as an excuse for unacceptable behavior. Unfortunately, you have used your potential to become a bully. Your response to life is that of an ungrateful child. You and your father believe you have become a man, but what I see is an immature soul with unrestrained use of the power he possesses. No, young lad, playing the victim to justify your actions only shows your cowardice, Lord Bredgin."

Gin's anger turned his face red. "I... I killed the Terra King. I'm positioned to take over his power with my father. I even defeated the mighty warrior Santorray. I'd say I've overcome the best, despite being used and deceived by those who were supposed to be in my corner!"

Shaking his head, Santorray finally realized the problem. "The error in your thinking is that success is a matter of defeating others."

"It is!" Gin shouted like the child he still was inside.

"No. A true warrior knows that you need not create an enemy if you can complete your task by showing some respect." Santorray recalled the fight that caused Nutrix's death. "We could have ended our training on good terms. Instead, you've stained them with the innocent blood of one who loved you like only a mother can."

Bredgin took a moment before retorting, in the calmest voice he could muster, "You lied to me and uprooted me from a path I was meant to follow. For that, I can never forgive you. Yet you spent years of your life training me to be a warrior. Because of that I now have skills I would not otherwise have. For this, I will give you the gift of sponging away this debt. It is an even trade, and we now have a clean slate." Leaning closer, he wanted to make his final point very clear. "Understand, my former teacher, that if we ever see each other again, I owe you nothing. So don't ever ask me for anything or attempt to stand in my way again!"

The two glared at each other until a side door opened, and Fenia was escorted in by Kaya.

"Santorray?" The young brandercat cautiously passed Gin and the guards as she approached her mother's friend. "I heard my mother perished on your mission, but I am grateful to see that you still live." Her voice was still filled with sorrow days after learning of her mother's fate.

Turning from Gin without any farewell, the blothrud motioned for Fenia to follow him. "Yes, your mother has fallen," he said as they started walking out of the great hall. "What you don't know is that she has given you the gift of freedom."

Stunned, she was unsure what that meant.

"Follow me. I'll explain once we're outside," he said before she could ask her questions. He wanted to be out of earshot as well as out of the fortress before he could relax enough to have this conversation.

Trusting him without any hesitation, she stayed quiet as they were escorted out.

Reaching the front gates, Santorray was humbled to see that all of Kaya's men and women were lined up on both sides of the exit. Standing at attention, they gave the blothrud a proper sendoff as each bowed their head in respect as he walked past them. One after another followed suit until Santorray reached the end of the drawbridge.

He then turned back to look upon all of them and recalled their time together: the frustrations, the difficult trainings, the battles, and the celebrations. They would all be missed.

Kaya stood before him with a straight back and her chin up. "It has been an honor, my friend."

The memories continued to flood his thoughts. "The honor has been all mine."

After a polite and respectful nod to each other, they parted ways.

Santorray then led Nutrix's daughter out of the only place in which she had ever lived. "I know of cities where you will be welcomed. Your mother's gift is for you to live a free life without a master." He then pulled a chain and crystal from a pouch. "This precious crystal will allow you to purchase a nice place to live and enough food and supplies for a lifetime." He then placed the necklace with the crystal over her head. He stepped back, and for a brief moment, instead of seeing Fenia, he saw Nutrix's image in his mind, and she was smiling.

Pleased with her new circumstances, Fenia stretched and breathed in the fresh air and changed the colors of her scales several times as she enjoyed the idea of being uninhibited by a master's expectations. "Thank you for this, Santorray."

"It was your mother's doing, not mine." He replied in a dry, unemotional tone.

"No, it wasn't," Fenia said. "She had no leverage to make this happen. Only you did."

"I once asked her what she wished for and her answer was freedom for the two of you. I am simply doing what I can to fulfill her wish."

"My mother was loving, and she would have treasured the idea of her and I being able to live without fear of a master. However, I know this was not her crystal, it is yours. You could live comfortably by selling it. Why give it to me?"

Struggling with her calling on him to tell the truth, he refused to start another path of deception. "Because she loved you more than anything. And for some unknown reason she believed in me and befriended me."

Fenia laughed at his struggles to say such things. "Of course she did. We all hold you in great esteem. Not just my mother and I, but nearly everyone in the fortress. You cared for our well being and pushed us to do better. Despite your harsh ways of doing it, we all knew your intent was to help us."

"I did no such thing. I was just passing through and simply corrected issues which I felt could be improved upon."

"No, you went out of your way to assist us and train our guards. You improved our water system and our weapon fabrication. You redesigned our hunting patterns to ensure we had ample game for years to come. You have no idea how many of us would follow you to Della Estovia and back."

Santorray gave a slight smile without realizing it. "That is the second time I've been told that today."

"Then believe it to be true."

"Why would anyone take such risks for me?"

"Because you have given us respect and hope in the future. You have changed our view of what could be."

"I seriously doubt that. I tried to change Gin's view of the world for years. All I ended up doing was strengthening Darkmere's values in him."

"Then it is Gin's loss, not your failure," she said. "My mother once told me that you can only provide opportunities for growth. It is up to others to accept and allow them to be nurtured and, yes, to be pruned when needed." She smiled at the thought of all the lives that Santorray had touched. "You don't have to be at someone's side all of the time to make a difference. You just need to care and be there for them when you are with them." She paused as she recalled his efforts over the years. "You have made our world a better place. Don't hold yourself responsible because a few simply can't accept what you've offered. And even if you didn't handle things the best way, at least you were engaged and tried to make a difference. That's more than most will ever do." Stopping, she looked up at him, just as her mother used to. "We all make mistakes. We must be willing to forgive ourselves. I do hope you will learn to forgive yourself, Santorray. My mother would have wanted that."

Santorray could see her mother's features in her face and hear the inflections of Nutrix's voice. Nodding to accept her words, he gave her a warm smile. "Let me tell you how special your mother was and how much she loved you."

BONUS

MATERIAL

A Short Story that takes place between "Betrayed" and "Hunted"

Blox

Altered Creatures
Epic Fantasy Adventures
presents the short story

A Deadly Venture
by
A.G. Wedgeworth

Chapter 1
Night Terror

As the sun fell behind the forest landscape, the locals scurried about within their little village. All valuables, wagons, crates, and supplies were moved inside homes and sheds in a race against time. Lanterns and torches were left unlit as darkness approached, and parents screamed for their children to run home. As the sunlight completed its journey beyond distant mountain ranges, the doors of homes and businesses slammed shut and were locked to keep them safe.

Within minutes, the bustling and thriving village had turned into a ghost town. Empty streets were eerily quiet, while the homes and shops appeared to be abandoned. Not so much as a single candle had been lit within any of them. Darkness had fallen and no one wanted the attention of the horrors that the full moon would bring.

A soft wind blew through the abandoned streets as leaves chased each other in little eddies that developed near the stone well in the center of town. The soft squeaking of chains holding up business signs filled the scene with an uneasy wind chime effect as the surrounding forest turned alarmingly quiet.

In one of many similar thatch-roofed homes, Lunn and Mara quietly pushed their table up against the front door before Lunn grabbed his weapon. They both backed into a far corner with their teenage son, Dru, as Lunn pulled an arrow from his leather quiver, but did not load it yet. "It was a damn fool thing to do!"

"It was my choice!" Dru attempted to protest, but the glare he received from his mother stopped him from going any further. Pulling a white stone sphere from his pocket, his face twisted from various emotions as he gazed upon it. "I thought you'd be proud of me."

"Not now, Dru," Mara said to stop the boy's explanation.

"Stop talking!" Lunn's voice was strong yet hushed. It was clear he wanted absolute silence. And that is exactly what he received, not only from within his own home, but as far outside as they could hear.

After several minutes of uncomfortable quiet, the sound of a deep growl rumbled through the streets and shook the villagers' nerves as they all waited for the event to be over.

Movement could be heard in the street as something large rushed through and then stopped at the home where Lunn, Mara, and Dru lived. Heavy breathing outside their door caused the family inside to hold one another as they prayed for the terror to end.

The answer to their prayers came in the form of a hard crash against their door, which was quickly followed by another. Mara screamed as she hid Dru's face in her robes to protect him. A third pounding of the door caused large cracks to appear as wooden splinters of the door fell inside the home.

Lunn stepped in front of his family and loaded his hunting bow. Mara grabbed a large butcher's knife with one hand, while she protected Dru with the other. They would fight to the death to protect their family.

The door blew apart upon the next attack from the beast and splinters were sprayed across the room inside. It was followed by a spine-tingling roar that made the family's knees shake.

As the unseen creature entered the home, the remaining parts of the door broke off and the pieces scattered on the floor were kicked about. Despite the fact that they could see the ramifications of the creature's movement in the faint moonlight, the creature itself was not visible.

"Stay back, demon!" Lunn launched the first of his arrows in the creature's general direction. The arrow sailed across the room and pierced the far wall. He had either missed, or the arrow flew straight through the invisible predator.

Before he could load a second arrow, he was hit from the side and tossed up against the wall. The unseen beast then pounced upon him, pinning Lunn to the ground before ripping one of his arms from his torso, causing him to convulse from the pain. Blood sprayed up from the open wound as a large chunk of flesh was devoured from the detached arm, like a dog would eat the meat off a chicken leg. The meat upon the arm quickly disappeared into the blood-covered mouth of the invisible invader. Rows of sharp teeth within a large powerful jaw floated above Lunn.

Fear and anger drove Mara into a rage as she plunged her knife forward, hoping to strike something. The blade landed deep into the unseen attacker, and blood showered her hand before she stepped back.

An unexpected cry from the beast turned into a growl as the visible red-stained teeth and gums turned to face her. The hint of two cat-like eyes opened from an invisible head as the creature stared her down.

Mara stepped back and pulled Dru behind her as the specter moved near her face and breathed heavily enough upon her to blow her hair behind her. Sweat dripped down her face while she stood firm, protecting her son.

The floating jaw opened as the soft light from the moon glimmered off the bloody teeth. It could easily take her entire head into its mouth. Each moment that passed allowed it to close in on her head as it prepared to crush her face with one powerful snap.

"Leave them alone!" Lunn yelled. With his one remaining hand, he grabbed the knife that appeared to be floating in midair. After pulling it out, he plunged it back in as hard as he could. He was weak from the creature's attack on him, but he refused to surrender.

The creature screamed into Mara's face before pulling back, closing its mouth, and disappearing before her eyes. Furniture flew about as the beast spun around and then knocked her husband back to the floor. And then, she watched her husband being picked up and dragged out of their home by his neck.

Without thinking twice, she bolted for the doorway and out into the street as her husband was dragged away by the invisible monster into the forest. Racing after them, she stopped at the edge of the village and listened to find a direction to go, only to hear the chomping of bones deep into the darkness.

Dru ran up to his mother and grabbed her, preventing her from following the creature. He held her tight until she fell to her knees where they both broke down and cried. They had lost him.

"I promise you, son," Mara said while holding his hand with both of hers. "I will avenge his death!" she yelled in anger, before lowering her head and sobbing.

Chapter 2
The Outsider

As the sound of the creature feasting upon his victim subsided, the musical tones of a whistle grew from the road that entered the village. Dru and Mara turned to see a traveler wander into their community completely unaware of the events unfolding.

Aside from the open vest, the man's shirtless attire exposed a large stomach that hung over the belt that held up his leather pants. His thick beard covered most of his chest while his head was completely bald. Items filled pockets on his pants, vest, and on the large pack he carried.

Stepping into the little village, he stopped as his whistle fell from a delightful tavern song to a questioning and inquisitive tone. "Where the blazes did these here people go?" he asked himself while he glanced down the main street.

Spotting two residents, he began to walk toward Mara and Dru. "Hello!" he yelled and gave a single wave of his arm. "I be lookin' for some drink and a bed ta sleep in. Preferably in that order."

Dru motioned to the stranger to stop talking, but quickly realized that his movements were having no effect on the man. "Mother, we have to get inside before it comes back." By the time he was able to get her to her feet, the stranger had arrived.

"Greetin's folks. I be Blox. What be your names?" He watched as the young man attempted to help his mother. She appeared dazed and confused. "Need a bit of help?"

"Please! We must hurry!" Dru told the outsider. "We have to get her to safety right away." Even though there was panic in his voice, the volume was oddly quiet.

Grabbing one of the woman's arms, he looked about to see what the danger was. "What ya be hiding from?"

"An evil spirit. We must hurry."

Thinking the young man was playing with him, he waited for the punch line of the joke. Not receiving one, he had to give his opinion. "There ain't such a thing as spirits and ghosts, lad."

As they prepared to move Mara, she turned back toward the forest and started screaming. "I'll kill you with my own hands!"

"Mother! We have to hide." Dru struggled to keep his voice down. "Father is gone. We need to go before it returns."

Blox looked at the confused woman as he put the pieces together. "Yer father's gone and yer mum is gonna kill him?"

"No. The spirit broke into our home and killed my father. I can't allow it to take my mother as well."

"Listen, lad, even if I believed in them things, what kind of spirit needs ta break into homes? Wouldn't it just be walkin' through the walls?" His doubt in the story prevented any effort to escort her down the street.

Glancing back toward the forest, Blox squinted his eyes to see anything odd. His expectation was he'd see the father standing out there. "Did your parents have too much ta drink that caused a bit of a tiff? Shall I be going out there and tellin' him it be okay to come home?"

"It was the spirit demon!" Dru insisted. "We need to make our way to the tavern. It's the strongest structure we have, and our leader, Kwenton, lives above it. He'll protect us."

Blox eyed the direction to the village's central well before giving another gander to the trees. "I'll be right back and then we be on our way to the tavern." Grabbing one of his torches from his pack, he lit it and made his way to the forest.

"Nothin' but a lovers' spat is all," Blox said to himself, but it was also loud enough for the boy to know he was on to the truth. "I'll just tell the cowering husband to grow a set and be gettin' back inta his house and apologize for whatever she thinks he did wrong." Walking confidently into the wooded area, he kicked at a few bushes to see where the man was hiding. Going a bit deeper, he saw the man's boot peeking out from his hiding spot. Grabbing hold of it, he gave it a hard tug to spook the man. Instead, he pulled up the man's boot and part of his leg. For a moment, he didn't understand what had happened until he realized that his leg had been chewed off.

"What in the…" He stepped in closer to find the lower half of a man's torso was shredded and lying on the forest floor. Blood was splattered across the nearby tree trunks, undergrowth, and dirt. Most of the body was missing.

Standing extremely still, he listened for any signs of what had mutilated the body. The still of the night gave off the faintest of sounds as he heard deep breathing in the distance. Blox spun around and held out his torch to see what was making the noise. Moments later, he heard the sound of small sticks breaking from the weight of a heavy creature circling his position. Turning to face the noise, he kept the flame of the torch far out in from of him. "I knows yer out there. Show yerself, ya bloody coward!"

Blox started backing out of the forest as the sounds of a pacing creature continued to stay at bay from the torch's flame. Once he was in the clearing, he increased his speed into the village, while holding the light toward the forest.

By the time he had reached the other two, they were already on their way down the street toward the largest building in the village. Across from the local well, the tavern was made of stone and had a wooden roof instead of the typical thatched roof.

Making their way past the well, they headed to the two strong wooden doors that had been placed in the center of the building's front wall. Blox's torch was the only light in the entire village and stood out like a lighthouse on a remote island. The traveler knew the risk of this, but he was not willing to move with haste without seeing where he was going.

A low growl from the edge of the forest echoed in the night, adding a bit more urgency to their steps.

"Put out the light!" Mara yelled as she attempted to grab it.

Pulling it back and up so she could not reach it, he had no plans to comply. "It be me weapon of choice."

Another growl was heard. This time it was closer and seemed to be coming from within the village.

Dru pulled at the doors, but found them to be locked. Cupping his hands around his mouth to focus his voice, he yelled through the slit between the doors. "Let us in!"

Mara knocked quickly as she also spoke into the door. "Hurry! Open these doors!"

Blox stood with his back to the doors with his torch out before him as he scanned the streets. "Show yer ugly mug," he said while waving the light about.

Within moments, he heard a soft footfall to his side and turned with the torch to see what he could. There, several yards before him, Blox could see a set of eyes reflecting the flames from his torch. Floating without a head or body to be seen, the eyes blinked, squinted, and then lowered before launching forward.

"He be jumpin'! Blox yelled as he threw himself backward to avoid being captured.

The eyes flew across as the beast missed the man. By the time it turned around, Blox, Mara, and Dru were inside the tavern. The doors had been unlocked and opened just as the outsider had leaped backward. And as fast as they opened, they were closed and locked afterward.

Falling to the floor of the tavern, Blox found the three of them to be safe as a loud slam hit the thick wooden doors. Everyone inside the tavern jumped from the sound as the vibration of the impact was sent through the entire building. There were nearly a dozen people inside, most of them holding onto loved ones, as they feared the unseen creature outside.

Chapter 3
Truths Revealed

B lox rolled his heavy body over and lifted himself up onto his knees. He then took a moment to rest before standing up. While there, he looked around at the frightened villagers staring at him. "I might be a pretty sight to the eyes, but I think yer overdoing it," he said with a laugh. Using a nearby table as leverage, he hoisted himself up onto his feet.

"Who are you? What do you want?" The tall, thin man asking the questions was the best dressed of the bunch.

"I'm Blox, and I be wanting somethin' ta drink and a bed ta sleep in, but I'm willin' ta just go with that there drink fer now." Licking his lips, he spotted a bottle on the bar that looked ripe for the taking.

The locals parted to make way for the chubby man to reach the bar and plant himself upon a stool. After taking the bottle in hand, he lifted it up to his lips and began to swallow his evening meal until the last drop poured out. Once complete, he slapped the side of his exposed belly and belched long and hard. "Now that ya know who I am, who the hell pissed off that there beastie?"

A loud roar from outside the double doors caused the locals to crouch with fear. It was followed by several heavier blows against the doors before stopping.

"Yeah, that's the beast I'm speakin' of," Blox said while grabbing the next closest bottle of liquor.

"Listen, sir. You should not be here. We have an evil spirit that is taking out its vengeance upon us." The thin man acted as though he spoke for everyone.

"Let me stop ya right there. Who the hell do ya think ya are, callin' me sir?" He wore the insult on his face for several seconds before being distracted by the new bottle.

"I am Kwenton, and this is my village!"

Dru stepped up to speak. "Kwenton, the spirit attacked our home and killed my father. Blox came into town just afterward and helped me save Mother."

Kwenton turned his glare from Blox to the young man and his mother. "I warned you this would happen. You're fortunate it didn't kill all three of you." Another roar from outside caused him to finish his thought. "And it still might. Now you've placed all of us in jeopardy."

Dru lowered his head. "I didn't mean to—"

"But you did," Kwenton interrupted, "and now your actions have already caused one death. Your father's death is on your hands, Dru."

Spilling a bit of his drink out onto his beard while pulling the bottle from his lips, Blox coughed at the comment. "Heavy burden ta be placin' on a young lad."

"This isn't of your concern!"

"Kwenton…" Mara slowly pulled herself out of her daze and glared at the village leader. "… don't you dare blame this on my son. He was trying to save us."

The leader stood tall to address her. "You can try to convince yourself otherwise, but his actions led to the death of your husband."

"You should have never allowed him the opportunity to make the challenge! He's too young!"

"He's of age. It wasn't my place to stop him. It was yours."

Mara bit her lip at his comment. "What would you have done if your son had accepted the challenge?"

"My son knows better." Kwenton's voice was pompous and demeaning. "And if not, I would have stopped him."

"We tried!" she yelled as she stepped closer to the thin man.

"Not until it was too late. By stopping him from carrying out his promise to take the challenge, you and Lunn have caused this threat just as much as Dru." Pointing at her and then her son, he finished his thought. "Your entire family is to be blamed for this horror we're now living with."

"My husband is dead. Can you show some compassion for him?"

"Lunn was always against the challenge and it is ironic that his attempt to stop it caused his own death. My hope is that this night will end soon, and we can all learn from his error to prevent future horrors." Kwenton knew she was expecting more compassion for her family. "My heart goes out to your family as they are taught a lesson for the rest of us to live by."

"You bastard!" Raising her fists, she decked him across the jaw before several others could restrain her. "If you were half the man you pretend to be, you would have accepted that challenge and taken that creature out!"

Holding his jaw as he moved it about to make sure nothing was broken, he walked up to her until he nearly had to look straight down at her. "I would love nothing more than that. However, I have attempted to make the challenge every month, but I have failed each time. I have not been granted the opportunity to select the white rock, for if I had I would have confronted this creature and put it out of its misery. But despite not being given the chance, I still took it upon myself to help. After every challenge had been made, I risked my own life to search out our challenger for days on end with hopes of finding them."

Finishing off his second bottle, which was only half full to begin with, Blox leaned back on the bar with a confused look upon his face. "What da hell are ya people talkin' about?"

Kwenton and Mara were too busy staring each other down to answer the outsider's question, so Dru did instead.

"It started several months ago, when Kwenton and a few of our best men were traveling in the Fesh-filled Marshlands. The demon spirit attacked them for entering its domain and informed them that the village would need to abandon their homes and leave the area. Not willing to surrender so easily, Kwenton refused to agree and the demon gave him an ultimatum. The price for staying would be the life of one of our villagers every full moon. If no one was sent, the spirit would take out its vengeance upon us. It was then that we decided to send one person to fight for our freedom each full moon."

Dru watched his mother and Kwenton slowly ease up and back away from one another. "Each month, we draw to see who will accept the challenge and fight for us." Pulling the off-white marble-sized sphere out of his pocket, he showed it to Blox. "To select the white stone is a sign of greatness from the Oracles. Therefore, they will be the one to challenge the demon before the next full moon."

Blox wiped his lips clean as he listened to the story. "So ya picked the lucky rock and were supposed ta fight that beast outside?"

Dru nodded. "My father was against this practice from the beginning. He claimed Kwenton was behind this as a way to get rid of those who opposed him as well as to gain power. My father refused to take part."

"Then why did ya go against yer father's wishes?"

"We were too poor to move away, but there is a promise of a purse of gold coins for the family who succeeds in a challenge. It would be enough for my parents to leave here and have a fresh start somewhere else."

"We didn't want a new life without you," Mara said to her son. "No amount of gold could replace you."

Dru smiled sheepishly at his mother before turning back to the newcomer. "My father found out that I had taken the challenge and that I had selected a white rock, but he forbad me to leave yesterday to defeat the demon."

Kwenton nodded in agreement with Dru as his eyes continued to be fixated upon Mara. "By preventing Dru from attempting to defeat it last night, Lunn has caused the beast to come here for its revenge. We've violated our terms. We know not what this night will bring in retaliation."

"I see," Blox said as he scratched the side of his extended belly. "What be yer options at this here point?"

Kwenton turned his glare to the young man. "Dru accepted the challenge and it was granted by the Oracles. He must face the beast for this to end."

"Never!" Mara yelled as she moved over and held onto her child.

"He must!" Kwenton ordered. "The Oracles granted him the white stone!"

Grabbing a third bottle, Blox returned to his stool. "Can he just give it ta someone else?"

"No!" Kwenton fired back. "It must be selected by the powers of the Oracles choosing the challenger."

Nodding, Blox looked about and counted heads. "We got enough in here to take the challenge. Drop that thing back in the bag and ya all can try yer hand at it to see who we send out there to face the beast."

Feelings about the idea filled their faces with mixed emotions.

Blox spoke up again. "If ya don't pick one, then we all be looking at dying on this night."

A smile grew on Kwenton's face as he eyed the sloppy man taking his first sip of his third bottle. "Will you also be taking this challenge?"

His sip stopped as he looked at all the eyes upon him. "This ain't me village. Why would I be riskin' me neck fer you folks?"

"As you said, if we don't all support this, then we may all end up dead."

"I be just passin' through this place."

Pointing toward the two large doors, Kwenton identified the exit. "Then be on your way."

"Right now? With that there thing out there?"

"You either leave now, or you take the challenge."

Frustrated, the outsider had limited options. "Is the purse of gold coins still the prize?"

"Yes, if you defeat the demon."

Taking a quick gulp from his bottle, Blox gave the village leader an evil eye. "Alright. I'll play yer game. Let's get this over with."

Kwenton motioned to the barkeep to grab the bag from behind the bar. Once he received the leather sack, he pulled on a few straps on top before opening it up for Dru.

With a nod of approval from his mother, Dru walked up and dropped his white rock inside.

Pulling the straps tight, the mouth of the sack closed up tight before the man shook it several times. "Who will be first?"

Dru stepped back up, but he was pulled back by his mother.

"No," she told him. "If this family will support this, then I will be the one to go." She then stepped up to Kwenton to make her selection.

Pulling on one of the straps, he lifted the bag high enough to prevent her from seeing inside. Then he opened the mouth of it and waited for her to select one.

Mara's hand trembled as she hung it above the opening, waiting for the courage to lower it and pull a stone from the sack. Taking a deep breath, she reached in and felt several options before selecting one and pulling it out. Holding it tight in her fist, she waited for the others to pull theirs out before they all revealed them at once.

A few more locals took their turn before Kwenton turned to Blox. Pulling the leather straps tight, he shook them again before pulling a strap and opening the top for Blox to reach into. A sinister glare grew upon his face as he waited for the outsider to take his turn. "A purse of gold coins could be waiting for you if you're selected and you vanquish the spirit."

"I ain't believin' in them spirits ya keep talkin' about, but I'm willin' ta take me turn ta get rid of that beast outside." Blox grinned as he held his hand over the sack and wiggled his pudgy fingers before dropping them inside. "It don't really matter which one, does it?" he asked Kwenton as he gave him a knowing wink.

The village leader arched back with an unsure concern of his statement. "What do you mean?"

"They're all the same color."

"If that were true, how has a white one shown up periodically amongst so many black stones?"

Blox pulled his hand out with the hidden stone tight in his fist. But before Kwenton could close the sack, the traveler snatched it away from him.

"What are you doing?"

"It be your turn. I'll be holding the sack fer you."

"This is outrageous! You have no authority to present this challenge to anyone."

"I got me more authority than a cheatin', double-dealin' Fesh like yerself."

"You, sir, are out of line!"

Blox opened his palm to expose a white stone that he had taken from the sack. "This here be a cheap trick played in many city markets."

"You have the white stone!" Dru announced the obvious without even thinking.

"Aye. They all be white stones on this side of the sack!" Emptying the contents onto the bar, several white spheres rolled around before Blox turned the leather sack back upright. He then shook it.

To the amazement of others, it sounded like the stones were still inside even though they witnessed him emptying it.

After pulling a few straps, he then emptied the rest into Dru's hands. They were all black.

"How could this be?" the young man asked.

Dropping the sack on top of the black rocks, the chubby man eyed Kwenton. "There be a divider inside that there sack. A tug of one of them straps one way or another determines which side you be grabbin' from."

It took a few seconds for the locals to understand what that meant, and once they did it was clear they were not pleased.

"You've been determining who would be sent to their deaths?" Mara asked their village leader as it continued to sink in. "You planned his death! You gave my son a white rock to punish Lunn for resisting your authority. You've given white rocks to everyone who has opposed you!"

Kwenton raised his hands to calm everyone down. "You're going to believe this fat little outsider over me? Have you lost your minds?"

Dru opened the sack and found the two compartments within it as well as the strap that closed off one side at a time. "It's true. It wasn't the will of the Oracles. You determined who would go." Tossing the leather sack to the side, he jumped at Kwenton to take his revenge. "My father is dead because of you!"

Attempting to hold back Mara, her son, and several others from becoming an angry mob, Kwenton stepped back around a table to keep some distance. "You don't know what you're talking about! This man has filled your minds with insane thoughts." His pointing at Blox did not seem to affect the mood in the room. "I am your leader. The larger we are, the stronger we are as a community. Why would I want to send anyone to their deaths?"

A momentary hush filled the tavern that was still tense with emotions.

Blox had no problem breaking the silence. "I think I be knowing the answer ta that."

"Oh really. And what grand story do you have to spin?"

"There only be one reason anyone would travel through the Fesh-filled Marshes instead of traveling around them." Taking another sip from his bottle, he leaned against the bar. "There be legend about a spring in them lands that gives ya great powers."

"The E'rudite Spring," Dru said as he turned back to the traveler. "My father told me about it. That was one of the reasons this village was first built here, to find the magical spring. But after several generations, it was realized that it didn't exist."

"Ah, but she does exist, in them Fesh-filled Marshes," Blox said. "And she be guarded by an ancient beast that fits the description of what we have outside these walls." Blox watched Kwenton become more nervous as the story continued. "Your leader here must have run into the beast and bargained for his life. My guess is that Kwenton promised ta send him fresh meat for the right to search his land for the E'rudite Spring."

"That is a lie!"

Mara glared at Kwenton. "You leave for several days after each of the challenges."

"I go to find them. I spend days searching for them in hopes they are still alive. I do this for you."

"You fool us into believing that the Oracle selects the stone we grab? You did this for us? You send us out to our deaths so you can search for your magical waters? This is also for us?" Her knuckles turned white from the tightness of her fists. "It's our turn now. I promised my son I would avenge his father's death, and I'm going to." Grabbing one of the white rocks off the bar, she slapped it into his palm. "There! Now you've been chosen to fight this spirit demon!"

Mara and the rest of the crowd escorted him to the door and then unlocked it. Before he could protest any more, they opened one of the doors and pushed him outside. Once the door was closed behind them, Mara broke down in tears. She was angry and crushed at the same time. Her family and village had been forever damaged by a lie.

Kwenton's banging on the door was accompanied by his pleading for them to let him back in, but all inside remained firm.

Dru sat by his mom's side as he held and comforted her. However, before he could say anything, the sound of the knocking suddenly stopped and Kwenton's screaming was heard for a few short seconds. It was followed by the loud cracking of bones and tearing of flesh. Within moments, their leader was no more.

Dru looked up at Blox. "Now what? Will it leave? If so, will it come back?"

Blox wiped his mouth with his sleeve as his drink ran down his chin and beard. "Good questions, lad. Fortunately, fer you, I've traveled around enough to know these legends and how ta end the terrors they bring."

He had the crowd's attention as they waited for him to go on.

"I have me some sacred items that when used right with the proper words, will get rid of that there beast." Pulling several items from his pack, he showed the gathering. "Now, which one of ya wants ta learn how?" His question caused everyone else to step back a bit.

Mara, on the other hand, stepped forward. "We can't take the risk of doing it wrong. You're the only one who can do this." Placing a gentle hand upon his shoulder, she wanted his full attention. "We need you to help us save this village. I need you to save my son."

Blox struggled to give in. "If I can learn it, how hard could it be?"

"Dru, go upstairs and get Kwenton's coin purse," Mara said to her son before returning to the traveler. "We believe that the Oracles send us what we need when we need it. The lies Kwenton made about the selection of white rocks do not diminish our trust in the greater power the Oracles have. They have sent you here for a purpose and we need you to fulfill it."

Blox looked into the eyes of Mara and then the rest of the villagers in the tavern before finally giving a slight nod. He then opened his pack and pulled out a few more expensive-looking items. After lighting the wick of a lantern, he placed his pack back over his shoulder. "I be needing a handful of salt, a rag, and another bottle of yer good stuff."

"I think you've had enough to drink," Mara told him as Dru returned with Kwenton's full purse and set it on the bar for the traveler to have after he defeated the creature.

Grabbing a fresh bottle from the bar, Blox smiled at Mara. "I've never had enough, but this here is fer our friend outside." Drenching the rag, he then fed part of it into the bottle. "I'll be lightin' that beast on fire to weaken it. Then I be using me tools to banish it from these lands."

Stepping next to the door, he prepared his plan. "If I don't return, hold off until daybreak and then leave this village forever."

Mara nodded. "Good luck."

"Just close that door behind me as fast as ya can so the beastie don't get in here."

Motioning everyone to stay quiet, Blox listened for movement outside the tavern before nodding that the coast was clear. Then, as soon as the door was unlocked and opened, he wedged his wide body through the opening. The door then slammed louder than they had hoped before they locked it up again. Blox knew the slam was too loud for the creature to not hear. It was simply a matter of time before it would approach the man with the lantern as he stood by himself in the dark street.

Stepping over a remaining detached limb of Kwenton, Blox held the lantern up high as he scouted the area for his enemy.

"Come on, ya cowardly critter!" he yelled into the air. "Ya killed Kwenton and yer deal with him is over. I know yer weakness, so yer no longer gonna be feastin' on these people." Continuing to rotate his body, he was keenly aware of every sound as he waited for an answer.

"If ya don't show yerself, I be huntin' ya down to yer lair." Blox scratched the side of his belly with the corner of the lantern as he waited for his answer."

A light breeze blew leaves about as a heavy breathing could be heard, which slowly grew in strength. It was unclear as to what direction it was coming from as the low vibration bounced between the buildings.

Blox could tell it was getting closer, but he struggled to determine from what direction. Lighting the rag hanging out of the bottle, he spun around as quickly as possible each time a noise grabbed his attention. If continued, he would easily lose his footing as he spun one way and then the other. A sudden rush of panic filled his body as he felt surrounded.

The villagers huddled against the door and waited to hear what would transpire. The shuffling of Blox's feet kept moving closer to the tavern before they heard an unexpected knock.

"I think it be gone," Blox urgently called through the door. "Open up!"

Dru began unlocking the door before Mara stopped him. "Blox, you can do this!"

"I'm sure you be right. I just need another drink to settle me nerves."

"No. You need to stand firm and carry out your plan."

An eerie quiet followed before Blox finally responded. "About that there plan…" He was suddenly distracted and forgot what he was saying. "Crap!" Blox yelled at the sound of a large creature landing near him.

Light shot under the doors and into the tavern as Blox's glass bottle crashed and exploded in a fiery blaze. The outsider yelled several phrases in ancient tongues between screaming in pain himself. By the end of the third round of his phrases a hideous screech erupted from the creature.

The locals covered their ears and closed their eyes as the piercing sound vibrated deep into their skin to the point that it was painful. The only relief they received was when it had to take a breath between cries.

After a moment of silence, the sounds of structures being demolished followed the continuing painful shrieks of the beast as it bolted out of the area through several of the homes in the village. Trees breaking under its weight were then heard as it tore through the forest to escape the spell Blox had placed upon it.

After a sigh of relief, Mara nodded to Dru to unlock the doors. Once completed, she slowly opened them to find the destruction outside.

Damaged walls left debris spewed out across the street, much of it still on fire from the battle that had taken place. Blox was leaning up against the central well with burn marks across his arms and hands. The items he had used had been broken and melted in the act of freeing the village. He had been successful, and he had survived.

Mara ran over to him and kneeled to help. "Are you injured?"

"Appears that I be burned a bit but I don't think me broke anything."

Attempting to help him sit up, she asked. "What can I get you?"

Blox sighed. "I just wanted a bit to drink and a bed ta sleep in."

A slight laugh slipped out before she smiled and nodded. "It's the least we can do for you."

Chapter 4
Back on the Road

The morning sunlight had a slight bite against the minor burns upon Blox's hands from the prior night. He had woken up late and had his fill of drink before leaving the village on his trek through the forest. Aside from a little sensitive skin and a few sore muscles, he enjoyed his walk down the dirt path toward new ventures.

Starting soft, his whistling of tavern songs became louder and brought back many memories. With a strong scratch to the side of his stomach he chuckled a bit at what he had seen over his years and the people he had run into. His home was wherever he slept that night and his friends were whoever would tolerate him for that evening. In his mind, he was free, and he had a grand life which he lived to the fullest.

As the forest path slowly turned, he noticed a dozen yards ahead that the dirt was being kicked about, but it was unclear as to the reason. Blox slowed his pace until he was only a few yards from it. He then stopped and stared at the unnatural movement of the topsoil. "What have we got here?

A pair of eyes opened before him from an invisible face attached to an unseen body. The creature from the night before was now standing before him out in the open. In fact, it had been waiting for the man to show up alone.

Pulling out the villagers' sack of gold coins, he showed it to the creature. "Not a bad haul fer one night of work, eh, Siver?" Blox asked the beast. "They bought the entire charade."

The creature shook its body to make itself visible to the man. Shaped like a large cat, it was covered in scales instead of hair. With its back at a height greater than that of Blox's hips, it had large fangs and powerful claws. Its scales allowed it to change colors and turn nearly invisible. It was by far one of the largest brandercats he had ever known.

Siver moaned at Blox and showed him the wound she had taken by Mara's knife.

"Got clumsy, did ya?" Blox shook his head with slight disappointment. I'll be havin' Natalya cast a few spells and fix ya right up, but her price will be comin' out of yer share of the gold we got last night."

The cat growled at the idea.

"Hey now. Ya got a free meal every full moon for months and even a snack last night. Although Kwenton didn't appear ta have a lot of meat on his bones." Blox patted Siver on the side. "Besides, we saved that there dysfunctional village from its greedy leader. Sure, there be a few unexpected casualties, but all in all we did them a favor and they'll be better off fer it."

Siver turned as they both started down the road away from the village.

"But did ya have ta eat Mara's husband? She seemed nice and the lad as well."

A soft roar rolled from the large cat's mouth.

"I hear ya. You were hungry. I'm like that with me drink. I stopped lookin' at labels a long time ago." Chuckling at his own joke, Blox shifted his pack one more time before the long walk to the next village. "Do ya think we've used that there E'rudite Spring legend too many times or shall we try it again?"

Stepping in front of Blox, the cat glared at him and showed a few teeth.

Blox stopped in his tracks. "Alright. No need ta get upset. A promise is a promise. Ya earned yer freedom. Once Natalya gets ya fixed up, yer on your own."

The cat relaxed and fell back in stride.

"Ya know, we make a good team. Ya might want ta stay on fer a few more adventures."

* * *

Blox continues his journey in the novel *Hunted*, where he teams up with a powerful witch to hunt down Santorray

Join us on more AC Epic Fantasy Adventures

CHARACTERS Pronunciation Guide

Alchemist: (al-kuh-mist) Expert users of magical spells and items

Ambrosius: (am-brō-zee-uhs) One of the Brothers of War, he and his brother ruled the Dovenar Kingdom until the Civil War.

Blox: (Bloks) Human Male, hunter, tracker, and conman

Civej: (siv-'ehj) A dark vaporish creature that can enter the mind of enemy of Civej's master and extract their thoughts.

Darkmere: (dahrk-meer) Born as Tarosius, he changed his name after being trained by Deleth. He and Ambrosius ruled the Dovenar Kingdom until the Civil War.

Deleth: (del-'eth) The Dark Oracle, one of the 3 ancient ones, once known as the Notarians

Ergrauth: (ur-grawth) The Demon of the Land and original ruler of all Del'Unday.

E'rudite: (ee-roo-dahyt) A group that have learned to manipulate and control the forces of nature.

Gin: (jin) Human, 13 year old young man

Javolo: (jah-vō-lō) Human Female, The Terra King's voice and personal assistant

Kaya: (kay-yah) Human Female, Leader of guards

Korin Swiph: (kor-in swif), Undead Human Male, leader of an ancient Dovenar Civil War army

Nutrix: (new-trix) Brandercat Female, Gin's nursemaid

Shrii: (shrē) Giant Black Panther

Terra King: (tehr-rah king) Human, Elder Male controlling the growth of his flock across the lands after the Civil War left them leaderless

Wittig: (wit-ehg) Human, Elder Male of the Bentree Village

LOCATIONS Pronunciation Guide

Bentree: (ben-trē) Small dirt road village comprised of general shops, a tavern, a stable, and some homes nestled in a remote dell.

Brushtower: (brush tow-er) Once a stronghold before the civil war, the remaining structures house a community trying to find it's path back to the power it once held.

Della Estovia: (del-lah ehs-tō-vē-ah) The underworld where the souls of the dead go to serve the demon Bakalor.

Dovenar: (doh-ven-ar) The Dovenar Kingdom was comprised of seven provinces until the twin heirs to the throne caused a civil war that divided and then dismantled the kingdom. The region is now filled with remaining regional governments and newly growing powers to obtain the land and resources.

Kiri Dunes: (kē-rē doons) Sandy desert region between the Volney River and the O'Sid Fields.

Luthralum: (loo-thrawl-uhm) The mighty lake that provides fresh water and life to the Dovenar Kingdom.

O'Sid Fields: (ō-sid fēldz) Grass plains between the Woodlen forests and the Guardian Mountain Range. Known for its vertical termite mounds and grazing chuttlebeasts.

Sandwell: (sand-wel) Typical well-established village with central community well, stone streets, and commerce that support the region.

Woodlen: (wood-len) Northernmost province of the Dovenar Kingdom

SPECIES Pronunciation Guide

Blothrud (AKA Ruds): blawth-ruhd

7' to 9' tall; Bony hairless dragon-like head; Red muscular human torso and arms; Sharp spikes extend out across shoulder blades, backs of arms, and backs of hands; Red hair covered waist and over two thick strong wolf legs. Blothruds are typically the highest class of the Del'Undays.

Brandercat: brand-er-kat

Large lion-sized cats that have scales instead of hair. They can change the color of their scales to turn nearly invisible.

Del'Unday: del-oon-dey

The Del'Unday are a collection of Altered Creatures who live in structured communities with rules and strong leadership. These include blothruds, wolvians, brandercats.

E'rudite: ee-roo-dahyt

The E'rudite aren't actually a species. They are typically humans that have been trained in the basic arts of the Notarian mind control powers which makes them much more powerful than others, but not nearly that of a Notarian.

Fesh'Unday: fesh-oon-dey

The Fesh'Unday are all of the Altered Creatures that roam freely without societies. Wolves, boars, raccoons, and most forest creatures are in this clan.

Gathler: gath-ler

6' to 8' tall; Giant sloth-like face and body; Gathlers are the spiritual leaders of the Ov'Undays. They are very curious creatures who take their time to investigate the true nature of things.

Human: hyoo-muhn

5' to 6' tall; pale to dark complexion; weight varies from anorexic to obese. Most live within the Dovenar Kingdom.

Krupe: kroop

6' to 8' tall; Covered from head to toe in black armor, these thick and heavy bipedal creatures move slow but are difficult to defeat. Few have seen what they look like under their armor. Krupes are the soldiers of the Del'Unday.

Mognin (AKA Mogs): mawg-nin

10' to 12' tall; Mognins are the tallest of the Ov'Unday. Dark hide-like skin with oversized hands that have 3 fingers between 2 thumbs.

Myth'Unday: mith-oon-dey

The Myth'Unday are a collection of Creatures brought to life by altering nature's plants and insects.

Notarian: noh-tawr-ee-in

These thin human-like creatures have semi-translucent skin and no natural hair anywhere on their bodies. Their motions are smooth and graceful and they have incredible mental powers that appear to be god-like to the other species.

Ov'Unday: ov-oon-dey

The Ov'Unday are a collection of Altered Creatures who believe in living as equals in peaceful communities. Typically pacifists. Species such as mognins and gathlers are part of this clan.

Polenum (AKA Nums): pol-uh-nuhm

4' to 5' tall; Human-like features; Very pale skin; Soul-markings cover their bodies in thin or thick lines as they mature. Exceptional eyesight.

www.AlteredCreatures.com

Historical Event		Published Novel
2nd Age Begins: Notarians Arrive		
Creation of Unday		
Training of E'rudites		
Creation of Notarian Structures		
Completion of Lu'Tythis Tower		TD5 Prey of Ambrosius
Fall of Notarians	2nd Age	TD6 Plea of Avanda
E'rudite & Alchemist War		SP5 Outraged
Mtn King Temple Established		TK1 Hidden Magic
Nomadic Living & Fighting		
Migration of the Ov'Unday		
Creation of Magical Items		TK2 Final Days
Creation of the Myth'Unday		
3rd Age Begins: Del'Unday Rule		
Del'Unday Expansion		
War of Del'Unday and Myth'Unday		
War of Del'Unday & Dragons	3rd Age	
Del'Unday Civil War		
Rise of the Alchemists		
Victor Dovenar's Revolution		
4th Age Begins: Dovenar 1st Wall		
7 Provinces Created in Kingdom		SP1 Exiled
Dovenar Kingdom Civil War		SP2 Captured
Assassination of Dovenar Knights		
Creation of the Grand Council		SP3 Betrayed
Matriarch's Cleansing	4th Age	SP4 Hunted
Destruction of the Grand Council		TD1 Fate of Thorik
Dovenar Provinces Secede		TD2 Sacrifice of Ericc
Reuniting against Del'Undays		TD3 Essence of Gluic
The Final Great Battle		TD4 Rise of Rummon
5th Age Begins: Frozen Lands		SP6 Defeated

Epic Fantasy

www.AlteredCreatures.com

AC's epic adventures continue with the following books:

Nums of Shoreview Series (Pre-Teen, Ages 9 to 12)
Stolen Orb (Book 1)
Unfair Trade (Book 2)
Slave Trade (Book 3)
Baka's Curse (Book 4)
Haunted Secrets (Book 5)
Rodent Buttes (Book 6)

Thorik Dain Series (Young Adult and Adult)
Treasure of Sorat (Prequel)
Fate of Thorik (Book 1)
Sacrifice of Ericc (Book 2)
Essence of Gluic (Book 3)
Rise of Rummon (Book 4)
Prey of Ambrosius (Book 5)
Plea of Avanda (Book 6)

Tilli of Kingsfoot Series (Adult)
Hidden Magic (Book 1)
Final Days (Book 2)

Santorray's Privations Series (Adult)
Exiled
Captured
Betrayed
Hunted
Outraged
Defeated

Look for other upcoming stories of
Santorray's Privations
Ambrosius
Tilli of Kingsfoot
Darkmere
Myth'Unday
Dragon & Del'Unday Wars
and more…

www.ingramcontent.com/pod-product-compliance
Lightning Source LLC
Chambersburg PA
CBHW071837020726
47502CB00004B/1404